VIOLET
DAWN

Other Books by Brandilyn Collins

Kanner Lake Series

1 | *Violet Dawn*

Hidden Faces Series

1 | *Brink of Death*

2 | *Stain of Guilt*

3 | *Dead of Night*

4 | *Web of Lies*

Bradleyville Series

1 | *Cast a Road Before Me*

2 | *Color the Sidewalk for Me*

3 | *Capture the Wind for Me*

Chelsea Adams Series

1 | *Eyes of Elisha*

2 | *Dread Champion*

BRANDILYN COLLINS

KANNER LAKE SERIES

VIOLET DAWN

BOOK I

ZONDERVAN®

GRAND RAPIDS, MICHIGAN 49530 USA

ZONDERVAN.COM/
AUTHORTRACKER

ZONDERVAN®

Violet Dawn
Copyright © 2006 by Brandilyn Collins

Requests for information should be addressed to:
Zondervan, *Grand Rapids, Michigan 49530*

Library of Congress Cataloging-in-Publication Data

Collins, Brandilyn.
    Violet dawn / Brandilyn Collins.
        p.   cm.—(Kanner Lake series ; bk. 1)
    Includes bibliographical references and index [if applicable].
    ISBN-13: 978-0-310-25223-8
    ISBN-10: 0-310-25223-7
    1. Young women—Fiction. 2. Murder—Fiction. 3. Idaho—Fiction.
I. Title. II. Series: Collins, Brandilyn. Kanner Lake series ; bk. 1.
PS3553.04747815V56   2006
813'.6—dc22

                              2006004764

Interior design by Beth Shagene

Printed in the United States of America

---

06 07 08 09 10 11 12 • 18 17 16 15 14 13 12 11 10 9 8 7 6 5 4 3

For Sister #1,
Dr. Sylvia Seamands.
Soft in heart
and a rock for our family.
You were there for me
when I was young and foolish.

God makes a home for the lonely.

PSALM 68:6 NASB

INTRODUCTION

Dear Reader,

Welcome to Kanner Lake. You'll find a warm, eclectic, and rather colorful community here. You'll also run across a few dead bodies.

I'm supposed to tell you that Kanner Lake is fictional. True, you won't find it on a map. But then, cartographers were never known for their imagination. Through *Violet Dawn* and future books in this series, you'll learn that Kanner Lake lies in the Idaho Panhandle a little east of Highway 41, about halfway between the towns of Spirit Lake and Priest River. Those familiar with this area will realize I've taken the audacious liberty of flattening the mountains just west of Spirit Lake Cutoff Road and replacing them with my lake. Ah, the power of a novelist! I've chosen the setting of Northern Idaho for an obvious reason. It is a gorgeous area of lakes, forests, and wildlife—just about the closest you can get to heaven on this earth.

Special note: two wonderful things found in Kanner Lake really do exist. Check the acknowledgments at the back to see what they are.

Okay. Now that you've got your bearings, it's time to climb aboard for another mind-rattling ride. You know the drill. Strap that seatbelt on tight, keep your hands inside the car, and
don't forget to *breathe*...

VIOLET DAWN

PART ONE

Targeted

ONE

Paige Williams harbored a restless kinship with the living dead.

Sleep, that nurturing, blessed state of subconsciousness, eluded her again this night. Almost 2:00 a.m., and rather than slumbering bliss, old memories nibbled at her like ragged-toothed wraiths.

With a defeated sigh she rose from bed.

Wrapped in a large towel, she moved through the darkened house, bare feet faintly scuffing across worn wood floors. Out of her room and down a short hall, passing the second bedroom—barren and needing to be filled—and the one bathroom, into the small kitchen.

She unlocked the sliding glass door. Stepped outside onto the back deck. The grating rhythm of cicadas rose to greet her. Scents from the woods—an almost sweet earthiness—wafted on a slight breeze.

The dry Idaho air was still warm.

A large hot tub sunk into the left corner of the deck was her destination—a soothing womb of heat to coddle and comfort. There, looking out over the forested hills and Kanner Lake, Paige could feel sheltered from the world. The closest neighbor on either side was a good quarter mile away.

But first, captivated by the night, she padded to the edge of the deck's top step and gazed up at the heavens.

A slivered moon hung askew, feeble and worn. Ice chip stars flung themselves in all directions. The Big Dipper tipped backward, pouring into Kanner Lake, which seemed to brood under the spangled sky. Across the sullen waters a few downtown lights resolutely twinkled.

Intense yearning welled so suddenly within Paige that she nearly staggered in its presence. She clutched the towel tighter around her body, swaddling herself. The universe was so vast, the world so small. A mere speck of dust, Earth churned and groaned in the spheres of infinity. Upon that speck, mothers and fathers, children and friends laughed and cried and celebrated one another. No bigger than dust mites they were, compared with the vastness of space. Their lives, their loves—insignificant.

So why did she long to be one of them?

Paige stared at the downtown lights across the water. In eight hours she would return there, among the families and the lovers. Surrounded by people who *belonged*. Separated from them by a mere two feet of counter space ... and a chasm. Behind the Simple Pleasures counter on Main Street, she would sell gift items and pretty home accessories to tourists and local residents. Parents with tagging children, couples, and friends. Sometimes from the corner of her eye she would watch them shopping, especially the young women. Pointing out an oil lamp candle to a girlfriend, exclaiming together over a glitz-studded handbag. And something inside her would swell and ache like bruised skin. God knew she wanted a friend like that more than anything else in the world, someone as close as a sister—

Stop it, Paige.

She lowered her chin and gazed at her feet. Slowly she turned away from the lake and town.

God, if You're up there, send me friends. Send me a sister—someone lonely, someone with a childhood as miserable as mine.

Her daily prayer. The one she'd brought with her to Kanner Lake. The one that had kept her going ever since she fled the Williams family hometown in Kansas.

Not that she deserved an answer.

As she edged across the deck, Paige consoled herself that all would be well. She might be parentless and alone, but wouldn't people expect a twenty-five-year-old to be capable of making friends? She'd settled in Kanner Lake only a month ago. She *would* make a life here, build her own family to love—

Your sister is coming very soon.

The stunning thought filled Paige's mind as forcefully as if the words had been shouted. Paige blinked, drew to a halt. For a moment she couldn't move. Could only tilt her head, listening. She must have imagined it.

But no. The knowledge bloomed within her all the more, as captivating as a vibrant flower in the desert. Her new friend, her sister, would soon enter her life. How Paige knew this, she couldn't begin to fathom. Where had such a strong premonition come from? Was it God's voice she'd heard?

She drew a hand across her forehead, anticipation mixing with perplexity. Whatever it was—God, fate, or some other force in the universe—she shouldn't question it. What if the power took back its promise as quickly as it had been sent?

Paige shivered in the warm night. She crossed to the hot tub, seeking its heat, her mind still singing with The Promise. What would her sister-friend be like? Had she grown up in Kanner Lake, or would she too be a newcomer? What kind of childhood had she experienced? What had happened in her life at age seven? Ten? In her teenage years? All these experiences—and the girl's secrets—Paige would soon share. They would encourage each other, do things together.

She would protect this "sister" with her life.

Paige reached the sunken hot tub, which protruded from the deck about one foot. A heavy vinyl cover, divided down the middle, rested over the tub, protecting its heat. Letting her towel fall, Paige leaned down and used both hands to fold back the cover, revealing half the water. No need to take the cover all the way off. It was heavy, and the tub was large enough that even half of it provided her with plenty room to relax. Inviting steam rose into her face. She would not turn on the jets—she never did. She wanted quiet solace, not roiling waters, as she thought about The Promise.

Paige held on to the smooth side and stepped into the tub. At that end a "couch" seat, formed like a recliner, ran its length. There she lay back, sinking up to her neck in the hot water and pillowing her head against the black vinyl headrest. She closed her eyes. Stretched out her legs and floated her arms in the warmth, her mind still filled with the prophetic words.

Her thigh tickled. Paige flicked her fingers over the spot.

Amid her new hope, persistent ghosts of old memories materialized. Whispering of her days in despair, nights on the run. *Even if you do find a sister, Paige, she too will be taken away.*

No. Not this time. Paige gazed with rising determination at the silver-studded sky. She would cling to The Promise with every fiber of her being—

Something sinuous brushed against Paige's knee. She jerked her leg away.

What was *that*?

She rose to a sitting position, groped around with her left hand.

Fine wisps wound themselves around her fingers.

Hair?

She yanked backward, but the tendrils clung. Something solid bumped her wrist.

16

Paige gasped. With one frantic motion she shook her arm free, grabbed the side of the hot tub, and heaved herself out.

Her body hit the deck with a wet *thud*. She rolled, whipped around to face the tub. Her eyes stabbed the black water. What was in there?

Paige pushed to her knees and cautiously leaned toward the hot tub.

A head surfaced.

TWO

A heavy *thud* on the bedroom floor startled Bailey Truitt awake. Her eyes flew open. She thrust a hand toward her husband's side of the bed. Empty.

Bailey jumped from beneath the covers, heart scudding. Her eyes couldn't see as well in the darkness as they used to. Why wasn't the night-light on? She felt her way down to the bottom of the mattress, around its corner. Passing the bed, she shuffled carefully, body bent and arms outstretched, searching the blackness of the floor. Near the bathroom door her fingers brushed a head.

John.

She hesitated, torn between the yearning to help her husband and her need for light. She felt his face, down to his shoulders. They were relaxed. *Thank you, God.* Probably a petit mal seizure. Scary enough, but it could have been so much worse.

Bailey stood upright, her exploring hands now leading her to the bathroom threshold. She grasped the wood, felt around the corner, and flipped on a switch. Sudden light pushed down her chin, squinted her eyes. Bailey blinked and turned back to John.

He lay on his side, knees bent, one arm out straight, clad only in his lightweight pajama bottoms. Apparently, in his fall one foot had caught their night-light and pulled it from its socket. It lay on the carpet near his toes. John wasn't moving. Bailey threw herself down beside him, laid a hand against his heart. Its steady beat against her palm flung tears into her eyes. He was unconscious, that was all.

Bailey pushed to her feet and hurried to the bed to fetch John's pillow. She laid it on the floor beside his head, then gently turned him onto his back. Lifting his neck, she fussed the pillow into position, then rose again to pull his winter robe from the closet to drape over him as a blanket.

"John?" Bailey whispered as she settled down beside him. She patted his shoulder beneath the robe, smoothed his cheek. In times like this she couldn't touch him enough. "I'm here."

No response. Bailey stroked his graying hair, waiting. Chiding herself for being such a sound sleeper. If only she'd woken up when he rose to use the bathroom. She imagined the small seizure hitting, John's arms flying toward the wall for support, while she lay just feet away. Not that she could have stopped the shaking, but maybe she would've reached his side before he fell.

Bailey gazed at her husband's face, drinking in every line of his forehead, the stubble on his strong chin. He looked so peaceful, so far removed from the multiple forms of epilepsy he'd fought so hard for the past five years. She knew that when he awoke, he would be disoriented. Extra tiredness would grip him as the morning dawned and the day wore on. He would need to sleep even more than usual. She sighed. John would be so disappointed with himself. He hadn't experienced a seizure in almost a month. Which was a godsend, considering the other things he'd had to deal with. For some reason his myoclonic seizures—those sudden jerks, as a normal person might experience when falling asleep—had increased. And Inderal, a new medication for him, had helped calm his Parkinson's-like tremors, but he'd gained twenty pounds as a side effect in the past month.

Lord, give him strength. Bailey smoothed back her husband's hair. *You know how hard it is for him, even though he always smiles.* Five years ago John had been a successful accountant and golf lover. But the car accident—and head injury—had changed his life. Now he couldn't even work, permanent disability his only income. Now he counted not dollars on a spreadsheet but pills into little plastic boxes for his daily doses. Big blue Depakot tablets and large white Klonopin ...

John's hand moved. His eyes opened, slowly blinking.

"Hi, sweetie, I'm here." Bailey touched his face.

He turned his head toward the sound of her voice, frowning. "Bailey?"

Her throat tightened. She forced a little grin. "And who else would it be in the middle of the night, with you half-dressed?"

He regarded her, eyes semiglazed. "What happened?"

"Just a little seizure, that's all. You fell coming back from the bathroom."

"Oh." A long sigh seeped from him. He closed his eyes.

Bailey checked the nightstand clock. A little past two. She would get John back to bed as soon as he felt strong enough to walk. He had plenty of hours yet to sleep. She would be extra quiet when she arose at six to dress for the day's work at Java Joint. Bailey hated to think of leaving John alone all day, but she had no one to help her at their coffee shop. Besides, they needed every dime Java Joint brought in to help pay their bills. Medical costs were eating through their savings.

"John, do you want some water?" She rubbed his arm.

"Yes, love. Thanks."

Bailey pushed to her feet to head for the bathroom, heart swelling at her husband's gentleness. Returning with the water, she helped John sit up. Pale-faced, he took the glass and raised it in a weary cheer. "Here's lookin' at ya, kid." Bailey watched him drink it.

She took the glass to the sink, then helped John to his feet. Picked up his pillow and walked beside him to the bed. Once he was settled, she plugged in their night-light, turned off the bathroom switch, and climbed in beside him. Her hand crept over to rest against his back. Already she could hear his even breaths of sleep.

For a long time Bailey lay awake, praying. For John. For more customers at Java Joint so they could afford his medicine. *I know the locals gossip there, Lord, and it seems nothing escapes their attention. But we need their business.* She thanked God for the extra money He had already provided through Edna San. As sleep eluded Bailey, the petitions expanded to their son and daughter, now moved away and raising their own families. And Sally, the young woman at church who'd suffered such a hard childhood and now yearned for meaning in her life. Then to Bailey's many friends. Finally drowsiness stole through her limbs.

Before sleep overtook her, Bailey Truitt's last request of God was for His protection from evil for her beloved Kanner Lake.

THREE

At the horrific sight, a scream ballooned in Paige's throat. She threw a hand over her mouth to hold it back. Her balance teetered and she fell from her knees to one side, palms smacking against the deck.

She froze, staring at the water.

The head eased into a slow roll. A shoulder appeared.

Paige's thoughts writhed in a jumbled mass. This couldn't *be*. She'd imagined everything. It was too dark to see...

She reached out, fingers trembling above the tub's light switch. Voices in her head shrieked — *Don't turn it on!* Her hand drew back, stretched out again. She pushed the switch.

Eerie blue lit the water. The top third of a body bobbed, facedown, the skin of its arms washed a pale, sickening aqua. Ash blonde hair floated around its head.

Paige scrabbled backward, heart slamming into double time. This couldn't be happening. It *couldn't*.

Minutes passed before she could move. Then, from deep inside, the old survival instincts kicked into gear. Paige licked her lips, shuffled toward the tub on her knees. Her brain chanted a manic mantra — *Get it out, get it out, get it out!*

She hugged her arms to her chest, trying to rein in her wild heartbeat. Her mind thrashed with questions. Was the rest of the body under the cover? What if it was only *part* of a body? What if a second person was under there? *Who* was it?

22

Calling 911 was out of the question. She had plenty of reasons not to trust the police. Whatever happened next, she'd have to do on her own. And there was only one thing she could do.

Somehow she managed to push to her feet, ankles like gelatin. She sidled down the side of the tub and reached trembling arms toward the cover. Gripped the warm, stiff edge and — before she lost her courage — wrenched it aside. It flopped over the two steps leading down to the lawn and landed with a heavy *poof* in the grass.

Through unwilling eyes Paige peeked at the water.

One body. Complete. A woman. Floating languidly, clad in a white short-sleeved blouse, red pants turned purple in the tinted light.

No.

Bile rose in Paige's throat. She forced it down. Backed away from the mind-numbing sight. Those pants — she'd seen them at work just today. And the blouse.

A dozen more questions bounced through her brain. How? When? *Why?*

Paige willed herself into logical thought. What should she do? Call 911 after all? But how to explain this? *"The body's just here ... I don't know how ... I had nothing to do with it ..."* Worse, the police and sheriff's deputies would descend. They'd tramp through her house, ask probing questions about her background — questions she'd have to *answer.* In the morning, the news would plague the streets of Kanner Lake. Folks would talk, ask questions of their own. And it wouldn't stop there. Reporters would hear. They'd hound her for details. Dissect her life. What if her face ended up on TV?

Paige's heart curled inward. Her hiding would be over. She'd end up dead herself.

Skin pebbling, she stared at the gruesome sight. Maybe it wasn't who she thought it was.

Whoever it is, Paige, it's still a dead body.

She would have to turn it over to be sure.

Paige gathered her courage—and put her mind on hold.

She stooped and reached her fingers into the liquid. Her hand brushed water-scaly skin, and a shudder palsied her limbs. Paige steeled herself. Gingerly she wrapped a thumb and two fingers around the body's elbow and pulled. The body skimmed sideways and bumped against the side of the hot tub.

Paige let go and drew back, breathing hard. How to turn it over? She needed leverage, but no way was she stepping into that water.

Maybe if it just pointed her direction, she could raise its head enough to see ...

Paige reached for a fistful of hair, then pushed the torso until it floated from her reach. Pulling the hair toward her, she nudged the body ninety degrees until its forehead bobbed against the edge of the tub. Bracing herself, she grabbed a handful of hair at the crown and pulled up.

The head rose, but not enough to see the face clearly.

She withdrew again, heart thumping. A sudden whiff of chlorine mixed with old perfume nauseated her. She knelt and turned her head away.

Maybe she *should* call the police. She would have to trust them.

But even if they were trustworthy, they would still ask their questions. And reporters would soon hear. Neither of those things could happen.

Paige, think.

Something clicked within her, like machinery gears sliding into place. She was on her own. A bomb had just exploded in her life—again—and she alone must pick up the pieces.

Okay, Paige. You can do this.

She stared at the body.

First things first. Before she made any further decisions, she needed to see the face of the corpse. Make sure who she was dealing with. And to do that, she had to get the thing out of her hot tub.

FOUR

Vince Edwards awoke to a deafening blast.

Eyes closed, the police chief of Kanner Lake turned over in bed and rubbed his temples. The imagined explosion echoed in his brain, trailing horrifying pictures of carnage and fire. Pictures of Tim.

Vince's muscles felt stiff. These days they were always tight. His headache throbbed just like the one he'd awakened to yesterday, and the day before. The pain had haunted him for about a month now. After dreaded Sunday—would it be gone?

Turning his head, he checked the digital clock by his side of the bed. Two fourteen. Great. Another sleepless night.

He listened for Nancy's breathing. It sounded slow and even. Good. At least one of them slept. Better it be Nancy. Vince didn't work on Saturdays, but she had to get up at four thirty to make her six o'clock nursing rounds at Deaconess Medical Center in Spokane. Despite that fact, a year ago he might have awakened her to talk. Just as Nancy might have awakened him when she couldn't sleep. Sometimes in the middle of the night they had worried about their son in Iraq. Was Tim safe? What was he doing? And they would take turns reassuring each other.

Those days were gone.

Vince stared at the ceiling, the familiar weight descending.

A year ago he and his high-school-sweetheart wife of twenty-six years had been as well tuned as the strings on the guitar she liked to play. Working in harmony, vibrating at each other's touch. But grief struck, with all its discordance. These days Vince couldn't even make the old metaphor fit. These days they trod the treacherous ground of a waterlogged hillside, deceptively solid at its surface, unstable underneath.

Vince massaged the back of his neck. After a few minutes restlessness drove him from bed. Treading quietly across the carpet so as not to wake Nancy, he fetched his lightweight robe from the chair near his dresser and slipped it on.

Out in the hall he closed the bedroom door without latching it. Then eased down the stairs and into the kitchen, where he took two aspirin and microwaved some herbal tea. He didn't particularly care for the taste, but peppermint tended to ease him back toward sleep. He carried it into the den.

A streetlight shone through the front window, casting a pale golden swath across the television and onto the hardwood floor. On the oak mantel above the fireplace, Vince could see the faint outline of a copper frame. In the darkness he couldn't make out the photo, but he knew it by heart. Every inch of it. Twenty-year-old Tim in his army uniform, leaning against a battered white wall with his arms folded and that ever-present lopsided grin. One cheek smudged, brown eyes squinted against the sun. By divine timing, one of Tim's buddies had snapped the picture last year. Three days before an insurgent's bomb blew Tim apart.

A year ago tomorrow.

Fresh anxiety rolled over Vince. He set his tea down on the long coffee table and sank onto the leather couch. Somewhere deep within him, battered and weary hope whispered of better days to come. Perhaps the hope sprang from others' words about the power of a year elapsed. By reputation, the first anniversary served as a Rubicon for the grieving. Vince wanted to believe it was true. Beyond that day he could no longer think, *A year ago*

Tim wrote me this letter . . . A year ago Tim arrived in Iraq . . . A year ago Tim shipped out . . .

Vince ran a hand along the smooth coolness of the sofa. Nancy absolutely dreaded the day. She'd made certain she would be off work, not trusting herself to rise from bed. She even declined the offer from their daughter, Heather, to drive over from Liberty Lake. Vince had promised to stay home with his wife to offer comfort. But laden with his own pain, what did he have to give? He could picture them both battling their private storms like wave-pitched ships on a roiling sea.

Worse, Sunday wasn't really the last of the one-year anniversaries. The following day would be the year mark of hearing the news. A few days later—the anniversary of Tim's remains arriving home. Then the funeral.

Maybe after that we can breathe again, he told himself. *Maybe then.*

Vince drank his tea.

His gaze wandered out the window, falling on the house across the street that had recently been bought—surprisingly—by a young married couple new to Kanner Lake. Quite a nice house for kids their age to afford. A dim light spilled from a pane in the upper level of the home. The nursery, Vince guessed. New mama was probably up tending her baby. The cycle of existence. There they celebrated new life. Here he and Nancy memorialized death.

Vince frowned. What was that young mother's name? Her husband's? Nancy would remember. By now friendly Nancy, even amid her grief, would know all about the couple, especially the wife. Where the young mother had grown up, where her family lived, her life story. A year ago Vince would have known too.

The tea had cooled a little. Vince took larger swallows, trying to suck down sleep.

Of its own accord Vince's gaze returned to the photo of his son. With eyes more adjusted to the darkness, he could make out the shape of Tim's body. The blond head Vince had teasingly buffed so many times. The shoulders he had hugged.

Vince stared at the picture as he drained his cup.

After some time sluggishness pulled itself through his veins. Leaving the mug on the table, Vince quietly mounted the stairs. Slipped into his room and out of his robe. Into bed.

Nancy slept on.

He faced her, part of him longing to pull her close, nestle in the softness of her body. Tell his wife how much he needed her and vow to close the growing chasm between them. The other part told him not to disturb her peace.

He turned onto his back and stared at the ceiling.

Coward.

As an undertow of weariness pulled Vince into the sea of sleep, he comforted himself with thoughts of the one strength that kept him going: his work as police chief. The job had become his lifeblood, his saving grace. The responsibility that managed, for bits of time, to turn his mind from the crushing loss. Truth was, he hadn't been able to protect his son from death. He didn't know how to revive his benumbed marriage. But Vince Edwards *could* protect his town. He *could* track down criminal behavior— and make sure it was prosecuted.

For Kanner Lake citizens' sake—and his own—what energy remained within him would be spent on that task.

FIVE

The woman was thin and not very tall, but she was also a dead weight.

Paige knelt a little to the right of the head. Holding her breath, she bent over the water. She plunged her arms into the heat, under the body's chest, and lifted. The woman came up and forward, but something snagged her head. With a groan Paige lifted higher until the head moved. Suddenly her strength gave way. She let go and the corpse started to sink, pulling the head back toward the water. She grabbed the woman's shoulders and held on.

Paige needed fresh air. Craning her neck to the side, she dragged deep breaths through her mouth. When she could summon more strength, she reached both arms beneath the woman's jutting ribcage. Lifted with all her might and pulled. The body barely moved. Paige tried again. No good.

She let the body go once more, her chest heaving. This time the woman's chin caught on the edge of the tub, securing her. Paige sat back on her haunches, waiting for her nerves to stop vibrating.

This wasn't going to work. She would have to get in the water.

Despite the warm night, goose bumps popped down her arms. Paige's mind spewed questions and terrors but she forced them away.

Pushing to her feet, she moved to the corner of the tub. Holding on to the side, she ventured, grit-teethed, into the blue-lit water. First she hunched upon the couch where she previously lay. Then she stepped off it, to the bottom. The woman's left hand floated beside her, long pink nails inches from her leg. Paige batted the hand away.

She edged forward, bent her knees, and stretched her arms beneath the woman's hips. Counted to three and lifted the corpse, shoving it forward until the shoulders lay on the edge of the hot tub. The head hung down toward the deck. Paige rested, then pulled up again. The body moved a little but the arms hooked on the edge. Cautiously Paige released her hold. The woman remained in place.

Paige climbed out of the tub, stood over the woman, and grasped both shoulders, hauling with all her might. The body slid out halfway, reached the pivot point, then shot out. Paige stumbled back and fell, the woman's torso landing on her legs. She shrieked and shoved it off. Scrambled to her feet, brain reeling with revulsion.

The woman teetered on her side, facing the opposite direction. Paige grasped a shoulder and pulled the body onto its back. A faint *slap* sounded as it shifted into place.

The glazed eyes of Edna San stared at the sky in violated shock.

The sight punched Paige in the gut. She jerked away, air rasping in her throat. Aged movie icon Edna San—the most famous, and infamous, citizen of Kanner Lake—here. Dead on her deck.

Paige had fallen asleep in bed after all. She hadn't come out here in the middle of the night, hadn't stumbled upon this shocking discovery.

This was a nightmare.

She forced her gaze back to the body, all too real. What was that on Edna San's neck? She squinted through the blue-illumined darkness. Angry marks, deep bruises. Strangulation?

Paige shoved a hand through her hair, thoughts kicking like dust in a sandstorm. Who did this? Most important, after the way this woman had accosted her in the store yesterday, who would believe she had nothing to do with it?

Fresh panic seized Paige by the throat. She bent over, dropped her hands in her face, wishing she could cry. But too much pain and too little rest had dried up her tears long ago. What should she do now? Run? *Again?*

She didn't want to run. She loved Kanner Lake already. The water, the beach, the forest and hills were soothing to her soul. She had just begun to build her new life here. All she had to do was lead a quiet existence and keep her face out of the papers. By this time, anyone looking for her was not likely to find her in this small tourist town a mere ninety minutes' drive from the Canadian border.

If they did find her, she didn't stand a chance.

But running would only make matters worse. Edna San's body found on her deck—and meanwhile she'd disappeared? Who in the world would believe in her innocence then? The police would hunt her down, discover her past. Plaster her picture on newspapers and television sets across the nation ...

No. She could not run.

Weakness flushed through Paige's limbs. She lifted her head toward the mocking heavens. *You're not real, God, are You?* If He existed up there, He floated in a cloud of indifference. Played chess with the angels, people as their pawns.

A crackle sounded from the woods. Paige spun, nerves tingling. Her eyes stabbed the darkness, seeing nothing. Only then did she remember her towel on the deck, the dim blue illumination upon her body. She sidestepped quickly toward the towel, wrapped it around her. Leaned down to punch off the light.

The deck fell into darkness.

Slowly Paige straightened, heart fluttering. She pierced the forest with her eyes once more. Was someone out there?

Silence.

Blood whooshed through her veins. Her gaze cut to the barely visible form of Edna San's body. She pictured the bruises around Edna's pale, bloated neck, remembered the water-wrinkled feel of her skin. Edna must have been in the hot tub for at least a couple hours. The sound in the forest was merely an animal. Whoever had carried Edna here was long gone, smirking that he'd staged the perfect frame for his deed.

Why me?

Was it someone who'd witnessed the scene between her and the actress? Who'd been in Simple Pleasures at the time? Other than the two sisters, Paige wouldn't recognize the other customers.

She pulled her arms across her chest, bowed her head. She had no one to help her, and Edna San's body could not be found here. There was only one thing to do now.

The reality of the night and all that must follow wrapped around Paige, cold and smothering. How many times before had she felt like this? Abandoned, vulnerable, time and the unknown stretching before her.

Time.

Paige yanked up her chin, surveyed the sky. How many hours did she have? Northern Idaho dawns came ridiculously early in July. When she'd first arrived, at summer solstice, she'd awakened at three thirty to see the first vestiges of light. Four weeks had passed since then. Now the most she could hope for was total darkness until a little past four o'clock. Nascent lightening of the sky would begin about that time, with sunrise around five.

Paige looked back to Edna San's body. It wasn't going to move by itself. She had to pull herself together. Do what had to be done.

She swiveled toward the house to get dressed.

SIX

In her bathroom Paige tossed her towel on the counter. A light *click* sounded by her feet. She jumped. Now what? She bent down, examining the floor. One of her golden heart earrings with the red stone in the middle lay by her toe. She picked it up and threw it into the top drawer.

From her dresser in the bedroom she pulled out black jeans and a black T-shirt. Good thing her short hair was black as well.

Paige dressed by the light of a muted television. Even though the nearest neighbor lived far away, the night seemed to loom with a thousand eyes. She could not risk some nocturnal snoop across the lake raising binoculars toward her house, spotting a light.

In the kitchen she fumbled for her purse on the counter, withdrew her car keys.

Her garage door opened with jarring loudness in the still night.

Paige backed out her old Ford Explorer, turned around at the end of her graveled driveway, and reversed into the garage. Once inside, she hit the button to close the garage door and slid from her car. Opened the hatchback, the vehicle's inside light turning on. This would be her only illumination when the automatic garage light switched off in one minute. Climbing inside the car, she unlocked the lever to each side of the divided backseat and laid the sections down flat. She slid out of the Explorer and stepped through the garage's rear entrance into her backyard, leaving the door open.

Heart churning, Paige turned right to mount the two side steps up to her deck and shuffled toward the dark lump. With a grimace she looked down, loath to touch that skin again, to smell it. How cold would it be now? Nausea snaked through her stomach. She needed gloves.

Moving as swiftly as she could in the darkness, she skirted the body, slid back the glass door that led into the kitchen. Feeling her way to the front hall, she opened the closet and groped on the top shelf for the black gloves she had bought on a summer sale, preparing ahead for winter. She found one; fingers scrambled for the second. Where *was* it? She pushed farther into the closet, burying her nose in the musty smell of a leather coat. Reached up and back as far as she could. *There.*

Back in the kitchen she pulled the gloves on.

Her pulse kicked up in her throat.

She stepped out on the deck, closed the sliding door. Stood over the body, thinking. If Edna had been such dead weight in the water, imagine how much worse it would be now. And if she just pulled the body off the deck, wouldn't it leave some kind of trail? Paige tried to imagine possible evidence. She did not expect anyone to come looking for signs of Edna here. The huge San estate lay across the lake, at the water's edge. Still, she could take no chances.

Paige went back into the house. When she returned, she carried a folded bedsheet. Stepping around the body, she spread it out on the deck. Then, turning off her mind, she grabbed Edna's arms and rolled the body onto the sheet.

She straightened, staring at the splayed sight. Had Edna San ever made a horror movie? Surely Paige had fallen headlong into one.

Paige bent again, gathered the end of the fabric into her fists. Pulling, she turned the corpse ninety degrees and thumped it feetfirst down the steps. On the grass, she dragged the load toward the garage, over the threshold, and onto the cement floor.

Now came the worst part. Getting the body into the back of the car.

She pressed her lips together. The corpse needed to stay on the sheet. It shouldn't lie on the hatchback floor. What if it left some tiny piece of skin or hair? Paige couldn't imagine anyone thinking to check her car for that kind of evidence.

Then again, neither would she have imagined this night.

Paige folded the material on either side of Edna over her body, covering her completely. Now—how to get this gruesome load into the hatchback?

Suddenly her resolute focus fell away, replaced by renewed terror. Paige pictured herself driving down the road with a wrapped body in the back of her car. At that point there would be no turning back. What if her car was stopped? What if she had an accident?

She flinched away, gloved knuckles against the sides of her cheeks. *I can't do this, I can't do this.* Maybe she *should* call the police. She could dump the body back into the hot tub, pretend she'd just discovered it.

Her thoughts segued to Whoever It Was out there who'd placed her in this position. He would be waiting for Edna to be found. And if she wasn't ...

So what's he going to do, Paige? Tell the police the corpse he dumped in your hot tub disappeared?

Paige straightened. Dawn approached and she had little time to waste.

With a deep breath she bent over the wrapped body. Struggling, she forced her arms underneath its back and legs and lifted it like a giant baby. Her knees staggered under the weight, the scent of chlorine-saturated skin, wet silk, and perfume wafting into her nostrils. She held her breath, heaved higher, until the body just cleared the open hatchback. Grunting, Paige shoved it farther into the car until she could close the door. An arm flopped out of the sheet, and wisps of hair. Paige crawled into the hatchback, pushed the limb and hair inside the sheet, making sure all was covered.

She backed out of the car, leaving the hatchback open so the Explorer's inside light would stay on. She pulled off her gloves, now tainted with the mixed scents of Edna's death, and tossed them beside the body.

For a moment she rested against the car. Then she hurried back outside, lugged the hot tub cover onto the deck and over the water. Paige stepped into the kitchen and locked the sliding glass door. From a drawer she fetched a heavy long-handled flashlight, then entered the garage once more. She closed and locked its back door.

Now for something to weight the body.

Her first week in the house she'd heard noises at night. Scratches. Heavy scampering. She knew the sound. Rats.

She could have gone to Mr. Ryskie, her elderly landlord, but he was hard of hearing and crotchety. Paige opted to take care of the problem herself. At the local hardware store, she asked for advice, then bought the suggested large traps. Peanut butter would serve as bait. The worst part involved crawling inside the smelly, low area under the house to place the traps. At least she'd done it in the daytime, when some light filtered in from the far window.

That's when she found the old-fashioned boat anchor attached to a thick chain. Long forgotten, it lay partially buried in the hard, packed dirt.

Paige walked to the crawl space door, pulled up its rusty latch, and dragged a filled trash can over to prop the door open. She knelt and peered inside. Pitch-dark. Paige turned on the Maglite and shone its beam into the gloom. The circle of light moved over dirt, rocks, the cavelike silence.

Paige shivered. She didn't want to go in there. A terrorizing scene fizzled through her mind. Somebody outside, watching through her garage window, breaking in to latch the crawl space door behind her, trapping her inside ...

If you can handle a slimy dead body, Paige, you can handle the dark. She squeezed her eyes shut, willed her heart to slow. *Think now. Where's the anchor?* She pictured herself crawling around, setting the traps ...

About halfway back and over to the left, near the wall. That's where she'd seen it. She aimed the flashlight beam in that direction, panning slowly, until a faint gleam of rusty metal caught her eye.

There. And time was ticking.

Paige steeled herself and crawled into the blackness.

SEVEN

"I found myself in the blackness of a little room. When my eyes got used to the dark, I saw it." Chelsea shivered. *"The walls were crawling."*

Leslie Brymes smacked the book closed and tossed it beside her on the bed. Second time she'd read Milt Waking's true crime, and it was proving just as creepy as the first. Especially after two in the morning.

She sat up straight from her multiple pillows and stretched. Even though she didn't have to work in the morning, she really ought to be turning out the light. But reading *Web of Lies* was like drinking a triple-shot mocha at Java Joint. Felt good going down and left you zinging afterward. For the millionth time Leslie told herself she'd give ol' Milt a run for his money one day. With his suave good looks and nose for a story, the FOX News correspondent had waded into the thick of *three* nationally watched cases. He'd managed to help solve two of them, netting exclusive footage of the bad guys going down. The final case, which had occurred just last September, he'd written a book about. Man. Leslie would settle for half his good fortune.

She dropped against her pillows with a sigh. The very thought of running down a major news story sent a quiver through her veins. *Serious* quiver, like when Dwight Lomas kissed her on the dance floor at senior prom two years ago. *Whooey.*

But even that magical night couldn't really compare. Under the glittering dance lights, clad in her satin blue gown and feeling Dwight's lips on hers, she'd known the moment was ephemeral. They'd be graduating in a month, and Dwight had his plans lined up—duffle bags packed, he'd be down at the bus station in June, going off to the army along with his buddy Tim Edwards.

His buddy who came home early, in pieces, for burial.

Leslie scrunched her eyes closed. No, she wasn't going to think about *that* right now. She was thinking about making it big as a reporter—for the rest of her life. The constant dream she pursued in her head, even as she slogged at her computer day after day in the drab and messy little *Kanner Lake Times* office, chasing down information on lost pets and fender benders and the occasional theft. Edna San's move to town had been Leslie's first thrill of a major story, but even that had fizzled over time.

Kanner Lake was too quiet. What Leslie needed was to move to some major city. No doubt she'd have to start at the bottom of the heap, but in time she'd work her way up to television news anchor. Hey, she had the looks for it, right? Blonde and petite? High-cheekboned. Large brown eyes and perfect lips.

Okay, that last one sounded arrogant, but fact was fact.

Hold on to that pseudo confidence, girl. You're gonna need it.

Reality washed over Leslie in a chilling wave. She thumped her hand on the book and drummed her fingers against its slick cover. Truth was, she didn't possess near the courage she feigned. Deep down she wasn't sure of herself at all. Flamboyance and verve on the outside—and a sticky marshmallow within. Besides, how would she ever pay her own way out in the world on a lowly reporter's salary? Living in her parents' home—now there was some cheap rent. She did have that one classmate who'd left town as soon as she could and moved to Seattle, but Leslie didn't know her very well. Not real conducive to picking up the phone and asking if the gal needed a roomie.

Drat it all.

Leslie folded her arms and made a face at Milt Waking's book. Then picked it up with frustrated resignation, flipping pages to where she'd left off. She found the chapter, read two lines, and threw the book down again. It bounced off the mattress and plopped on the floor. Oh well. She'd let it lie until morning. Right now it was time for some serious *z*'s.

She threw all but one pillow off the bed and reached to turn off the reading lamp. Settled down in the darkness, seeking sleep. A little rejuvenation was all she needed. By morning Leslie Brymes would have her mojo back.

EIGHT

The smell hit Paige in the face. Dusty, stale. Rank with old rat droppings and the cutting, metallic scent of pipes and dirt. Darkness cloaked her with a palpable and ominous cold. As she crawled, the flashlight in her right hand banged against hard dirt, its circle of light jumping. Through her pants the uneven ground scratched at her knees. The farther she moved from the entrance, the more the blackness swallowed her whole.

Wait.

She stopped. She *had* taken out all the rat traps, hadn't she?

Balancing on her left hand, she shone the flashlight over the ground. Ridges and loose pieces of earth materialized under the arcing light, then faded. She saw no traps. Paige raised the flashlight a little, searching again for that telltale shine from the anchor. *There.* About twenty feet away. She held the flashlight in that direction and crawled forward.

The air chilled, the darkness congealing like cooling tar. Were the walls closing in? Paige resisted the urge to turn her head, check how far she'd come from the opening. If she looked back, she just might panic—

Something pierced her left palm. Paige gasped, drew back her hand. Tipped the light upon it. A small, sharp rock stuck into her skin. She set the flashlight down, lowered her hand into its beam, and used a shaking thumb and forefinger to pluck it out.

Why hadn't she kept her gloves on?

Picking up the flashlight, she forced herself forward. When she thought she could stand no more, she reached the anchor. She put the flashlight on the ground and studied the rusted metal. The long, thick chain was attached to its top. Its bottom lay more deeply buried than she remembered. The whole thing leaned to one side, only partly visible. What if she couldn't pull it out?

Her fingers tested the surrounding earth. Packed down tight. She balanced awkwardly on her knees, put one hand under each side of the anchor's bent horizontal section and lifted.

It didn't budge.

She tried again. No movement. A third time, her arm and pectoral muscles straining. The anchor didn't move an inch. It might as well have been cemented down.

Fresh fear cleated up Paige's chest. She *had* to get this thing out now. Dawn approached and she had nothing to weigh down the body she must bury in the lake. Paige imagined the sun rising— and herself stuck with Edna San's corpse. She would have no choice but to put it back in her hot tub, call the police.

Her life would be over.

Oh, please, God—somebody—help me.

She wrapped her fingers around the top of the anchor and alternately pushed and pulled, trying to loosen it. It gave way a tiny bit. She yanked the thing back and forth, harder, harder, beads of sweat itching her forehead. Still it hardly budged.

Paige dropped her hands and bent over her knees, drawing in rancid air, her chest heaving. She needed some kind of digging tool. She jerked up the flashlight, pointed it at her watch. Almost three thirty.

She had little more than thirty minutes of fully covering night.

With a small cry she shuffled around and crawled as fast as she could toward the opening. The knuckled ground beat at her hands, her knees, but she gave it no heed. Far ahead through the door she could see the dark-blue side of her car, its inside light on. The flashlight banged and bumped in her gripping fingers. She endured the suffocating darkness, the smell, her fear as she scuttled like the rats she'd once hunted. By the time she reached the crawl space door, her palms burned from scrapes.

Paige burst through the opening onto cold garage floor, gulping fresh air. She pushed to teetering feet, feeling the cramp of muscles too quickly extended. Stumbling around the car, averting her eyes from its gruesome cargo, she headed for Ryskie's heavy metal cabinet of garden tools in the far corner of the garage. The cabinet was a near antique and rusty, sitting on two-inch metal legs. Its door squeaked as she pulled it open. Her eyes darted across the shelves, over rakes and hoes, gardening shears and gloves. There—a hand trowel. Sharp at the end, meant for digging. She snatched it up, trotted back to the car, and retrieved her gloves. Might as well save what skin she had left on her palms.

At the crawl space door she sucked in fresh air, then into the blackness she returned, veering to the left, toward the anchor that would save her. The flashlight and trowel bumped and jostled against her glove-protected hands, the smell of ancient rodent droppings welcoming her back, mixing with the odor of her own terror-sluiced sweat. She pulled up to the anchor, breathing hard, little sounds spilling from her lips.

How much time had passed? Five minutes?

Dig, Paige.

She set down the flashlight and attacked the hardened earth with furious strokes of the trowel, both fists gripping its wooden handle. Again and again she stabbed the dirt, chipping, chipping away, around the front of the anchor, its sides. Perspiration rolled down her temples, the *thunk*, *thunk* of blade against stubborn ground ringing in her ears.

She threw down the trowel and yanked the anchor. Back and forth, back and forth, working it loose from the ground's mouth like a giant tooth.

Paige jerked up the trowel and hacked at the dirt once more, chunks flying. A particle landed in her eye and clawed. She let out a hiss, dropped her tool and smacked a hand over the eye, blinking rapidly, willing the cleansing tears to come. Her world blurred as she blink-pushed the dirt out. Then back to her digging, her movements increasingly jerky, panic-stricken. Minutes ticktocked, and soon the sun would thrust impatient fingers through the curtain of night.

Paige, dig!

She dropped the trowel to the ground. Wrapping both hands around the sides of the anchor, she breathed a prayer to the fates of the universe and pulled. The surrounding ground shifted, then split as if assaulted by an earthquake. Paige rocked again, harder—and the anchor gave way.

The force sent her tumbling onto her side.

No time to celebrate. She scrambled back to her knees, grabbed the flashlight. What to do with the trowel? She only had two hands. She awkwardly threw the trowel near the opening. It thumped somewhere in the darkness. She would find it on her way out.

She clutched the flashlight in one fist and dragged the anchor with the other, grunting at the heavy burden. Paige scuffled toward the garage and Edna San, seconds clickety-clacking in her head. As she neared the door, the flashlight beam hit the trowel. She grabbed it and threw it out of the crawl space. It landed on the garage floor with a loud clatter. Head down, Paige birthed like a frenzied woman-baby from the black chamber into the dim garage. She sprang to her feet and dragged the anchor and chain across the cement, wincing at the clanging it made.

At the gaping hatchback she set the flashlight on the garage floor, picked up the anchor and thunked it inside the car beside Edna's body. Gathered up the snaking chain and rattled it inside as well.

Paige glanced at her watch: 3:45.

She banged the hatchback door closed. Snatched up her flashlight with gloved hands. Ran to the driver's seat, slid inside, and hit the garage door button. No time for anything now. No time for second thoughts or fears or meticulous planning. The waning minutes of night mocked her, dared her to falter. She would not.

Paige started the car, memories of The Promise jumping into her mind. Was it less than two hours ago she'd believed some sugar-sweet premonition that she would soon find a sister? What a laugh. She'd found something all right—a dead woman in her hot tub.

The garage door stopped rolling. Paige set her jaw and drove into the diminishing darkness.

NINE

She has spilled sugar on the floor.

Seven-year-old Rachel Brandt stares at the white mess. What's she going to do? Her mommy's down the hall asleep on her bed. It's the middle of the afternoon on a Saturday. She stayed up with those people all Friday night, laughing and drinking and sniffing white powder stuff up her nose. The noise kept Rachel awake. She cleaned up the messes from the party this morning, but she's just hit the bag of sugar when she went to put away a plate and now the bag is on the floor, and sugar's everywhere, and her mommy will be *mad*. Mommy will hit her for sure. And in three days, on February 24, it's Rachel's birthday. What if Mommy won't buy her a present like she promised?

Well. *So what?*

Rachel shakes her head, making her long bangs bounce against her eyes. *I don't care, I don't care, I don't care.* So what if Mommy hits her? It's nothing new.

Rachel puts a hand on her hip, fingers sticking into her flesh. Maybe if she pushes them deep enough, she'll make a little hole through her skin, right to her bones. And maybe that will hurt enough so if Mommy beats her, she can think about her hip and won't feel the slaps as much.

She pushes her fingers in harder. Her hip begins to hurt. Too much. Rachel pulls her fingers away.

48

She stares at the spilled sugar. After a minute she puts the look on her face that her mommy calls "defiant." She's not sure what defiant means, but it must have something to do with her mouth feeling tight and her eyes getting slitty. Her muscles go hard, like to protect her body and her heart. Then suddenly all the hardness goes away, and she feels empty and cold and *caring* again. Caring that Mommy's blue eyes will look at Rachel with hate, and her cheekbones will stick out even more, and she'll hiss like a cat. Then she'll raise her arm and start slapping ...

Rachel bites her lip and looks at the sugar mess. She needs to fix this — quick.

Bending over, she yanks up the pink sugar bag. Plops it on the counter, far back from the edge. Then turns toward the sink and grabs the sponge. She wets it and gets down on her hands and knees, picking up sugar. When the sponge is full, she rinses it and pulls it across the floor again. She does this two more times.

She hears a sound from down the hall. A squeak from Mommy's bed.

Rachel's heart beats harder. There's a lot of sugar to clean, and she better get it all. *Stay asleep, Mommy, stay asleep.* She works faster, her mouth open so she can breathe all the air she needs, because suddenly she's feeling like she needs a *lot.*

More squeaks.

Rachel hears a bad word. Feet hitting bare floor.

Please.

Maybe her mommy will lie down again. Fall over on the bed like she does after she takes the drugs. Then Rachel will have time to clean up the mess, and Mommy will never know. Maybe she'll even have time to do something else for Mommy, like throw away old food in the refrigerator and clean the stove ...

A moan.

Uh-oh. Mommy has one of her "after party" headaches.

And the headaches make her mean.

Go, Rachel, go! She tries to work faster. But her eyes burn and the world goes blurry and she can't *see*. The floor feels hard on her knees, and the smell of dirty sponge makes her feel kind of sick. Her breath comes in little puffs as she wipes the floor, shoves to her feet and rinses the sponge. Back down again. Clean more sugar ... back on her feet to rinse ... down again.

The feet are walking. Down the hall, toward the kitchen.

No, no, no.

Rachel starts to make noises in her throat—noises she doesn't want to make but can't help. Hearing them only makes her more scared. Because now she knows what's going to happen, and she's *caring* so very much that she can't even find her defiant face. Her hand shakes, and she shoves the sponge back and forth, trying to find every little piece of sugar, knowing she'll never get it all.

"*What* are you doing?" Mommy spits the words.

Rachel's skin goes burning cold, like when you put a wet finger on ice and can't let go. She opens her mouth but can't make a sound.

"Rachel! I'm *talking* to you!"

Rachel's chest gets tight. She wants to keep her back toward Mommy to hide what she's doing, but then she won't know if a hand's coming down ...

She moves around on her knees, her fingers tight on the icky, smelly sponge. Mommy's hands are at the sides of her head. Her T-shirt has a purple stain on it. Her white-blonde hair sticks out like straw, and her cheeks look gray. She makes a bad face at Rachel.

Rachel wishes she were small like an ant so she could run away. "I'm just cleaning the floor."

Her mommy makes a noise like that dog did last year when it bit Rachel, and Mommy's boyfriend with the ponytail laughed because Rachel cried so hard, and she vowed she'd never cry again. "Why'd you pour sugar on it?"

Rachel pulls back, her heart going real hard. "I–I didn't pour it. It just spilled."

"All by itself?"

"No, it–"

"Don't lie to me, girl. *Ever.* You know what I have to do when you lie to me."

"But–"

"Nobody in this world loves you but your mommy." She points a finger at Rachel, the red nail polish chipped mostly off. Her voice gets louder. "I *won't* let you be a bad kid. I have to teach you right in this world."

"I already–"

Mommy moves so fast, Rachel doesn't have time to run. Her arm is yanked up–hard. Her head jerks back and her teeth hit together. Mommy pulls Rachel to her feet, the nails biting into her skin. Mommy's arm goes back, her fingers spread.

The slaps come. They *hurt.* Rachel wants to cry but she won't. She looks down inside herself, real deep, and pulls up her defiant face. The hard mouth and the slitty eyes. She will not cry.

Mommy hits again. And again. Pain rips at Rachel. But she doesn't care. She *doesn't.*

Not caring takes the hurt away.

Just a little.

TEN

Gravel popped beneath the tires as the SUV surged down the driveway toward Lakeshore Road. Paige remembered she hadn't closed the garage door, and had to stop abruptly and back up for the remote to work.

A precious minute lost.

Having explored the whole of Lakeshore Road, she knew where she was headed. Four miles winding south, then a left turn onto an old and rutted logging road—a curved, descending path through forest down close to the water's edge. There the lake was shallow for the first ten feet from shore, and then the bottom dropped away to a depth of about thirty feet. Locals had once used the area for a swimming hole, Paige had been told, but that was long ago, before a child stepped off that cliff and drowned.

On the road, the car's headlights cut through the darkness, illuminating flexuous asphalt with woods on either side. She bent over the wheel, shoulders taut, riding the accelerator and hard-braking for curves. Her wheels could not eat the pavement fast enough.

Questions and fears swirled through her brain. What if someone passed her, recognized the car? If pressed in the days to come, what reason could she possibly give for being out at this hour—on the night Edna San disappeared? Or what if she had an accident—rolled the car or couldn't restart the engine?

Paige slowed down.

Her eyes cut to the odometer. She'd gone one mile.

She pictured herself behind the counter of Simple Pleasures in just a few hours. Dead on her feet, scanning faces with paranoia. Trying to appear normal. Who out there would be watching her ... waiting ... wondering when Edna's body would be found? He — or maybe even she — wouldn't know Paige had been to the hot tub in the middle of the night. How many days before he began to suspect the truth?

Maybe it wouldn't matter. Maybe the mysterious disappearance of Edna's body would serve him just as well.

But he would know what Paige had done. Surely he'd be amazed, shocked. And he'd wonder why. What would he do?

What *could* he do? He'd trapped himself in his own fatal game.

A second mile gone.

Paige tight-rounded a curve in her Explorer-turned-hearse. In the hatchback the anchor's chain slinked and rattled. The sound sent shudders up her spine. She still had to drive another mile and a half. By the time she got down the logging road, did what she had to do, surely the sky would be lighting. She would have to make up some story in case someone saw her —

Headlights.

Paige braked, squinted through the trees to her left. Up ahead, where the road curved back on itself — hadn't she seen a wash of illumination?

Her pulse skidded. Paige clutched the steering wheel, jaw clenched. There, again, through the trees.

A car was coming.

Paige had no time to think, nowhere to go. The car would be around the bend in thirty seconds. She could only drive on, heart pounding in her ears. If she did anything else, it would look suspicious. The Explorer hit the top of the hairpin curve and she rotated the wheel, wishing, wishing she could turn her head away. The car approached, for a split second its headlights angled through her window into her eyes. Instinctively she drew back, squinting. The second stretched out, Paige imagining the stare of the other driver—a stare filled with the subliminal sense that something wasn't right.

The moment strained, then whipped by, Paige's death vehicle hurtling on into night.

Her throat constricted. What was she *doing*? What had she been thinking? In a day or two, when the town talked of nothing but Edna San's disappearance, when this night and this hour soared in significance, the driver she had just passed would not fail to remember this moment.

Still, Lakeshore Road wound around the entire lake, a twenty-six-mile route, with many homes set back from it on this side of the water. If the person hadn't seen her face or noticed her make or color of car, police should find the lead of little worth.

The turnoff approached. Paige slowed, afraid to miss it. The logging road's entrance was overgrown and easy to overlook, even in daylight. She spotted it almost too late, braked hard, and cranked the steering wheel to the left. The car bounced over rough terrain, the anchor chain rattling ... and something thumping. Edna's body, shifting? Paige's nerves pricked with the bites of a thousand fire ants. A horror movie scene materialized in her mind: *Edna's limbs jerking alive, her eyeballs darting. Up, up she rises, sitting straight, turning about, seeking a target for vengeance. She drags her zombie limbs over the back of the rear seat, clawlike hands reaching for her captor ...*

Paige checked the rearview mirror, seeking movement—

The Explorer's wheels hit a deep rut. Paige jounced, hit her left elbow on the door. She cursed at the pain through clenched teeth. Pushing the brake harder, she eased around a curve. One more bend and she would reach the lake. She had to stop now, unwilling to chance some early riser across the water noticing her headlights.

Paige halted the car. Cut the engine and the lights. The world fell into darkness.

She could hear her own heartbeat.

Paige felt for the flashlight on the passenger seat. Before exiting the car, she hit the switch to the dome light so it wouldn't turn on. She slid out quickly and shut the door. Turning on the flashlight, she aimed it at the ground and picked her way to the rear of the car. Opened the hatchback.

Seconds ticked away. She could feel them slipping, slipping through her fingers. *Get moving!*

Still she hesitated. She would have to drag Edna around the bend and down to the water. Should she wrap the anchor up with the body, try to move it all at once? Or make two trips?

Paige bit her lip, forcing her frenetic mind to think clearly.

No time for two trips. She would have to take care of the chaining here.

And no time for any slipups. Or fear or disgust at what she must do.

Paige set the flashlight down on its side in the car, aimed at the body. First she hauled the anchor onto the packed and rocky dirt at her feet, followed by the length of its chain. She tried desperately to be quiet, but the anchor and chain clanked in the still night. She froze a moment, listening.

Nothing. No cicadas even. The noises had frightened them into anxious silence.

Gathering the end of the bedsheet in both hands, Paige set her jaw, dug her heels into the ground, and pulled backward. Edna's body slid over the edge of the hatchback and thumped in a white mummified slash upon the grayed road. Paige snatched up the flashlight and set it on the ground. Its illumination caught a slivered opening in the sheet around Edna's face. An accusing eye gleamed at her.

"Ah!" Paige jerked backed, every nerve tingling. Fighting the irrational terror that any moment Edna's hands would reach for her throat.

She swallowed hard. *Don't think. Just do.*

She reached up to shut the hatchback door.

Paige pulled the sheet folds away from the corpse. She rolled the body on its side, then pulled the anchor and chain up close. Sweat slid into her eyes, and she wiped it away with the back of a gloved hand.

Only then did the difficulty of the task hit her. How to weight the body so it wouldn't work loose from the chain underwater?

Fresh panic surged up her throat. She couldn't do this. How many murder trials had been built upon the stubborn rising of a body from a watery grave? Edna San needed to *stay* at the bottom of the lake. If she was pulled up a day, a week, even months later, wouldn't they find evidence? What if the police sent divers down and they discovered the anchor? Could they trace it to Paige's rented home? Would Mr. Ryskie recognize it?

Paige let out a strangled cry. She hadn't thought this through. Not at all. And now she was running out of time.

She glanced up at the sky—and saw the first blush of light.

ELEVEN

Draped upon his couch, Black Mamba's hooded eyes gazed out the window at the first streak of light across dark water. He'd pulled a throw blanket over himself for warmth. Even in summer weather he despised the predawn chill. True brother to his cold-blooded namesake, he preferred basking in the sun at noon.

But he'd been given the title for far different reasons.

Black mamba—one of the world's deadliest snakes. Even its head is coffin-shaped. Its neurotoxic bite is one hundred percent fatal without antivenin. It's also the world's swiftest snake, reaching up to seven miles an hour in short bursts. Fast enough to catch a fleeing child.

The snake plays with its prey. It bites with the longest of fangs, then waits. Confident. Silent. Watching the slowly paralyzed squirrel or rat stagger away, hide in a burrow. Then, uncurling its sleek body—up to fourteen feet long—it smugly slides after the animal. Drags it out. And swallows it whole.

Mamba approved of this name.

He reveled in the deed finally done. His slim body felt almost fat and slothful with satiety, as would a snake engorged after its meal. For the next hour he wanted nothing but to coil up and watch the coming dawn.

A pretty town, Kanner Lake. An innocent place. Open and welcoming, unaware of his stealthy slither among its denizens. Idly he wondered what would become of Kanner Lake once the news hit. People were scurrilously fickle. One black mark against a delightful retreat, and visitors could melt away like snails in the sun.

Even cautious Edna San had fallen prey to the area's laid-back ways. Her driveway was gated, but the surrounding forest was not. Her house was equipped with an alarm, yet it remained deactivated while she was home during the day. Mamba lifted his head, stretching his neck muscles from side to side. Actually, he shouldn't be surprised at that. Even avid night users didn't turn on a system during the day, when a warning chime would sound every time someone opened a door or window. This had worked in his favor on many an occasion. What good is an alarm if an intruder has already breached the house before it's set?

He smiled.

Some years ago he'd faced the unfortunate but necessary task of removing the key witness for the upcoming murder trial of one of his business associates. The woman was the victim's grieving wife—around thirty-five, mother of three young children. Highly paranoid since the death of her husband, she fortressed herself and the kids in her extensively alarmed house. But they owned a cat. One night the cat slipped outside, right through the legs of the three-year-old girl. She and her older brother ran to catch it.

Mamba slid inside the house.

He hugged shadowed corners and silent rooms, waiting, listening as the nervous mother herded her children back into the house, locked the doors.

Before she could activate the alarm, he struck. As she lay moaning, pleading for her children, he urged the alarm's code from her lips.

He was forced to kill the children too. They'd seen his face. But they died quickly, painlessly.

The strewn bodies were discovered two days later in the locked house with the burglar alarm activated. No sign of forced entry, reported the media. No foreign fingerprints.

By then Mamba was sunning himself at the beach.

Without the witness, the prosecution's case took a fatal hit. Mamba's colleague walked free.

He stretched his languid limbs. Those killings had been more of an annoyance. But *this* one was for him. Others among his secret associates could have done the job, but they lacked the patience to stalk, to scheme an ingenious plan. He needed to do just that to prove himself to his superiors. What he had lost through letting down his guard, he would regain.

They would applaud his creativity.

He sighed with satisfaction, gazing at the lake. The water glimmered under the faint moon like cooling obsidian. The sight lulled him, drugged him. His eyelids drooped ...

Black Mamba slipped off the couch and into bed, where he succumbed to a blissful and well-deserved sleep.

TWELVE

Amazing how the mind conceals unfathomed depths of strength. Two hours ago Paige could not have conceived of herself in such a ghoulish situation. Now her brain hummed and churned, pushing aside emotion, seeking new pathways of action.

She needed to wrap the body. Fast. Drag the chain around and around from neck to feet, over chest and under spine, down the legs. And pray it would never come loose.

She would start with the anchor end.

For long seconds Paige pawed at the chain, pulling the anchor close to Edna's shoulder. She heaped the bulk of the chain over the body, raised Edna's arms high, and worked the first taut links right up to the armpits. The smell of rust, dirt, and wet, death-perfumed silk swept into her nose.

Paige rocked Edna's body toward her own and pushed the length of the chain underneath Edna's side as far as possible. Then she rocked the body the other way, fingers scrabbling to work the chain beneath the torso. Back and forth, back and forth she maneuvered the body, wrapping the chain around two, three, four times. She tugged and rolled, her slackened lips puffing. When the chain looped around the torso five times, she ran it around another five, this time pinning the arms. Then she turned the body onto its back and threaded the links underneath the thighs, up and over the tops of both legs. Again and again she pushed and tightened the chain, taking it down to the knees, the calves, the ankles.

About two feet of chain remained.

Sweating profusely, Paige wove the extra links in and out of the leg coils until she reached the end.

She sat back and gazed at her work.

The indignity of murder. Edna San, revered seventy-something actress, stunning beauty in her day, lay on her back, eyes piercing the heavens with glittering violation. Her bleached hair was matted and snarled, her body swathed in rusted links.

Paige's eyes narrowed. What if the job was too sloppy? What if the chain worked free?

She should have brought a lock. At least she could have secured that last link to a coil. Too late. What was done was done.

Now to get the body into the water.

Paige pushed to her feet. Above Edna's head she bunched the extra sheet together in both hands and prepared to tug backward—

The flashlight.

Paige pulled up short. How was she going to hold the flashlight and move Edna's body at the same time? She needed both hands to pull. Gazing past the soaring treetops, she studied the sky. Was it just her imagination, or was it lightening with every second?

She grabbed the flashlight. Hurrying past the car to the top of the bend, she aimed the illuminating arc down the rocky road and toward the water some thirty feet away, memorizing ruts in her path. The road ended about eight feet from the water. Then down a slight hill and she would enter the lake.

It would be cold. Replenished in spring from the winter snow's runoff, Kanner Lake had the reputation of not warming completely until August. But Paige didn't care how chilly the lake would be. Her muscles burned, and she almost longed for the shock of frigid water.

She checked the sky again.

Paige set down the flashlight, aiming its beam in the direction she would go. She scurried back to the body, wrapped her hands around the bedsheet, and pulled.

Edna San began to slide.

Paige moved backward on the balls of her feet, picking up speed. Her teeth clenched, and she could feel the cords of her neck pushing out, pulsing. The body moved a foot, then two. Three. Four. A chant rose in her brain—*Go, go, go, go.* Paige's arm and shoulder ligaments burned, but she couldn't lose her momentum. Back she shuffled, looking over her shoulder for direction, Edna's iron-wrapped body and the anchor scraping and clanking over protesting earth. The flashlight now aimed at Edna's bouncing feet as if to say, *Look, see the crime being committed, the evil performed!*

Paige's jaw creaked open, air piercing like nails in her throat. *Don't stop now. Go, go, go!* The flashlight receded with every step. Sweat trickled down Paige's forehead and into her eyes. She blinked hard and kept moving.

She stumbled off the road onto soft earth, fought to regain her balance, then fell hard, teeth clacking. Scrambling up, she swept up the sheet once more and pulled until Edna's entire body left the road. A second's rest, then Paige hauled again. *Chink-chink* went the chain and anchor.

Paige's right foot splashed into water. No time to flinch, no time to *think.* She stepped backward, trying to watch her footing. The water wrapped cold fingers around her ankles, her shins. For a moment Paige could almost believe the lake had come alive, sought to draw both her and Edna into its grave. She fought to push the thought away, focus only on the splashing of her legs, the chill creeping up to her knees. The squishy *chink* of

Edna's body sliding from dirt into the expectant and carnivorous Kanner Lake.

The corpse sank immediately into the soft mud of the shallow lake bottom.

Paige clung to the sheet, feeling the pull of Edna's body. She shook and tugged then, trying to yank the sheet from under the corpse. Edna's hair floated up like fine seaweed, tickling Paige's legs as it had in the hot tub. She fisted the sheet little by little, and with the help of the water, rocked Edna off.

The sheet came free. Paige gathered up the sopping fabric, waded a few steps toward shore, and tossed it onto the dirt. Only then did she realize—she could *see* the dirt better than before, and the lapping water.

Daylight was coming.

Paige threw herself into the lake, its chill smacking her in the chest, the neck. She thrashed around, seeking Edna's body. Her fingers brushed skin. She sensed the form of a cheek, two of her fingers slipping into an open mouth, scraping teeth. Paige gasped, her mind filling with a vision of Edna biting off her fingers. She snatched back her hand, caught Edna by the chain links around her shoulders, and pulled.

The body came easily now, already growing accustomed to the lesser gravity of its coffin. Paige waded until the water reached her waist, preparing herself for the sudden drop of earth beneath her feet. One final heave backward, and Paige found herself swimming a one-handed dog paddle, still gripping the chain. The body's legs scraped the mud before the cliff. Paige treaded the frigid water, angling her head up to breathe, seeking leverage to pull.

Two more hand strokes, and Edna's corpse launched itself off the cliff.

The sudden weight yanked Paige under.

Water shot up her nose. Her body jolted to its side, pulled down by her left hand. The world muffled; hard bubbles pinged against her ears. Her eyes opened wide in terror but she saw only blackness. She struggled to pull Edna up, wanting to take her further from shore, but the drag was too vicious.

Let go!

Paige's fingers uncurled but the chain caught her knuckles. She shook her arm violently, trying to wrench away. The metal clutched her hand like some ravenous monster come to life.

More bubbles echoed in Paige's ears. Rolled in taunting little balls up her face.

Time flattened into a long, dark void.

As Paige sank, as she fought, her mind screamed against the irony. In death, Edna San had found a way to destroy her. Paige was going to die here, now. Die for the choice she made to save herself.

THIRTEEN

Mom has brought a new boyfriend home to live.

Rachel sits cross-legged on her bed, trying to do math home-work. Loud music from the den beats through her thin bedroom walls. R. Kelly — Mr. "Bump 'n' Grind." Rachel hates R. Kelly.

How many boyfriends does this make? Rachel has lost count. Only ten years old, and surely she's seen her mother with at least a dozen different ones. They've been fat, skinny, tall, short.

All have been ugly, as far as she's concerned.

Every time it ends the same. Her mom and the guy have some huge fight, and he knocks her around, and she slaps him and pulls his hair. They both scream nasty names at each other. He bangs out the door, yelling that he's had it with her, and she can just blankety-blank pay her own rent from now on.

Until the next guy comes along, it's quiet in the house. Well, as quiet as it can be, living with a mother like Rosa Brandt. At least then Rachel only has to worry about being hit by one adult instead of two.

This new guy's name is Wayne. No last name. Just Wayne.

He's tall and skinny like a telephone pole. Has a mean look in his beady eyes. He smokes cigarettes all day and his breath stinks. He's got needle marks on his arm and the knobbiest knees Rachel has ever seen.

What does her mother see in this guy?

Not that it's any of Rachel's business. She goes to school, does her homework, cleans the house, waits on her mom and the boy-friend-of-the-month, and otherwise tries to stay out of the way. Most of the time she's in her room. There she dreams about being popular and having friends come over after school. Living in a big, pretty house with a nice mom who lets her have sleepovers. On Saturdays she goes swimming with her dozens of friends, maybe to the movies. They watch TV at night and eat popcorn. And three or four boys, all very cute, like her at once ...

Thump-thump pounds the bass drum, going right into her chest. Rachel presses her hands over her ears and reads the math prob-lem for the fifth time.

"Raachell!"

She jerks up straight at the screeching voice. Anger rises within her so quickly, it scares her. She jumps off the bed, opens her bedroom door. The music hits her in the face. She trots down the hall into the den. Her mom and Wayne are slouched on the sofa, eyes slitted open. How can they *stand* the noise? Rachel has to yell over it.

"What?"

Wayne scratches his scruffy face slowly, like he's thinking very wise and wondrous thoughts. Rachel fastens on the long nail of his little finger. His mouth moves. Rachel can't hear what he's saying. She turns down the volume on the stereo.

"Hey!" Mom's voice sounds thick. "Turn that music back up, *now.*"

Rachel surveys her mom, calculating. The woman's too high to move very fast. Wayne doesn't look much better. But Rachel doesn't know him well enough yet. He could surprise her.

Wayne waves a hand at her. "Get me some food, girl."

Rachel sets her jaw. "What do you want?"

One day she will be free from this.

"A turkey sandwich. Put lots of mayonnaise on it, and some pickles. And make it quick — I'm starving."

Rachel's gaze slides to her mom. She's slumping against Wayne, eyes closed. Head slightly swaying. "Do it, Rachel, or I'll beat the tar outta ya." The words flow like cold syrup.

In Rachel's mind she tells Wayne to make his own bleeping sandwich. Then like Superwoman she picks him up, hauls him to the door, and kicks him outside. Mom soon comes out of her fog and realizes how terribly she's treated Rachel, and she breaks down and cries and cries, saying she'll be the best mom in the whole world from now on, and ever after that she walks Rachel to school and helps with her homework and packs homemade cookies in her lunch —

"Rachel!" Wayne glares at her. "Go."

She turns toward the kitchen, her own anger bubbling.

At the battered refrigerator she pulls out leftover turkey, a loaf of bread, the mayonnaise. There are no pickles.

Don't hit me for that, Wayne; it's not my fault.

"Rachel! Get in here and put the music back up!"

She closes her eyes and sighs. Returns to the den, ratchets up the music. The noise slices through her head.

Back in the kitchen Rachel pulls out a knife to spread the mayonnaise thickly. She hopes she uses the right amount. If not, she'll pay.

She cleans up after herself, then takes the sandwich on a plate to Wayne. "Here." The bitter word drops from her mouth like stone.

Wayne's head comes off the couch. He narrows his eyes.

Fear prickles the back of Rachel's neck. What on earth was she thinking? She forces a smile. "Hope you like —"

Wayne's arm jerks out and catches her wrist. The sandwich flies off the plate and lands on the floor. He yanks Rachel close, his cigarette breath stale in her face. "Don't *ever* talk to me in that tone of voice. You hear?"

He shoves her backward. Rachel stumbles and falls, one arm whacking the coffee table. Pain shoots up her shoulder.

A minute later Rachel is back in the kitchen, teeth gritted, making another sandwich.

FOURTEEN

Paige's lungs shrieked for air. Any second now they would burst apart, exploding her trapped body into a million pieces. She shook her arm harder, desperately stroking upward with the other hand, fighting for even an inch of water and gaining none.

Still she sank.

In a final desperate move, she ceased fighting with her free hand. Paige plummeted faster. She forced her right arm down into the water, fumbling and pulling at the revengeful links that captured her left fingers. Yanking her knuckles from their grip.

The chain loosened.

Edna San's body slipped away.

Too late to reach the surface. Paige knew that. But her primal instinct would not heed impossibility. Frantically she swam upward in the darkness, lungs packed with pressure. Up and up, knowing her sin would sink her to the bottom of Kanner Lake to lie with Edna San—the telltale sheet and her car left at the scene.

Her mouth opened. Bubbles bounced upward with a muted clatter.

Paige stroked harder.

Like a launched missile, she erupted from the surface. Choking, thrashing furiously. She went under again, fought her way back up and broke into the night. Air stutter-creaked into her throat. Paige dropped her jaw, sucking precious oxygen. She started to sink a third time. Somehow her arms churned into a tread. Fighting to keep her head above water, she groaned in more air. Not enough. Never enough. Paige breathed and stroked, breathed and stroked.

Her limbs were weakening.

In a final defiance of death, Paige twisted her body toward shore. She threw out her arms, dragged her aching body toward safety.

Her kicking feet sank, seeking the feel of blessed earth.

Nothing.

Two more strokes.

Three.

Her toes hit the cliff. She heaved herself forward and let her legs sink. One foot touched bottom. The second.

Spluttering, Paige came to rest on squishy earth. For long, rending minutes she gulped air. Her limbs threatened to give way. She had to gather herself, get out of the lake. She sneezed and coughed. Pulled in more oxygen. Rubbed water from her eyes.

Mid-breath, the airflow stopped. Paige looked ahead, her heart stalling. The forest, the road. They were much lighter.

Paige threw herself toward shore, pushing through the water. It receded to her thighs, her knees. She splashed through the last ounces of it, hit shore and stumbled over the sheet. With an awkward two-step she caught herself, grabbed up the sodden, cold fabric, and scurried up to her car, wetness squishing in her shoes, goose bumps popping down her chilled arms. Her ears hurt from the cold.

She reached the Explorer, flung the sheet into the hatchback, then jumped into the driver's seat. Only when she slammed the door did her eyes fall on the path she'd created with Edna's body, as if some giant slug had dragged itself down the road. Air hitched in her throat. She stared at the signs of passage, then gazed at the sky.

No time. She had to get *out* of there.

Paige started the car, turned around, and sped up the road, bouncing, teeth clamped and heart racing. She'd done it now, no taking it back, and all she could do this day and forever was hope against hope that her deed would not be discovered.

Her near-death experience replayed in her brain.

Eons passed before she hit Lakeshore, turned right. She leaned on the accelerator, praying that no one would appear from the opposite direction. Her tires ate up the ground as she slouched over the steering wheel, already thinking that perhaps the following night she should return, dive into darkness, and somehow, some way drag Edna's body out farther, where it wouldn't be found …

After an eternity she reached her house. She'd passed no one.

She nudged into her garage before the door stopped rolling up. Shut off the engine.

Paige flung herself through the house, cleaning up after the deed. Tearing off her wet clothes, throwing them onto the bathroom floor along with the sheet and gloves. In her pajamas, she turned on the back deck light and trotted out to make sure she'd covered the hot tub. Checked briefly for any remaining bits of Edna San on the deck—a hair, a wayward piece of fabric. After a shower she would have to sweep the deck clean. She even remembered to run back into the garage, pick up the trowel and put it away. All these tasks she performed with her mind on hold, pushing her enervated body beyond its limits.

By the time she dragged herself into the kitchen for some much needed water, it was nearly five o'clock. Suddenly, as if a plug within her had disintegrated, her adrenaline and strength drained away. Paige sagged against the counter, knees weakening. Chills came, tearing into her body with a predator's fury. Wrapping trembling fingers around the lip of the sink, she found the stubbornness to stay on her feet.

Paige shook.

Twice she threw up in the sink.

Finally she stopped quivering. Paige straightened slowly. Whatever would become of her now? How could she live with this secret, with the constant fear of its discovery? She raised dull eyes to the window, the view of the lake that had once seemed so beautiful. No more. Parting the night sky were the pointing fingers of an accusing violet dawn.

Not until she was in the shower, scrubbing away the odor of Edna San, did Paige realize she'd left her flashlight at the lake.

PART TWO

Hunted

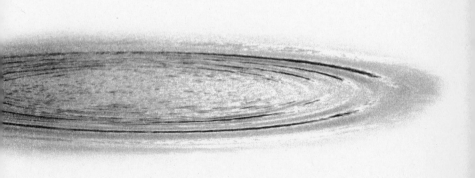

FIFTEEN

At seven thirty Vince Edwards pulled himself from bed with a sigh. Nancy had left for work over two hours ago. He hadn't woken to tell her good-bye. Vince's muscles were still tight and he barely felt rested. But the sun shone through his window and his inner clock ticked. He would find no more sleep this morning.

His headache lingered.

He planned to work around the house on this day off. Everyone in town knew tomorrow was the anniversary of Tim's death, and Vince didn't want to face their empathy, the sorrow in their eyes.

In the shower he dropped a new bar of soap, and the *thwap* against tile triggered the bomb in his head for the millionth time.

He raked up the soap, stuck it back into its silver holder. Hot water pound-pounded his body but could not wash away the pictures of Tim in his mind.

By rote he dressed. Khaki pants, a tucked-in brown golf shirt. Vince studied his face in the fading fog of the bathroom mirror, wondering how he could look so old at forty-five. He had a strong Roman nose, a wide jaw. A smile that once was quick. Women used to think him handsome. Now look at him. Lines around his eyes, down each side of his mouth. An expression of weariness and pain.

He reached into the medicine cabinet for two aspirin.

In his kitchen of country blue, Vince fried two eggs and three pieces of bacon. He pulled out a wooden chair from the table, its legs sputtering over the white tile. The salty, rich smell of his breakfast drifted up as he set down his meal and sank into his seat.

He'd taken three bites when the phone rang.

Vince glanced at it, chewing. He rose from his chair, reached toward the countertop for the phone. "Vince here."

"Hi, Chief. Sorry to bother you at home, but I've got something you'll want to know about."

Frank West's voice—the fresh-faced young police officer who would've reported for his shift at six a.m.

Vince set down his fork, dubious of the thinly veiled excitement in Frank's tone. The kid was solid enough, but he was only six months on the job and had a tendency toward the dramatic. Probably had something to do with those paperback crime novels he always read. "Okay, shoot."

"Edna San is missing."

Vince blinked. "Define 'missing.'"

"*Missing*, as in not where she's supposed to be. Which is at home."

"Who reported it?"

"Dispatch called a few minutes ago. Ms. San's assistant—you know that woman who's always driving her around?—was the one who phoned 911. Her name's Francesca Galvin. I just called her to get the story. Thought I should know a few details before I bothered you."

"Good thinking. Yeah, I know Francesca." Vince eyed his eggs. "What'd you find out?" He picked up his fork, slid a large bite into his mouth.

"Okay. She lives on Ms. San's property in a guest cottage. According to her, Ms. San takes breakfast in bed at seven o'clock —*every* morning. But today Ms. Galvin walked over to find an empty house. The burglar alarm wasn't on and some back door was unlocked. Things she said Ms. San would never allow. The master bedroom door was open. All Ms. San's stuff seemed to be there, even her purse. And her car's in the garage. But the bed hasn't been slept in."

Vince swallowed, not overly concerned. Edna San would likely turn up soon. Most missing people did. And this woman certainly had a mind of her own. "All right. Who's on duty this morning with you—Jim?"

With a population of seventeen hundred, Kanner Lake employed only five officers, including Vince. The four men under him worked ten-hour shifts, four days a week.

"Yeah. You want to meet me at the San estate, or you want him to go with me?"

No way could he stay home on this one, Vince thought. Movie Queen was just a little too famous. He didn't want any pointing fingers accusing that he'd taken Frank's call too lightly. Besides, if something really had happened to her, he'd feel terrible for not checking into it sooner. "No, I'd better get out there with you."

"Okay." Frank hesitated. "Chief, I think this might really *be* something. Ms. Galvin insisted this is highly unlike Ms. San. Said the woman just wouldn't go anywhere on her own, especially on foot."

Vince considered that. Edna San had managed to make numerous enemies in town before she even moved to Kanner Lake. With the sheer force of her reputation she'd managed to convince old, half-senile Wally Keller to part with a prime twenty acres of land long owned by his family. Poor man had wept buckets since then, claiming she'd snookered him in a weak moment. Everyone in town felt sorry for Wally, decrying that the price she'd paid was a fraction of what she should have offered—and could well afford.

Vince glanced at the sunflower clock on the kitchen wall—a present he'd surprised Nancy with years ago. She'd gotten teary-eyed at the gesture. It was almost eight o'clock. "Well, Frank, we'll check it out. I'll meet you at the San estate at eight fifteen. I'll bring a tape recorder. You bring your notebook and the camera."

Vince was used to running out of the house at a moment's notice. In short shrift he wolfed down his remaining breakfast, brushed his teeth, and changed into his uniform. He gathered his tape recorder and cell phone, locked up the house, and slid into his black-and-white police car. Soon, he hoped, Edna San would show up—and he could beat it back home.

He headed down Spram Street, where he and Nancy had lived for the past twenty years. They'd raised their daughter, Heather, in that home. And Tim.

Vince focused on the road, trying to push away the pictures in his mind. Tim as a little towhead, batting his first ball ... Tim riding his first bike ... On the lake with his dad, catching his first fish. Poor kid had gotten a terrible sunburn, and Nancy had been furious at Vince. Tim didn't care—he'd proudly displayed his three small fish, crimson face split with a grin ... Tim grown up, strapping and ready to take on the world. "Dad, I've enlisted. It's the right thing to do ..." Catching the bus to report for duty ... Hugging his dad for what would be the last time ...

The familiar hot laser seared Vince's gut.

Three quarters of a mile from his house he passed Main Street, home of downtown Kanner Lake—all four blocks of it. He headed toward Lakeshore Road and turned east. On his right the top end of the lake sparkled under morning sun, calm before the Jet Skiers and boaters churned its waves. Vince passed the city beach, also quiet at this early hour. Tourists would occupy it soon enough, venturing from the many B and Bs throughout town and around the lake. The temperature was supposed to reach eighty-nine today, and the air was already warm. Vince drove with his front windows down. Evergreen trees slid by. The northern Idaho smell of timber — sort of sweet, with a tang to it — drifted into the car.

He rounded the top of the lake and headed south. After about eight more minutes of driving, he reached Edna San's estate.

The ostentatious gate had been enough to rile many a Kanner Lake citizen. And surely not a local existed who hadn't driven out here to ogle the thing. It was made of heavy wrought iron, ornate enough for an English castle. A smoothly paved driveway, lined on either side with multicolored flowers, disappeared into the woods beyond the gate. Every inch of the surrounding forest floor was cleaned of dead branches and debris. A natural habitat, yes, but one pristine enough for Disneyland.

Red warning signs — Idaho Prime Security System — were affixed on either side of the gate. Another sign read Caution! Guard Dog on Duty. Vince glanced down the driveway but saw no dog. He hoped Francesca Galvin had thought to chain up the animal.

He climbed out of his car. Next to the gate he spotted a small bell. He pushed it.

"Yes?" A disembodied female voice sounded from a small speaker.

"It's Chief Edwards."

"Oh, good."

The gate swung open.

Seconds later Vince was easing down the perfectly poured driveway into the actress's private domain.

SIXTEEN

Paige swept the garage, her body numb with the mix of adrenaline and exhaustion. Around seven o'clock she'd tried to sleep for thirty minutes but ended up tossing and turning, realizing all the cleaning she had yet to do. Her final deed of the dawn certainly hadn't helped her relax. Horrified at her stupidity, she'd leapt out of the shower, thrown on clothes, and driven back to the mocking water to retrieve the flashlight, praying the whole way that no one would pass her on Lakeshore.

Two cars had. She had no idea who the drivers were. And now she refused to think about it. What was done was done.

She'd put the heavy flashlight away in the garage's metal cabinet.

Frowning, Paige concentrated on her work. Plenty remained to be cleaned, and by nine fifteen at the very latest she needed to be getting ready for work. She also had to eat some breakfast. Not that food had any appeal on this terrible morning, but she couldn't afford to faint behind the Simple Pleasures counter.

Right now every bit of dust on the garage floor, every piece of lint, had to be swept into a bin and thrown away in the forest. If the worst happened and someone did come here looking for clues of Edna, they would find none.

Paige leaned the broom against the wall. She'd swept from the back door to the car and now needed to move the Explorer to the driveway. She hit the button and the front door slid open.

The morning greeted her with a pine-scented breeze, the twittering of birds.

Another beautiful day in peaceful Kanner Lake.

She tipped back her head and closed her eyes. With the sunny sky and clear air, she wished she could convince herself that last night had been a nightmare. Terrifying and vivid but nothing more.

Not a chance. Even now the talons of its memory sank into her skin.

She climbed into the Explorer, all its windows down, and sniffed experimentally. The lingering smell was nearly gone. Earlier when she'd vacuumed the car, Paige had been aghast at the clinging odor—a nauseating combination of hot tub chemicals, wet silk, sodden perfume, and something akin to rotting vegetables. She'd rolled down all the windows in a hurry, praying the smell hadn't seeped into the damp carpet in back. The leather on the driver's seat had been toweled off, but the hatchback area would have to dry on its own. In the arid Idaho air, it shouldn't take long.

With the Explorer in the driveway, she returned to her sweeping. She could leave no sign of the path Edna's corpse had forged when she dragged it across the garage. And no piece of dirt tracked out from the crawl space. Paige clutched the broom handle hard, arms swinging. Her shoulders already ached from the work she'd performed last night. But she gave the discomfort little heed.

How long before they discovered Edna was missing?

Paige knew Edna had a live-in assistant—the gray-haired woman who drove her around town in the black Mercedes with tinted windows. Who shopped for her in the grocery store, took her clothes to the cleaners. Paige had never talked to this woman and knew little of Edna's habits other than the whispers she'd heard. Would the assistant think Edna had merely taken a walk in the woods? Or driven somewhere by herself—if her car was gone?

One thing Paige had learned during her month in Kanner Lake—Edna San was legendary in the area. Perhaps some liked the woman, but most citizens resented her mean-spiritedness and arrogance. Edna San seemed to think the small town was hers to run, apparently since Hollywood had worshiped her for so many years.

Whenever the news of her disappearance hit, Kanner Lake would be abuzz. And word would quickly spread. Reporters would descend—no stopping that.

Paige just had to lie low. Keep her face off camera. That shouldn't be hard. Who was she anyway but a new girl in town, the quiet and considerate helper in Simple Pleasures?

By eight forty-five Paige was satisfied that the garage floor lay clean.

Half an hour left to finish her tasks.

SEVENTEEN

Vince rounded the last bend of Edna San's driveway—and her magnificent house swept into view.

Wow.

His imaginings of this place hadn't done it justice. Under huge trees, perfectly groomed green lawns were edged with lush flowers of every color. The massive house of beige wood and stone rose two stories, with a pillared porch running its entire length. Arched, mullioned windows. To the right of the house Vince caught a glimpse of the backyard and the sparkling lake some one hundred yards beyond. To the left and in the trees some distance away, he spotted a small house made of similar stone.

Frank West's car was parked in the circular driveway. No doubt the kid was inside, trying his best to look professional as he ogled the place. Vince parked behind the vehicle and got out of his car, carrying his tape recorder. Mounting the three curved flagstone steps, he trod across the porch and rang the bell. Westminster chimes pealed in rich tones.

He winced. The sounds reminded him of the music at Tim's funeral. That horrible day, with the closed casket. The folding of the flag. Nancy's sobs.

From inside the house came footsteps. The huge carved door pulled back to reveal Francesca Galvin, looking as worn and worried as Vince had ever seen her. Francesca was a small, wiry woman in perhaps her midsixties, with the quick, efficient movements of a bird building a nest. Vince had talked to her on various occasions as she shopped or ran errands for Edna San. With her focused, no-nonsense attitude, the gray-haired assistant always appeared in calm control of any situation. But not so this morning.

"Come in, come in." She beckoned him with a fluttering hand, her forehead etched. The minute he stepped over the threshold, she shut the door with a leery glance outside, as if he were chased by phantoms. He glanced around, noting the gleaming tile floor of the entryway, a curving staircase to the left, formal living room to the right—

"Hi, Chief." Frank West appeared through a door directly ahead, walking straight-backed and with an air of solemn efficiency. He carried a notebook with a pen stuck in its spiral binding, camera slung over his shoulder. One hand rested on his hip, close to his gun. His serious expression mixed focused intent with an almost boyish anticipation.

"Morning, Frank."

The kid ran a hand through his short-cropped brown hair. "I was just looking around the kitchen. Ms. Galvin"—he nodded toward Francesca—"informed me that the keys to Ms. San's Benz are always kept in a certain drawer, and they're there. And the car's in the garage."

Francesca ran her tongue over her lips, thrust her right hand to the base of her neck. Tangible anxiety emanated from her, nudging her other hand to pull at the fabric of her tan slacks. Vince nodded to her. "I know you've been over some things already, but I need to hear it from the beginning. Where's a good place for us to sit?"

"Yes." Francesca's nervous fingers roamed to her blouse. "Come this way. We'll talk at the dining room table."

Vince and Frank exchanged a glance as she scurried ahead of them, leading the way. In a missing person's case, the last one to

see the person was always the first suspect. Vince had been picking up Francesca's nonverbal cues since she opened the door.
The woman was clearly uneasy. Could be no more than concern
for her employer. Could be more.

Vince's head pounded. He hoped the aspirin would kick in
soon.

Francesca led them down a short, wide hall off the kitchen
and into the formal dining room. A gleaming cherrywood table
rested beneath a crystal chandelier, and a matching hutch displayed china and finely fluted goblets. Vince hesitated at the
table, afraid his tape recorder would scratch it.

"Wait, please." Francesca pulled a blue silk placemat from a
drawer of the hutch and laid it on the table. "Here." She shot him
a tight smile.

"Thanks." He placed the tape recorder on the mat and pulled
out a chair. Frank sat at the end of the table, leaving Francesca
to sit opposite Vince.

"Don't let this bother you." Vince pointed to the machine.
"It's just routine. This way we won't miss anything you say. It's a
backup to Officer West's notes."

Francesca placed her elbows on the table, hands clasped, and
nodded.

Vince started the tape, stating the obligatory introduction of
time, date, place, and names of those present. His first objective
was to learn the habits of Ms. San—any piece of information that
might become relevant should the woman fail to appear soon.
He opened with the standard general questions for a missing
person of Ms. San's age. Did she have illnesses? Was she on any
medication? Any sign or diagnosis of Alzheimer's? How about
stroke? Had she ever disappeared like this before? Did she tend
to go off for walks by herself?

According to Francesca, Ms. San was in perfect health and
extremely proud of it. "Not even medication for cholesterol," she

said. And no, Ms. San would not disappear like this; it was highly irregular; and would they *please* do something about it *now*?

Francesca drew a breath. "Another important thing I haven't had the chance to tell you—the dog is missing."

Frank looked up from his notes, eyebrows rising. "We saw the sign out front. What kind of dog?"

"A trained Doberman." Francesca's gaze roamed to the window overlooking the backyard. "His name is Bravo. I feed him every morning on the back patio. He's always there, waiting for me. But not this morning. I called and called for him."

Vince rubbed his forehead. This didn't sound good. Dogs were habitual creatures, not likely to miss a meal.

"Would Ms. San take him on a walk?"

"No, never. Edna doesn't like dogs. Bravo wasn't a companion. He was a servant."

A servant. Something in her voice as she spoke the word. Bitterness?

Francesca's tone remained tight. "And the french doors in the kitchen that lead out to the patio were unlocked, and the burglar alarm deactivated, even though it's always on at night. I turn it off when I arrive each morning." She locked eyes with Vince. "Please. You have to start looking for Ms. San."

"I understand your concern. But it's important we gather all the facts first." He held Francesca's gaze. "All right?"

Briefly she nodded.

"Back to the dog." Vince shifted in his chair. "Anyone but you and Ms. San know Bravo? Anyone else he'd be friendly with?"

"No. He was trained to be vicious with anyone who set foot on the property. He would bark and snarl, and attack if I or Ms. San gave the command."

"What about gardeners? You must have a lot of people taking care of property like this."

Francesca nodded. "A crew of three comes once a week and spends most of the afternoon. I put Bravo in the garage while they're here."

"What's the name of their company?"

"Sprenger Lawn and Garden. They're out of Spokane."

Spokane. How like Edna San to hire a gardening crew from that far away when there were plenty in the area. Part of her "Keep your distance, Kanner Lake" persona.

"All right." Vince waited while Frank caught up with his notes. "Ms. Galvin, Officer West indicated that you have a routine with Ms. San. Tell us what you did last night and what happened this morning."

Francesca launched into her story, revealing Ms. San's pampered lifestyle. Francesca's last responsibility each day was to draw a bath to be ready at 9:00 p.m. Ms. San would take the bath, then read in bed until she fell asleep. Last night all seemed normal. About 9:15 Francesca retired to her own quarters, the house Vince had seen tucked in the trees. Upon leaving the main house, she ensured that the alarm was on. In her own home, she felt tired and went to bed soon. At 6:00 a.m. she got up, letting herself into Edna's house about 6:40. The warning beep for the alarm did not sound when she opened a side door with her key. At the control pad in the kitchen, she discovered the alarm had been deactivated. She also noticed the french doors hanging slightly open.

As Francesca talked, Vince watched her body language, her eye movements, for any sign of deception. He glanced at her carotid artery. Was her pulse beating faster than normal? Didn't seem to be. Sometimes a woman's neck would show telltale red blotches, but Vince noticed nothing of that nature either. And lying eyes tended to pull toward the dominant side. Francesca was clearly right-handed, but a number of times she glanced left when thinking.

Normally, Francesca continued, she would first feed the dog, who would be waiting with impatience for his one meal of the day. But this morning—no Bravo. She walked out to the deck, called his name. He failed to appear. She could have begun preparing breakfast—a bagel with cream cheese, fresh fruit compote, and black coffee, but the unusual circumstances alarmed her. Francesca mounted the stairs to check on Ms. San. The master bedroom door stood wide open. The bed was still made from yesterday. Francesca looked about the room but noticed nothing missing. In the closet sat Ms. San's purse with sunglasses inside. "She'd never go anywhere in the summer without those sunglasses," she added.

Frank tapped his pen against the notebook. "About the bed. Any chance she'd have gotten up and made it herself?"

Francesca gave a small smile. "Ms. San wouldn't know how to make a bed if her life depended on it."

There was that tone again—that something. Resentment toward Ms. San? "Was the bathwater still in the tub?"

"Yes. But that's typical. I let it out in the morning and clean the tub. I also take care of the clothes she's dropped on the floor. But today—no clothes."

"Is the water still there?"

"Of course. I hardly worried about letting it out, what with my concern for Ms. San."

"Good." Vince could see her rising impatience. "Almost done here, and then we'll check around. First—anything unusual in the house lately? Any threatening phone calls? Someone trying to get on the property? Maybe someone in town threatening Ms. San?"

Francesca's gaze dropped to the table, her forehead creasing. "There is something. I wouldn't have thought much about it, except now ..." She hesitated. "Ms. San tends to be abrasive. No doubt you know that. A lot of people don't know how to talk to her, and small things set her off." She raised her eyes to Vince, mouth tightening. Small wrinkles puckered above her lips. "There was an unfortunate incident in town yesterday morning. I wasn't present when it occurred, but I certainly heard about it—all the way home. Ms. San was absolutely livid."

Frank's pen poised over his notebook, questions on his face. Vince looked from him to Francesca, feeling a little tug in his gut—that inexplicable prescience he often felt when on the verge of hearing important information. "What happened?"

Francesca lifted her chin. "According to Ms. San, the girl who works at Simple Pleasures threatened to kill her."

EIGHTEEN

Rachel is sneaking out of the house.

She stands in front of the mirror, checking herself out. Not bad. She's thirteen but is dressed to look sixteen. At least. Makeup's done pretty decent. The black liner makes her eyes look extra big. Mascara lengthens her lashes. Her light-brown hair looks good against the red shirt, and her jeans are tight.

A towel is rolled up and pushed against her bedroom door, blocking any spill of light. She's supposed to be asleep.

Sure — on a Saturday night. While Rosa and latest boyfriend Jack get high with their druggie friends in the den.

Rachel's radio is quietly playing the Backstreet Boys — "Quit Playing Games with My Heart." She mouths the words, watching herself in the mirror as she churns her hips. Yeah. She moves like she knows what she's doing.

She glances at the clock radio's red digits. Nearly midnight. Time to skip this joint.

Off goes the music. And the light. A streetlamp sheds a dull circle of illumination through her open window — enough to see the bedcovers plumped up with pillows. Rachel slips the long strap of a small purse over her head and shoulder so the purse rests against the opposite hip. At the window she thrusts one leg out over the sill, leans low so she won't scrape her back, brings out the other leg, and drops four feet to the ground with a light thump. Hunched over, she scurries toward the street.

Suddenly — headlights. A latecomer to the Rosa Brandt party.

Rachel jerks back, heart thudding. Presses herself against the side of the house. If the person sees her and tells Rosa, she'll get beat for sure. A vision fills her head of the punches and how much they'll hurt. Jack will probably help ...

Yeah, well, things could be worse, the way he's been looking at her lately.

Rachel closes her eyes. Swallows hard. Waiting. Daring to pray. Even though God probably won't listen to a nobody teenager, especially when she's trying to slip out at night. Then again, if there is a God, He's put her in this position, so He owes her *something.*

Please, God. Don't let me be caught.

Rosa's raucous laughter tumbles through the night. Rachel pictures her mother in the yellow short skirt, spilling out of her low-cut blue top. Rosa's hair is now double-bleached, almost pure white. Stiff as straw. She's taken to wearing "dazzling pink" lipstick that borders on purple. And her blue eyes, once so pretty, now have a watery look.

The newcomers — sounds like a couple — greet Rosa. The man makes some lewd comment about her clothes, and Rosa responds with fake disapproval that drips with private pleasure. Rachel's heard that tone a thousand times, but tonight it sends a knife through her chest. The stab is sudden and brutal, and the pain radiates through her body. Hiding in the dark with the house's siding pressed against her back, Rachel feels the world open up and swallow her — the world with all its disappointment and hurt and overwhelming loneliness. For a crazy moment she longs to be with Rosa and the partying crowd, to laugh and drug it up and dance the night away, just so she can belong.

That's crazy, Rachel; you do belong. To her friends who await her at the beach. Carey and Stacey and Kim will be there, and that new guy in school, Brandon. Plus a dozen or so others. But something way down deep in Rachel's soul cries that they're all misfits just like she is. That none of them have parents who care, that they too are all desperately seeking *something* ...

Footsteps on the porch. Rosa and the couple are heading inside. The front door shuts.

Music kicks on.

Rachel lets out a shaky breath. And with it she blows out the nutty thoughts in her head. The pain in her chest disappears, and there's no knife, none at all. In fact, there is nothing left in its place but a sort of deadness.

Her friends are waiting.

She lingers another minute just to make sure all is clear. Then she runs diagonally toward the street, away from the hated house with its peeling paint and two wooden slats broken on the little porch. What is *wrong* with her, thinking even for a second she wanted to be a part of her mother's world?

She hits a corner and turns left. Down a block, walking swiftly now, and a right turn. As she spots the beach ahead, Rachel knows that somebody will bring weed for sure. They'll all sit in the circle, passing the joint. Rachel will sit with them but she won't smoke it. She hopes no one will make fun of her. So far everybody's been cool. But even if they do, she won't take one puff. The mere thought terrifies her. Rachel has seen and heard and *felt* what drugs have done to Rosa.

And if there's one person I never want to be like, it's my mother.

NINETEEN

Paige rubbed her forehead, fighting her tiredness and the vivid scenes flashing in her brain.

The tickle and bump of something in the hot tub.

Edna San's glazed eyes.

She shook her head. No time for remorse now, and certainly no time to slow down. She still had to clean the deck.

Paige forced herself through the garage back door, carrying the broom, and stopped in her tracks. *The grass.* Flat and smooth. The perfect path of Edna's body, from deck to door. In the dark, she hadn't noticed. Paige closed her eyes. Why had she thought merely using a sheet could keep this from happening? The makeshift gurney had only bent the grass all the more.

She let go of the broom. It fell onto the grass with a *shoosh*. Back in the garage she fetched a rake from the metal cabinet. Beginning just outside the garage door, she raked the flattened blades, nudging them to stand proud, point their chins toward the sun. She was careful not to dig too hard into the dirt. Kicking that up into the grass would leave its own telltale marks.

Marks.

In her house, her car. They were now being cleaned and swept away. But the stain in her mind and heart—wouldn't it be there forever?

For the millionth time Paige wished for that sister to talk to. She pushed away the thought. Even if The Promise she'd believed last night came true, she couldn't tell the closest friend in the world what she'd done. How wrong it would be to weight someone else with such a secret. That person would either have to tell or become a part of the crime herself.

Exactly what crime had she committed? Paige raked on, frowning. Tampering with evidence? Obstruction of justice? She'd heard the terms on TV but wasn't sure what they meant. One thing she did suspect—whatever the names for what she'd done, she'd go to jail if they caught her. Probably for a long time.

Paige backed up, raked another area. After a few minutes she stopped to check her work with narrowed eyes. It was better but certainly not perfect. There was no way to return every blade of grass to its former position.

She just had to hope nobody came looking.

She checked her watch. *Oh no.* Ten minutes after nine.

Swiftly Paige put away the rake, then returned outside to pick up the broom. She swept the deck with ferocity, taking extra care around the hot tub. When that was done, she hurried to the bathroom, peeled off her pajamas and threw them along with the clothes she'd worn last night—still wet and crumpled on the floor—into the washing machine. These were followed by the gloves she'd used and the sheet. She dumped in soap, pulled the silver knob. Water whooshed out as the cycle began.

In her bedroom Paige dressed for work in her typical under-stated colors. Dark jeans, flat sandals, a cream-colored knit top. Sarah Wray, her boss, would stand out in stark contrast, donned in bright hues of pink or orange or green, with sparkly shoes and chunky jewelry. Paige's short black hair had long since dried from her shower. She crossed to the bathroom to apply gel, working the strands upward into spikes. Next, makeup. With her smooth and tanned skin, she needed no foundation. Just a little blusher. She spent most of the time on her eyes—her best feature—donning various tones of shadow, liner, and mascara.

She pulled back from the mirror and studied herself. Green-blue eyes looked back at her. Were they the same as yesterday? Could anyone see the new secrets they held?

Paige picked up her watch, lying on the bathroom counter: nine forty-five.

Time to drive into town—and feign her way through an ordinary day.

TWENTY

Vince leaned back in his chair, studying Francesca's face. She had spoken of the alleged death threat toward Edna San with such factuality that for a moment Vince thought he'd misunderstood her words.

"The girl at Simple Pleasures?" Frank frowned at Vince. "Know who that is?"

Vince's gaze drifted to the tape recorder. "I've seen her a couple times. She's new in town."

And she wasn't easy to forget. Vince guessed she was in her early to midtwenties. A classic beauty with black hair cut far too short for his taste and the most incredible eyes he'd ever seen. They were a light, almost translucent green-blue. He'd nodded to the girl once at Java Joint, the coffee shop across the street from Simple Pleasures. She'd nodded back, then looked quickly away. Something about her had tugged at Vince. He'd sensed a painfulness about the girl, a loneliness.

He cleared his throat and looked to Francesca. "Tell us what you know about the incident."

She nodded. "As I said, I didn't see what happened. I was driving the car around for Ms. San, as there were no parking spaces directly outside. She had impulsively decided to go into Simple Pleasures to see if they had any silk flower arrangements. Why, I don't know. As I pulled up to the curb, she was waiting on the sidewalk absolutely *fuming*. Saying the—" Francesca tilted her head—"I won't say the name she called the girl. Saying the girl had been clumsy and should be fired. Ms. San had said as much to the owner of the store. When Ms. San was walking out, this girl apparently muttered the threat at her back—loud enough for others to hear. Words to the effect of wanting to strangle Ms. San."

Vince raised his eyebrows. "Do you know who was present to hear this, other than Ms. San and Sarah Wray?"

"No idea. I didn't even look into the store when I drove up. I don't know how far inside I could have seen through the windows anyway."

Vince exchanged a glance with Frank. This wasn't much to go on, but they'd have to investigate. He checked his watch. Time was ticking. "Ms. Galvin, all right if we go take a look at Ms. San's bedroom?"

"Yes, please." She pushed back her chair. "It's on the second floor."

As Vince rose, he realized his headache was gone. For now, anyway.

He picked up the tape recorder. Frank brought his notebook and camera. Francesca led them up the wide and lustrous staircase with sheened banister. Lining one wall of the staircase were photos of the Hollywood elite posed with Ms. San, dating years back. Vince recognized the faces of Audrey Hepburn, Cary Grant, Bette Davis, Doris Day. All of them perfectly poised and glamorous and arrayed. Not one family picture. Vince knew Ms. San had long ago divorced all four of her husbands but she did have two grown children. The coldness of that egocentric display of photos crept into Vince's veins, and he turned his eyes away. His thoughts skipped to his married daughter, Heather, and her little girl, Christy. How long had it been since he'd spent time with his granddaughter?

At the top of the staircase Francesca turned left, treading over a thick Persian rug. "Ms. San's quarters fill this side of the house," she said over her shoulder. They reached the open door and she stood aside, allowing them to enter.

Vince stepped inside, his gaze cruising the room. Edna San's "quarters" stretched long and wide, immaculately clean. Gold-colored drapes closed off all the windows, casting a rich glow across the white carpet. No piece of dirt or lint on the floor that he could see. No noticeable footprints. The gold comforter and pillows of the queen-size bed looked crisp and smoothed. Not so much as an indentation from someone sitting on the edge. The furniture was heavy and ornate, of polished cherrywood. An armoire and two matching dressers, all drawers closed. On the far wall hung a full-length mirror with a gold filigree frame. No immediately visible prints on the glass. To his right an over-stuffed armchair and small end table complete with lamp faced a marble fireplace. Two books lay on the table.

"Are the curtains typically closed like this?" Vince gestured toward the windows.

"Yes." Francesca stood with her arms folded and tight, as if to protect herself from the emptiness of the room. "I close them at night when I prepare Ms. San's bath. She doesn't like the summer sun coming in so early in the morning. It wakes her up."

Frank began taking photos of the room from various angles. They ventured next into the bathroom, Vince's eyes roaming, his brain cataloging every piece of information as Frank jotted notes.

The bathroom was enormous, with white tile, dual sinks with gold fixtures, and a Jacuzzi tub big enough for two. One corner housed a large shower. The toilet was in a separate room. A makeup counter and mirror ran the length of one wall. Vince and Frank walked to the tub and studied the water. Vince held the tape recorder in one hand and tested the temperature with his other. It was cold.

He straightened. "Do you put anything in the water for Ms. San? Bubble bath? Oil?"

"Some bubble bath, yes. Here, I'll show you." Francesca strode to a closet and withdrew a lavender bottle, handing it to Vince.

He set down the tape recorder and opened the bottle, sniffed it, then gave it back to her. Looked to the tub once more. Any bubbles were long since gone, but it seemed to him if Edna San had taken a bath in this water, the tub would be sporting more of a ring. "Ms. Galvin, what was she wearing when you last saw her?"

"Red pants and a white silk blouse."

"And you indicated if she had taken the bath, she'd have left these clothes on the floor?"

"Yes, actually here." Francesca pointed to about three feet of tile between the tub and wall.

"What about her closet?"

"We passed it, right before the bathroom." She turned and walked to a door, opened it wide.

"Zowie," Frank said under his breath as he peered inside. "Place is big enough to park a truck."

Vince retrieved his recorder before he and Frank stepped through the door. He spotted a hamper to his right and opened the lid. He saw some items, but no red pants and white blouse. He looked around at the racks and racks of clothes and shoes. Everything looked pristine and ordered.

They spent some time photographing the bathroom, tub, and closet. Then on to a thorough search of the house, Vince leaving the tape recorder on the kitchen table. They looked at the alarm system, making notes of how it worked and where the central keypad was located. Just in case they had to send out techs later that day, Vince asked Francesca for a plastic grocery store bag and tape. These he used to seal off the keypad, ensuring that any fingerprints upon it wouldn't be tainted.

As they searched the rest of the house, Vince questioned Francesca about Edna's son and daughter. Grant Wyman, son from Edna's first marriage, lived in Hillsborough, located in the Bay Area of California. Daughter Arela Clifford, product of Edna's second marriage, lived in San Diego. According to Francesca, their relationships with their mother were strained.

Vince's poker face remained intact but the word seared. Why had God chosen *his* son, one so close to him, to take away?

Next they checked the french doors off the kitchen. No sign of forced entry there. Neither had any other door or window been forced.

They stepped through the french doors onto the tiled patio in back. Near the edge, some fifteen feet away, Vince spotted something glinting in the sun. He walked over, Frank on his heels, and stooped. It was a stud earring, made for a pierced ear, with a golden heart. In the middle of the heart lay a small red stone.

Francesca bent over beside them, peering down at their find.

Vince looked up at her. "You recognize this?"

She shook her head. "It's certainly too cheap to be Ms. San's. And it isn't mine."

Vince looked back to the earring. Most likely a woman's piece. Then again, these days men wore some pretty odd things.

Frank shot Vince an excited glance. "I'll get a bag from my car." He pushed to his feet and hurried into the house. A moment later he returned with a paper evidence bag and gloves. Vince donned the right glove, then laid a long edge of the bag beside the earring. With his index finger he nudged the piece of jewelry inside.

A careful search around the patio and grass did not turn up the backing to the earring.

Shortly before ten o'clock the two men walked out the front door to search the immediate grounds, including the beach area, four-car garage, and a storage shed. They found nothing more. Following this, with Francesca along, they looked through her one-bedroom house.

No sign of Edna.

The woods remained. Not to mention a large lake.

Vince stood outside Francesca's house with hands on his hips, eyes scanning the deeper forest, his mind going a dozen directions. Francesca started on her way back to the main house, just in case someone with information about Ms. San should call. Frank waited for her to be out of earshot, then turned to Vince.

"Want me to run a background check on her now?"

"Yeah, go ahead. Also, call Sarah Wray at Simple Pleasures and find out the name of the girl working there yesterday. Just don't tell Sarah why you're asking. Run the girl's name too. Use your cell phone for now. Might as well keep this thing under wraps as long as we can."

"Okay." Frank pulled out his phone and started dialing.

The media tended to listen to police scanners, including the folks at the *Kanner Lake Times. Especially* the folks at *Kanner Lake Times.* Jared Moore had to find something to fill his six-page weekly paper. His assistant, Leslie Brymes, a childhood friend of Tim's, was particularly nosey. Came with the territory of being young and ambitious.

As Frank talked into his cell, Vince's eyes roamed the forest. *Where* was Edna San? Had she just walked into the woods at night with her dog? Maybe, but after finding that earring, Vince wasn't willing to take any chances. As soon as Frank's background checks were done, they'd need to call dispatch for search and rescue. One handler and a dog, plus one observer, should be able to cover the twenty acres in about an hour. In the meantime, in case this was foul play, they might as well go ahead and call Fairchild Air Force Base to put their thermal imaging chopper on standby. With its heat-seeking scanner, the helicopter could detect a body once it started to decompose—

His gaze fixed upon a black-brown object on the forest floor some distance away. *What is that?*

He strode toward it, eyes trained on the lump. As he grew closer, it took shape.

A dog. Lying on its side.

He hurried to it and bent down. Flies buzzed around his face.

The Doberman lay dead, shot between the eyes.

TWENTY-ONE

Paige sat on her stool behind the counter, watching the store customers with pretended calm. Sarah was in the back room, searching for a box to package an item. Paige could only hope no one would notice her frozen muscles. The sleepless night and fear of discovery nauseated her. Every sense felt on edge. The store's soft track lighting was too bright, voices too loud, the feel of the wood beneath her too hard.

Edna's body on the sheet, thumping down her deck steps. The blackness, the smell of rat droppings in the crawl space.

How could she live day after day with this terror of being caught?

A family wandered into the store—a couple trailing a bored-looking son of perhaps eleven and a daughter around thirteen. After a quick glance around, father and son announced they would wait outside. The girl drew Paige's eyes. She had long brown hair, a pixie face, and sported turquoise-colored braces.

"Good morning." Paige forced a smile.

"Hi." The woman glanced at Paige, then turned away to browse. Paige remained on her stool, vibrating with tension, and watched the woman feel the soft texture of a green woven throw blanket, pick up a painted goblet.

Who killed Edna San? The question bounced through Paige's head. It could be a woman, but she doubted it. Wouldn't a man's strength be needed to carry the body to her hot tub?

Was the man a tourist? Or did he live here?

Was he watching her?

"Excuse me. Could you tell me about these candles?"

Paige jumped at the voice. "Oh, sorry. Of course." She slid from her stool and walked around the counter, feeling the weight of her body with each step, the guilt that surely emanated from her. If this woman knew what her hands had done only hours before, she'd grab her daughter and run. Paige hoped her scraped palms wouldn't be noticed.

The daughter sidled up to Paige, staring openly. Paige's heart skipped a beat.

"You have such pretty eyes." The girl regarded her with a mixture of awe and wistfulness.

The words hit Paige in the chest. She'd heard the compliment many times before, but on this fateful morning it was the last thing she'd expected. The ancient ache rolled through her, sudden and swift. This young girl, with life stretching ahead, with a mother and father who loved her enough to take her on vacation, put braces on her teeth—did she know what she *had*? Paige felt herself smile, and before she knew it, she'd reached out to touch the girl's hair. "Thank you."

The girl grinned back, pleasure flushing her face. For a moment they locked gazes, until the hurt in Paige's throat forced her to blink away. She turned toward the girl's mother.

"These are oil lamp candles." Paige laid her hand against one of the largest, the color of sea green. "Beautiful, aren't they? They're one of our most popular items." She pulled out the wick, feeling the eyes of the girl upon her. "You pour the liquid paraffin in here, put the wick back on, and light it. You can also choose to add any of these oils for fragrance." Paige pointed to small bottles. The girl picked up one labeled Jasmine. "The candles look like ordinary wax candles, but they never burn down. No smoke, no dripping." She nodded to the girl. "Go ahead and open the bottle to smell, if you like."

The phone rang. Paige turned, searching for Sarah, who appeared from the back room, square white box in hand. "I'll get it, Paige." She hurried to the counter and picked up the receiver.

Paige continued talking to the mother and her daughter, answering further questions, chatting about their vacation in Kanner Lake. Sarah's voice faded to the background. Until a vague *something* caused Paige to glance over her shoulder at Sarah's face.

Had she heard her own name spoken?

Sarah's eyes cut to hers with alarm. Then abruptly she turned her back, bent over the phone. Her voice lowered.

Apprehension washed through Paige like acid.

She forced her gaze back to the mother and daughter, barely hearing their words. By rote she answered, mouth upturned, as if the world had not suddenly tilted on its axis.

Sarah hung up the phone. Paige dared not look at her. A young man who'd been perusing the store asked Sarah to help him choose a bracelet for his girlfriend, and she walked over to help.

Paige felt Sarah's eyes graze her profile as she passed.

Mother and daughter wanted three candles in various sizes and colors. A bottle of liquid paraffin. Fragrances of vanilla and lavender. Paige helped gather the items, place them on the counter. A smile pasted on her face, she wrapped and boxed the candles and accessories with the hands that had chained Edna San's body and dragged her into the lake. Then everything had to be tallied, placed into a bag. The bill paid. As she thanked the two customers, smiled one last time at the girl, Paige's ankles began to shake.

She sat on the stool, wondering if her rapid heartbeat could be seen through her shirt.

An eternity passed as the young man Sarah was helping wavered between selections.

Paige cast furtive glances toward Sarah's substantial figure. The woman's summery pants outfit of lime green and peach breathed of freshness and her ever-present sense of fun, but Paige sensed she was troubled. It was in her distracted answers to the customer, the thrust of fingers into her gray curls.

Finally the man made his choice. Paid for the bracelet. And left.

Paige felt frozen to her seat.

Sarah leaned against the counter to face her with a concerned expression, one hand playing with her chunky necklace of peach and green squares.

"What?" Paige forced innocent lightness into her tone.

Sarah eyed her. "Well, I'm not supposed to say anything, but now I'm worried about you. Is everything all right? Because a policeman just called, wanting to know your name."

TWENTY-TWO

Sunshine filtering through the closed curtains awoke Black Mamba. He found himself on his side, legs drawn up tight. In slow focus, his eyes sought the digital clock radio next to his bed: 10:06. How nice to sleep in on his day off.

Slowly he uncoiled himself, rolled onto his back.

For a few minutes he stared at the ceiling, sensations of the night an intoxicating susurration in his head. He reveled in the whispers, the memories of texture and smell, skin against skin as fingers encircled throat. The expression of terror, the proud brought low.

He would not have guessed how much he'd enjoy the deed.

Today would bring further pursuits.

He slid out of bed and pulled back the curtains. Blessed light streamed in, pooling on the hardwood floor. Mamba moved into the sun, basking in the warmth upon his shoulders. He remained there until thoroughly heated.

As he proceeded to the shower, his thoughts shifted to his planned movement through Kanner Lake. Stealth was not difficult for him. When he wanted to move unseen, he could glide with the perfect quiet of a snake through swamp, hugging shadows with lithe grace. And in public, at his weekly job about town, he maneuvered unsuspected. Black Mamba did not appear a killer any more than the snake looked its name. The serpent mamba wasn't really black. It was brownish gray, with a light-colored belly. Its name arose from the purple-black lining of its fatal mouth, which it displayed when threatened.

This Black Mamba had his own threats to carry out today. A certain young woman was going to pay for the sin of killing Edna San.

Shower done, he dressed, focusing on his tasks with the intensity of a hunter fixed on his prey. As he slipped outside to head for downtown Kanner Lake, hunger slunk through his stomach.

TWENTY-THREE

Bailey Truitt held the metal container of milk under her espresso machine and expertly whipped up foam. Her nose tickled from the biting smell of strong coffee blended with scents of cinnamon, pastries, and the unmistakable flowery perfume of real estate agent Carla Radling, who perched at the counter impatiently tapping her long red fingernails. *Tap, tap, tap.* Even over the gurgle of the latte in-the-making, the sound pecked at Bailey's nerves.

Lord, I'm so tired. Give me patience today. You know I need it.

"Would you cut that out!" Wilbur Hucks groused, and Carla's tapping stopped.

"Well, excuse me, Mr. Got Out of Bed on the Wrong Side." Carla sleeked her shiny black hair behind her ears and frowned at him.

"Hey, you two, no fighting at my counter." Bailey eased a good-natured tone into her words. "Do I have to tell you that every morning?" She poured the nonfat, biggie double latte into a to-go cup and set it before Carla. "There you are, fuel for the day. Where are you off to?"

Carla slipped a protective holder over the cup, flicking an annoyed blue-eyed glance at Wilbur. "I'm meeting some clients at ten thirty to show them property on Priest River, and I have a ton of paperwork to do before then." She stood up, gathering her

109

purse and latte, and leaned close to Wilbur's scruffy face. "And no, I *don't* want to see your scar."

He drew back with all the indignation his seventy-seven years could muster. "I didn't say a *word* about my scar this morning, you little pip-squeak." He mugged a face. "But now that you mention it ..." His hands went to his worn-out "I'd rather be hunting" shirt.

"Oh no, I'm out of here." Carla turned away just as the shirt began to reveal Wilbur's potbelly. "Don't scare the Ts off, Wilbur!" she called over her shoulder.

"Don't scare the Ts off, Wilbur," he singsonged, wagging his head. With a "humph" he hunched over his black cup of coffee, forearms flat against the counter and roughened red elbows sticking out. "If anybody scares the tourists around here, it's S-Man."

Bailey wiped down the espresso machine. "Come on now, Ted's entertaining and you know it."

Wilbur snorted. "So are monkeys, but they're locked in a zoo."

"Oh, Wilbur. You need a pastry this morning to sweeten you up."

"You say that every day. Just trying to take my hard-earned money, you are."

Bailey shook her head, her eyes roving over the coffee shop customers. Bev and Angie, both retired teachers, sat at their table by the door, discussing the day with serious intent. A colorful pair, as always. Bev's blue-white hair looked a bit frazzled. Tuesday, Bailey knew, she'd visit Phoebe's for her weekly shampoo and style. Angie's purple pants and red top screamed in stark contrast against Java Joint's yellow walls. Two tables down, Sidney Rykes, new shelf stocker at the IGA grocery store, read the *Spokesman Review* and sipped his caramel mocha. Catty-cornered from him, a young couple lingered over crumb-strewn plates with the languid postures of folks on vacation. Bailey heard snatches of their conversation. They were discussing which to do first, rent Jet Skis or go for a bike ride.

"Mornin' there, Belle Bailey." Hank Detcher walked in on schedule.

"Morning, Pastor." Bailey smiled at him, automatically reaching for a middler-size cup to make his double latte. Hank was in his fifties, a good-ol'-boy, love-everybody kind of guy, and the only man in town who could get away with calling Wilbur old. Bailey thought Hank's brown eyes, even with their early crow's-feet and tendency to squint nearly closed when he laughed, were the kindest she'd ever seen.

"How's the blogging going?" he asked.

Bailey had recently started a blog about Kanner Lake, posting Monday through Friday. Her goal was to introduce more people around the country to the town, subtly encouraging them to come for a visit. More tourists meant more business for her—and she needed that.

"Good. Don't know whether anybody out there's reading the thing yet, but people are having fun posting. You'll be seeing all kinds of stories from various townsfolk. It's fun. I'm determined to get a post from you up there soon."

"All right, keep houndin' me." Hank touched the bill of his faded red baseball cap and slid into the stool next to Wilbur. "Hey, old man, how ya healing?"

"Pretty good." Wilbur leaned away from Hank and pulled his shirt up high, revealing his gray-haired chest.

Hank inspected closely, drawing down the sides of his mouth, then nodded.

"Been four weeks now and my heart's stronger 'n a bull pup." Wilbur lowered his shirt with pride. "Can't keep a good man down, I'm telling ya, not even with a triple bypass."

"That's the truth." Hank turned to Bailey. "How's John today?"

Unexpected tears bit Bailey's eyes. She focused on her work and blinked them away, then forced a smile. "He had a mild seizure last night and passed out. He's extra tired this morning. I gave him breakfast in bed, and he was still resting when I left." She set the latte before Hank.

Wilbur grunted. "Sorry, Bailey, I didn't know."

Hank gazed at her with concern. "Bailey, I'm so sorry. I know you hate to leave him on a day like this. How about if I drop in on him before lunch?" He pulled out his typical four dollars to pay for the three-dollar drink.

Bailey nodded, her throat tight. "I would appreciate that so much."

A familiar thump sounded at the open door. "Shnakvorum rikoyoch!"

"Oh boy, here he comes." Hitching his shoulders, Wilbur sank lower over his coffee.

"Hey, S-Man." Hank turned to greet him.

"Hi, Ted." Bailey watched the logger-turned-author gimp inside using his single crutch, his casted leg thunking on the tile. The two Ts in the shop watched him curiously. Over his shoulder hung the ever-present black computer case. S-Man's shaggy brown hair and wide mouth lent him a Stephen King kind of look, further bolstered by his intensity when he talked about his science fiction world. From that world—Sauria—had come his nickname. "You want donuts or cinnamon rolls today?" Bailey asked.

"Rolls, and heat 'em up." Ted made his way over to his usual table against the far wall, a man on a mission. He muttered to himself as he slid the computer bag off his shoulder and placed it on the table.

As Bailey fetched a biggie cup, she saw Bev and Angie roll their eyes at each other and giggle. Ted paid them no heed.

Wilbur shot Bailey a mischievous look. "So S-Man." He swayed toward Ted. "How's Sauria today?"

Ted held up a *hold-on* finger, still muttering to himself. He unzipped his black bag, withdrew the computer, and turned it on. At its musical tone he clumped to the counter, crutchless. "We got major trouble today on two fronts." He sank against a counter stool, hands waving. "This Saurian character keeps insisting his name isn't Gruln when I know it is, and that he's only three *aboyoch* old—mighty young for a shopkeeper. And he informs me he has just one leg—" Ted's eyes widened, his hands hanging in the air. "Wait!" he blinked rapidly. "The hatchling Rathe saved during his training had its leg bitten off, and *he* would be about three aboyoch right now!" His mouth rounded, possible consequences of the new story twist flitting across his face. Pushing away from the counter, he gave Bailey a grim look. "Oooh, Rathe isn't going to like this one bit."

He swung toward his table, forgetting the latte and cinnamon rolls Bailey placed on the counter. Wilbur watched, slowly shaking his head, as if Ted were some mental patient on the loose.

"Hey," Hank called to S-Man, "you said trouble on two fronts. What's the second?"

Ted halted. "Oh yeah." He turned, clomped back to the counter, and leaned against it, lowering his voice conspiratorially. "Edna San is missing."

Bailey stared at him. Only Ted, preoccupied with his Saurian world, could forget such stunning news. "Huh?"

Wilbur screwed up his face. "Boy, what are you talking about?"

"It's true." Ted checked over his shoulder, making sure no tourists were in earshot. "I just came from the post office. Saw Taylor Hodges there. He'd just been to the IGA, where Marge O'Reilly told him. She said Lester just got a call from the police to bring his dog out to Edna San's estate. Edna's assistant—you know that woman Francesca something-or-other—apparently called 911 this morning and reported she's flat-out gone."

Silence. Bailey, Hank, and Wilbur exchanged nonplused glances. Marge O'Reilly's husband, Lester, and his dog, Trace, formed one of the best search and rescue pairs in north Idaho. If they'd been called, something was wrong for sure.

Wilbur shook his head. "Yeah, well, let's not get our hopes up."

Bailey shot him a disapproving look.

Hank hit a knuckle against the counter. "Hope she's all right. Not like Edna to—"

"Hey, everybody!" Sixty-five-year-old Jake Tremaine scurried into Java Joint, skinny arms pumping. His bug-eyed gaze danced around the shop, registering the presence of Ts. With an *oops* hitch of his shoulders, he made a beeline for the counter. He flattened both palms against the Formica and swayed in close enough for Bailey to smell garlic sausage on his breath. "The ol' bat—she's gone AWOL."

"We heard." Bailey was too busy trying to make sense of it to frown at his favorite name for Edna San.

Ted regarded Jake absentmindedly, then picked up his rolls and drink and clumped back to his table. Enough of the real world—his mind had apparently returned to Sauria.

Jake sagged, clearly disappointed he'd been beat out as first news bearer. Then gathered himself for a second round. "Well, I just talked to Maude, who just saw Marge at the grocery store. And Marge had just been on the phone for the second time with Lester, so this is the *very latest*." His tone turned deadly serious. "Lester wasn't sure of the details, but he heard something about Edna San's *dog* being missing too."

"A dog?" Wilbur shook his head. "Now *that's* sad."

A couple of Ts drifted in, and Bailey moved down the counter to wait on them. Wilbur, Jake, and Hank continued to discuss the situation in low tones. Bailey knew Hank wouldn't say anything against Edna, even though the woman had disdained his every move at friendship, muttering how she hated "hypocrite preachers." Only Bailey herself had somehow gotten through to the actress. Maybe it was the free mocha Bailey offered the one and only time Edna showed her face in Java Joint, shortly after she'd moved to the area. Not that the woman needed any kind of charity. But Bailey had seen the sadness behind her suspicious eyes, a world-weariness that spoke of an aesthete, a life hard lived and hard loved. Despite their vast differences, chemistry had sparked between them, Edna staying a few minutes to talk about the town. For Edna, Bailey had since learned, that was a *lot*. Six months later when the *Kanner Lake Times* ran a story about John's turn for the worse with epilepsy, Edna's assistant had appeared on Bailey's doorstep, shoved an envelope embossed with Edna's name into her hands, and left without a word. The envelope contained a thousand dollars in cash. Every month since then, Francesca had shown up with an identical gift, and none of Bailey's protests had been able to stop her.

Truth was, what would she have done without that money? With John's spiraling medical costs and the coffee shop's slim profits, those gifts had helped keep them afloat.

More tourists and townsfolk on their day off entered Java Joint in a sudden rush. Bailey hurried about, pasting a smile on her face, trying to wait on them all at once. As she frothed milk again in the espresso machine, she wondered where Edna San could have gone. *Please, God, keep her safe.* Another thought nudged its way into her head, one that shamed her for its appalling selfishness. Immediately she pushed it away, but it refused to go far.

God forgive her, but Bailey couldn't help but fear for herself and her beloved John if those gifts stopped coming.

TWENTY-FOUR

The police calling? Paige turned to ice as she locked eyes with Sarah. How could they possibly have any reason—and so *soon*?

"They asked about me? I have no idea why." Paige's voice felt brittle.

The anchor chain rattling in the back of her Explorer. Edna San's body thunking onto the rutted road.

Sarah gave a little shrug. "Well, who knows? It was Officer Frank West who phoned. Know him?"

Paige shook her head.

"Young guy, only a few years older than you." Sarah raised an eyebrow. "Not married, and really a looker. He's tall, with short brown hair and big green eyes. Tell you, makes me wish I was a younger woman." She grinned. "Maybe he's seen you around and is interested."

Hands twisting in her lap, Paige tried to smile. A cop, interested in her? That was crazy. But under the circumstances it was the best reason she could imagine.

"My, what a shy smile." Sarah looked askance at Paige. "I've seen plenty a young man wander in here and give you a second look, but you never seem to notice. You already have a boyfriend? Back in Kansas?"

More questions. That's the way it had been with vivacious Sarah from day one. Where was Paige from? What was her family like? Why had she moved to Kanner Lake all alone? Sarah never apologized for her curiosity. A naturally trusting soul, thanks to a loving childhood and supportive husband, no doubt, she had no clue about the seamier side of life. When Paige had reluctantly told her a few chosen details, Sarah was clearly astounded. Orphaned at three? Six foster homes? How could such things happen? And in *Kansas*?

Paige studied the floor, her gaze landing on a stray little piece of blue ribbon. "No, no boyfriend."

"Hmm, a girl as pretty as you? You want one, don't you?"

Paige's eyes fastened on the ribbon, its edge so keenly cut. She licked her lips. "I had a boyfriend once." Her voice was low.

"What happened?"

Paige's lips firmed. Shadowed sequences played through her head. She dared a look into Sarah's face, hoping her own frayed expression would preclude any further probing. "I lost him."

She held Sarah's gaze, watched the woman's mouth open, then close. Sarah looked away, sadness brushing over her face. Then it was gone, replaced with determined optimism. "Well, you'll find one in Kanner Lake, I predict." She waved a hand. "That's why you've come here, Paige Williams. You just don't know it yet. You came to the right place to find a boyfriend, and friends, and a whole new family. That's what Kanner Lake's all about—community."

Paige searched for a response but found none. She was saved by a customer entering the store.

"Marie!" Sarah bustled from around the counter to hug the woman. "I haven't seen you for so long!"

As the women fell into lively chatter, Paige sat on her stool, tuning them out, wanting to fade to nothingness. Her eyes returned to the bit of ribbon. Why had a policeman called about her? *Today?*

She slipped off the stool, bent to pick up the piece of trash, and threw it away.

The woman named Marie said something in a low voice. Paige caught "Edna San" and "missing."

Paige stilled. The word was out.

And police had already called.

Edna's eye gleaming in the arc of the flashlight.

Another fleeting vision whisked through Paige's mind: herself, digging up the metal box buried in her backyard and fleeing Kanner Lake before life beat her down once more. Maybe she should leave work right now. Claim a headache. Go home, clean out her belongings, and *run.*

Paige, you thought about this last night. How far do you think you'd get before the police found you?

She'd been fortunate when she fled her past two months ago. Four weeks on the road, traveling through states and gathering pieces of a life, until she'd found quiet little Kanner Lake. She could rest here—as long as she stayed out of the public eye.

The police. What did they want?

More customers wandered in—a couple and their little girl.

Somehow Paige collected herself. Stood to greet them, smiling, ready to chat and appear helpful, while her limbs shook and her insides withered like blossoms under scorching sun.

TWENTY-FIVE

Rosa has a new pair of expensive designer jeans.

Rachel climbs the two front porch steps after school, thinking about those jeans, nagging thoughts that chew on her mind. Rosa also bought a new blouse — made of silk. She's never worn silk before because of its expense. How is she supposed to afford dry-cleaning it? But these things obviously don't concern Rosa. She strutted like some vain lioness in her outfit this morning as she left for work.

Come to think of it, Rosa seems to have a lot of new things lately, Rachel realizes as she steps inside the house. Rosa's even bought a few things for her — a new purse, a pair of earrings. Rachel knows her mother makes little more than minimum wage from her checkout job at the convenience store. So where's the money coming from? Certainly not Tony, Rosa's new live-in, who hangs around the house all day. Rachel can't stand to come home from school and see him slouched on the sofa, beer in hand and a cigarette dangling from his lips. Tony is short and muscular, with a crooked nose, apparently once broken. He listens to country music all day long. That's a new one. Rosa hates country music.

Rachel passes the back of the couch, Tony slumped on its cushions as usual. Her backpack weights her shoulders, and her stomach is grumbling. She had no time to grab anything for lunch when she ran out of the house this morning. She says nothing to Tony as

119

she goes by, and he says nothing to her. Two people in the same house with zero to give each other.

Rachel heads into the kitchen, slips her backpack onto the counter. She makes herself a salami sandwich, trying to ignore the twangy croon of the stereo. She thinks about her creative writing assignment — a three-page paper about her plans for the future. *What a laugh.* Although she's good in English, she can't think of more than a few sentences to sum up her life plans. *Graduate from high school. Get out of this black hole of a house.* She finishes her task, washes off the knife, and puts the ingredients away. The sandwich goes on a plate. She slugs her backpack over one arm and awkwardly carries it, bumping against one leg, out of the kitchen and down the hall, sandwich in her other hand. She is almost to her room when the front door opens and she hears Rosa's voice.

Rachel slows at her bedroom door, hearing Rosa's high heels clatter over the worn bare floor of the entry. She and Tony exchange greetings as if it's no surprise that she's home at three-thirty, when she doesn't get off work until five.

Fear trickles down Rachel's spine. Something is happening here, and it can't be good.

She stands still for a moment, gathering little pieces of strength scattered through her weary soul. She pushes through her bedroom door, thumps down her backpack, sets down the sandwich. Already the feeling is growing stronger — the sense that her unsteady world is about to be further rocked.

Back in the hall, she keeps her footsteps quiet.

In the den Rosa is perched on the edge of the couch, smacking Tony on the leg with rugged affection and talking animatedly. Her voice has that hard smoker's edge and her laugh is almost caustic. "It feels so *good* to get out of that place! Why didn't you tell me to quit sooner?" She leans over and play-strangles Tony, who's grinning at her like an idiot.

The sight sickens Rachel.

"What are you doing home?" The words blurt from her, etched with anxiety. She hates that her tone has revealed her fear, and her jaw hardens. She stops at the door, distancing herself.

"Well, hello to you too." Rosa turns to look at Rachel over the back of the couch. Her white-blonde bangs hang in her eyes, and her lipstick is worn off, leaving a jagged ring of liner around her mouth. She tosses her head with supreme satisfaction, and her loop earrings swing.

Rachel only glares, her silence demanding an answer. Rosa cocks her head and wiggles her plucked eyebrows. She's apparently so very happy with life at the moment that even her daughter's cynicism won't bring her down.

A year ago Rachel wouldn't have been so bold. But something happened when she turned sixteen three months ago. Rosa stopped hitting her. Maybe because she finally stood as tall as her mother. Or maybe because of the hardness Rachel pretended to have built around herself, like some fiberglass wall. Whatever the reason, Rosa has mellowed. Sometimes Rachel almost misses the beatings. At least Rosa was playing mother, however bad she was at the role. Now she treats Rachel more like an irritating little sister.

Rachel tries to tell herself she doesn't care.

"What's wrong with you?" Rosa makes a face at her.

Rachel holds her stare. She will not show any more weakness. "You quit your *job*?"

Rosa lifts her arms in the air, as if thanking the heavens. "Yes! No more slaving in that dump!"

The news washes through Rachel like cold rain. One thing about Rosa — as tripped-out and selfish as the woman can be, she's also paranoid. For as long as Rachel can remember, she has fretted about not being able to pay bills, losing their house. It's one of the reasons why one man after another has lived with them. The second income has kept a roof, however saggy, over their heads.

Rachel swallows. Her eyes slide to Tony, who's up on one elbow. His bulldog expression holds a certain smug satisfaction. Rachel allows distaste to cross her face, then looks, tight-lipped, back to Rosa. "How do you expect to pay the bills around here? *He* certainly isn't helping."

"We're sending you out on the streets." Tony guffaws at his own joke.

Rosa fakes an *Oh, you bad boy* frown and smacks him on the leg. "Don't you worry about it, Rachel." Her tone mixes pride and irritation. "Tony and me together are gonna make more money than you've ever seen. I'll be able to buy you more things. You should be happy, so wipe that accusing look off your face."

Tony — make money? Whatever scheme he's concocted is sure to fall through soon. Worse, it probably isn't legal. In quick succession Rachel pictures Rosa and herself losing their house, forced out on the streets.

"How are you going to make money?" Rachel wishes she could relax, feign indifference. But her chest is tightening more and more.

"None of your business." Tony sits up and glares at her. "Just go hide in your room like you always do. I don't see you doing anything around here to help."

The words shoot fire through Rachel's veins. "*I* don't do anything? How about cleaning the house and doing all the cooking and dishes and laundry? What do you do, Mr. Lie on the Couch?"

Tony is on his feet in an instant, mouth curling. He pushes Rosa aside, lunges for Rachel. "I'll teach you to talk to me like—"

Rosa grabs the back of his shirt. "Forget it, Tony. Leave her alone."

He yanks away, points a finger at Rosa. "No, I'm gonna teach her this time. I'm *sick* of the way she looks at me."

Rachel backs up toward the front door, eyes on Tony. Every muscle in her body is poised to turn and run. If he's going to beat her, he'll have to chase her down the street in front of everybody. *Let's just see how fast you land in jail, Mr. Big Man.*

"Tony!" Rosa pushes off the couch and grasps his wrist. "I said leave her alone."

Rachel shuffles back two more steps. A third. Rosa and Tony argue, exchanging curses, Rosa's voice shrilling and Tony's hoarse with anger. "Okay, Rosa!" he finally yells, thrusting his face in hers. "You control your brat yourself, hear me? Or I'm outta here, and the deals go with me. *Then* where will you be?"

Rosa glares at him, breathing hard. Abruptly she snaps toward Rachel. "Look what you've done! You want us out on the street?" She pushes around the end of the couch and stomps into the entryway. Stops two feet from Rachel, cheeks flaring red. "You want to know where the money's coming from, Little Miss Smart Aleck? Fine, I'll tell you. We're passing some products along; that's all you need to know. Satisfied?"

Rachel freezes. Two, maybe three seconds pass as she stares at Rosa, a harsh wind blowing through her head. A dozen thoughts bombard her at once—the realization that her mother has resorted to selling drugs and could be arrested, that she and Rosa are now inextricably tied to Tony because if he falls they both go down with him, that Rosa and Tony could wind up in jail and Rachel would be left alone.

Truly alone.

"Answer me, girl." Rosa grabs Rachel's shoulders and shakes her.

Rachel jerks away from the hated touch. "Fine, Rosa, do whatever you want. Just don't get caught, okay? You need to think about that."

Rosa's anger turns to smugness. "You think we're stupid? Tony knows people, cops included. We got nothin' to worry about."

"And *you*"—Tony points at her—"keep your mouth shut. Or I'll shut it for ya."

Rachel looks from him to Rosa, overwhelming loneliness wrapping around her heart. They are a team. United, with a mission. She is the outsider. Now more than ever before.

She pulls in her shoulders. Turns away so they won't see the pain on her face. "Just who in my life would I have to tell?"

TWENTY-SIX

"Jared, I'm out of here."

And I can't believe this is happening!

Leslie had practically freaked when her boss called with the news of Edna San's disappearance. She'd been dressed in her bathing suit—a red two-piece that made her look fine indeed, thank you very much—preparing to lie out in the sun and contemplate her move from Kanner Lake. Within ten minutes after hanging up the phone, she'd thrown on some makeup and pulled on a light-blue cotton top and fitted jeans studded with rhinestones. She'd raced downtown in her bright yellow VW bug with a large pink daisy on each side to pick up her steno pad and camera. The camera was now slung over her shoulder along with her purse, the notebook clutched in her hands. Adrenaline zinged her nerves. Her train to fame had finally come, and she was catching it, oh yeah, baby. *Ahead* of all other media. Heaven knew they'd come running soon enough.

Jared paced behind his gray steel desk, hands jingling coins in his pockets. From the animated expression on his wizened features, Leslie knew he shared her excitement, although he'd die before admitting it. Jared had owned the *Times* so long he considered himself a veteran of sleuth reporting, and a poker face came with the territory.

"All right, girl, now I want you to phone me at every turn, hear?" Jared pointed a long, bony finger, his blue eyes glimmering.

"Try my cell phone if you can't get through on the land line. I'll be making calls, getting all the background information I can. We've got to work fast. If this thing keeps going, we'll turn out an extra paper on Monday."

"I'm on it." Leslie reached into her purse for her car keys. Her fingers closed around the large rubber sunflower attached to her key chain. She yanked it out.

"Don't let those big-time Spokane reporters push you around!"

"No way, this story's *mine*." She threw the words at him as she shoved through the door. On the sidewalk she squinted in the bright sun, then turned left to trot down the block to her car.

Carpe diem and all that. Leslie intended to seize this day like it was the last one of her life.

In high gear she walked past Hamburgers on Main, The Leather Shop, and Java Joint, her peripheral vision registering the regular gang inside the coffee shop.

Extra ears.

Leslie skidded to a halt. Swung around and skittered into the café. Numerous Ts dotted the tables, lolling over their lattes and pastries as if this day weren't a world-changing event.

"Hi, Leslie," Bailey called. "Love your jeans."

"Hey!" Jake Tremaine leaned toward her with raised eyebrows, Adam's apple bobbing in his scrawny throat. "You heard about Ed—"

"Shh!" Leslie flung a meaningful glance toward the tourists. She scurried to the counter, pushing in between Wilbur and Hank, lowering her breathless voice. "Yes, I've heard. I'm headed out to the San estate now. I want you all to call me if you hear any rumors, okay? And *don't* talk to any Spokane reporters."

"Go, Leslie, you're our girl." Wilbur grinned, showing crooked teeth.

The rest chimed in with their support. Leslie gave them a thumbs-up and pushed away from the counter.

As she turned toward the door, Terry Branton, her high school writing teacher, entered the café. Mr. Branton was a tall and gangling sort of man with an angular, serious-looking face that belied his bookishness. "Hi, Leslie." His thin lips stretched widely. "How's my best student doing today?"

Best student. She'd been out of high school for two years and still he called her that. Probably would until doomsday. Not that Leslie minded. Mr. Branton had always believed in her, and that belief had helped her through many a day. "Great, Mr. Branton." Leslie drew close to him and lowered her voice. "I'm onto something big. You always told me I'd make it—maybe this is it!" As his mouth started to open, she jerked a thumb toward the counter. "If you haven't heard, they'll fill you in." She squeezed his arm and hurried for the exit.

"Hey, Les!"

S-Man's voice. Leslie pulled up short, impatience tightening her expression. "What?"

He leaned back from his computer, bushy brows almost touching each other. Slowly he raised a hand from the keyboard, tapped the side of his computer screen. "Rakjear says, 'Nizer benduh rillin.'"

A few tourists eyed him in wonder.

Leslie sighed. "What on earth does *that* mean?"

He shot her a look of dark warning. "Not on earth. On Sauria. And it means—*be verrry careful.*" He drew out the phrase.

Strange. Funny as Ted may have sounded, something about those words writhed in Leslie's brain. She stared at S-Man, wondering how he'd cast such a pall on her. Maybe it was his bony face, the intensity of his gaze. Whatever quality, it was ... spooky.

Hey, Les, this ain't The Twilight Zone.

She raised her hands, palms out. "Sure, Ted. Don't you worry."

Leslie turned on her heel, out of there. Two seconds later she was back on the sidewalk, making for her train to fame.

TWENTY-SEVEN

Frank's background checks on Francesca and Paige came up clean. Vince considered neither off the hook, however. His gut told him Francesca hadn't lied to him. As for Paige, the first minute he could question her, he would.

That earring they'd found weighed on his mind. It was at the lab already, being checked for prints.

Shortly after eleven o'clock Vince heard the distant *thwap-thwap* of the chopper from the air force base. Standing next to Frank in Edna San's driveway, he surveyed the sky.

"There." Frank pointed, eagerness in his voice. "Over the lake."

Vince nodded. The search had begun. He'd told the chopper crew about Bravo's body in the woods, since the dog had not yet been moved.

Once he'd found Bravo shot in the head, Vince strongly suspected he was dealing with foul play. No point in guessing Edna San had wandered off on a jaunt—unless she'd gone crazy enough to kill her own dog. Vince decided to request the chopper at the same time he called for the SAR team. No time to waste now. They had a famous woman to find, and the media would come running in a hurry, which could complicate matters. Vince knew for a fact that the *Kanner Lake Times* never turned off its eavesdropping police scanner, even on a weekend. Jared Moore probably figured he'd hit a gold mine.

Francesca stepped out onto the porch, face pallid and hands tightly clasped. Her color had not returned since she heard about Bravo. "The men are here with the search dog. I just opened the gate for them."

"All right, thanks." Vince turned to look up the driveway and spotted Lester O'Reilly's familiar white pickup. He peered at the windshield. "Good, looks like he's got Mick Rummin with him." He was glad these men were available. They formed the best SAR team around.

Frank watched the hound. "Dog looks ready to go."

No doubt about it. Lester's bloodhound, Trace, roamed the back of the pickup with impatience, tail crooked and high. The dog was ready to play. Sniff, trail, find ... receive reward—that's what the dog knew.

Lester waved, pulling up behind Vince's police car. Lester and Mick climbed out of the truck, leaving the dog to his pacing while the four men gathered to confer about the task.

"Morning, Lester, Mick." Vince shook hands with the Mutt and Jeff pair. Lester was in his midforties, standing six foot three and lanky, with a nose that never quite set straight after he broke it during a high school softball game. Mick, pushing fifty, was a good six inches shorter and muscular, his round cheeks already red from the heat.

Vince gestured toward the house. Francesca remained near the front door, ready for her cue to lead the searchers to Edna's bedroom to retrieve a piece of the missing woman's clothing. "We had an unlocked back door leading from the kitchen out to the patio. Probably the exit point. A good place for you two to start."

"All right, we're ready." Lester waved a fly away from his face.

Vince showed them a crude map he'd drawn of the San estate. The property ran down to the water, with about two hundred feet of cleared beach, then extended into natural forest on either side. Most of the acreage lay to the left of the men as they stood facing the house.

As the chopper cruised the sky in search of a body, Lester and Trace, with Mick as observer, began their search. Lester carried a blouse worn by Edna San the day before she disappeared. On the back patio he let Trace sniff the clothing. The dog then followed his nose along the ground for a moment—and quickly picked up the scent. He headed off, straining at his lead, an amazing olfactory machine capable of filtering out all other stimuli to hone in on the one he sought. Lester trotted to keep up.

The dog cut straight south from the patio, toward the woods. "That's it, boy, find her," Vince whispered as he watched them disappear into the trees. Mick carried a radio. Vince would be informed if they made a discovery.

Discovery.

Vince catapulted back in time to a camping trip years ago with ten-year-old Tim, his son's face flushed with anguish. "Dad, Dad, come see what I found in the woods!"

He'd discovered a baby osprey, wing broken and unable to fly. It fluttered weakly, then froze as they drew near, heartbeat visibly pulsing in its little chest.

"Can we help him?" Tim bent over the bird, hands on his knees, his forehead wrinkled. Vince could smell the familiar scent of him—the sun-drenched skin and young boy sweat that spoke of summer and life and wide-eyed vitality. "Please, Dad, we have to do *something.*"

They captured the bird, took it to the vet, even though Vince knew there was no hope. The osprey died within a day.

Vince blinked hard. Standing now amid the opulence of Edna San's back patio, he flinched at the soul-wrenching poverty of his loss.

It occurred to him, now that the time had passed, how blessed the last two hours had been, the tyranny of the task at hand blocking thoughts of Tim. This was what life had reduced him to. Either he writhed under pressing grief or mourned blissfully distracted moments already passed.

"Hey, Chief."

Vince brought his gaze around to his young colleague. "Yeah."

Frank stood with feet apart and arms crossed, one leg jiggling. "I can start trying to locate Ms. San's son and daughter." He glanced toward the kitchen. "Maybe park myself at the table there, or in the library, and make the calls."

Edna San's adult children might be able to shed some light on what may have happened to their mother. Their whereabouts during the past night also needed to be checked. Either one of them probably stood to inherit a handsome sum upon their mother's death, provided they weren't so estranged, as Francesca had put it, that they'd been cut out of the family will.

At the same time, in the space of one minute Vince could list a good twenty people in Kanner Lake who wouldn't mourn Edna San's passing.

"Yeah, go ahead." Vince turned back to peer at the woods, even though the SAR team had long faded from sight. Thoughts of Tim still sprayed his mind. "First call Wally Keller and inform him of the search. I forgot to do that. If the team keeps heading in that direction, they'll end up on his property. No doubt he'll give us permission to be there, but we still need to ask. I'll head out front to meet the coroner's wagon."

The county coroner's office was sending a wagon to pick up Bravo and take his body back to the morgue. They would remove the bullet and have it sent to the lab for analysis, plus perform an autopsy to determine cause of death. Sure looked like the dog had died from the bullet wound, but what if he'd been poisoned first? A certain poison traced to a point of purchase might offer a lead to the perpetrator.

Vince and Frank stepped through the french doors into the kitchen. Vince made his way toward the front door.

"Mr. Edwards." Francesca hustled toward him in the hallway, her face grim. "A reporter's already at the front gate. Said her name is Leslie Brymes. I didn't let her in, of course, but I thought you should know."

Vince sighed. "Wish I could tell you she'll be the only one."

"No matter." Francesca waved a hand, drawing herself up to her full height, a territorial hardness defining her jaw. "I'll dispatch with the lot of them if I have to. We have No Trespassing signs posted everywhere. Anyone who walks in through the woods will have charges pressed against them."

Vince suppressed a smile. "Don't worry, we'll help you handle it. The media can be a pain sometimes, but they can also offer tremendous help if we need to get word out to the public. It's just a matter of knowing how to work 'em."

Francesca harrumphed. A two-note bell sounded and she tossed Vince a worn look. "That's the gate again."

"Better answer—it may be the coroner's wagon."

It was. For the next half hour Vince remained busy, leading the coroner's assistant to Bravo and helping load the dog. As they worked, he could hear the chopper making passes in its pattern overhead. No word yet that the medic aboard with his scanner had spotted any sign of Edna San.

Mick and Lester radioed in a couple times, reporting that Trace still followed the scent. "Looks like an old logging road up ahead," Mick noted in his second call, which came in as the coroner's wagon was rolling up Edna San's driveway toward the gate. Between one dead canine and one live one, they just might get some leads on this case. "I think we're off the San property and on Wally's at this point."

"Yeah, Mick, you are. Wait just a minute." Vince hurried into the house and back to the kitchen, where Frank sat at the table, talking on the phone and taking notes. He motioned to Frank to interrupt him.

"You talk with Wally?"

"Yeah, it's okay."

Vince nodded and raised the radio to his mouth. "Mick, you're fine. Keller's not gonna come shootin' at you."

"That's good to know." Mick's words rode on puffs of air. "But Trace bore left a minute ago and we're on Lakeshore Road."

Vince sagged against the counter. "Don't tell me he's headed down the pavement."

"Yup," Mick huffed. "'Fraid so."

"Roger." Vince couldn't keep the disappointment from his voice. "Keep me informed."

He adjusted his weight against the counter, vaguely listening as Frank talked to one of Edna San's children. Vince could picture Trace tugging Lester down Lakeshore, Mick throwing glances side to side as he hurried to keep up. If their search ended as Vince suspected, they'd keep to the road for two to three miles, maybe more, then Trace would lose the scent. Which would only mean one thing. Edna had been taken to a vehicle on that road and driven away. A bloodhound's incredible nose could track a scent as it flowed through air vents in a car or truck, but not forever. Maybe five miles at most, given the number of hours that had passed.

Frank hung up the phone and looked to him with a slight shrug. "If this all checks out, their whereabouts are accounted for." He shuffled through his notes. "I talked to Grant Wyman at his home in Hillsborough, California. He was in his office at his law firm yesterday and at a dinner party last night in San Francisco with his wife until nearly eleven o'clock. Ms. San's daughter, Arela Clifford, was also home—in San Diego. She's an interior decorator, recently divorced. Yesterday she met with two clients in their homes. Last night she attended a play with a female friend. She returned to her house around eleven thirty."

"Any reason they can think of that their mother might be missing? Thoughts about who might do something?"

Frank shook his head. "Nothing concrete. They both admitted their mother 'had her enemies.' But they said it was old stuff. Like jealousies from other actresses in her day, things like that. Neither of them has seen their mother since she moved here." He pulled down one side of his mouth. "Apparently, no loving holiday get-togethers for this family."

At the word *holiday*, thoughts of Tim came screaming back. Vince took a deep breath. "All right. Let's see if the SAR team comes up with anything."

Within the hour they heard the news. Trace had followed the scent nearly three miles down Lakeshore Road, then lost it. And the chopper had found nothing.

Frank prepared to head back to the station to put out a description and photo of Edna San to the local media. People would be encouraged to call with any tips, anonymous or otherwise. But Kanner Lake being the small community it was, Vince knew word was already blowing through the streets. Calls would start flowing into the station long before the story hit the Spokane evening news or tomorrow's newspapers.

Vince needed to return to the station and set up his incident command. He would list on the board what had been done so far, what information had been uncovered, who would be in charge of what next. They had to enlarge the search, call in a cadaver dog and as many volunteers as they could find. A lot of forest still required thorough searching. If someone had abducted Edna San and killed her, the body might be lying in the woods adjacent to Lakeshore Road. She also could have been dumped in the lake, but as yet they had no clear indication of where to search the water. And they needed to call the techs. Edna San's property was about to become a crime scene, complete with yellow tape and a policeman guarding its entrance.

"Frank." Vince stopped the kid before he slid into his vehicle. "Call in Al and Roger. Afraid their day off just went out the window. You three and Jim can start lining up the searchers and securing this crime scene. Jim's senior, so he'll be in charge. Get the techs over here as fast as you can. Before this town gets too crazy and every pair of eyes is watching me, I want to follow our one lead."

"Okay."

The young officer had one hand on his open door, the other at his hip. Kid looked a combination of somberness and anticipation. It was his first big case. Possibly a homicide. Vince couldn't blame him for his humming energy.

Frank slid into his car and took off up the driveway.

As Vince watched him drive away, the memory of Tim and the broken-winged osprey burned anew.

Vince turned back toward the house. For a few minutes he reassured Francesca that they were doing all they could to find Edna San. What he didn't tell her was that they'd go over every bit of her interview, looking for any inconsistency that might pop up.

But first the most pressing task at hand.

He'd stop by the station, check in with his men. And pick up the tiny tape recorder that could be concealed on his body. In Idaho it was legal to record a conversation clandestinely, as long as one person involved in the conversation knew about the taping. That person would be him.

As he'd done with Francesca, Vince would watch Paige Williams closely for physical clues while she answered questions. He'd ask closed-end questions, requiring a mere yes or no answer. Often when a person lied, he or she would elaborate when it wasn't necessary. Slowly he would lead to more pointed questions. But he'd keep it friendly, the atmosphere easy. He'd take her somewhere quiet, where she'd feel comfortable. Buy her a can of soda.

Vince Edwards might be a small-town cop, but he'd worked hard during his twenty-four-year career to keep on top of his game. He'd spent plenty of his own money, time, and energy on continuing classes, held as far away as Vegas. Courses on forensics, crime scene investigation, the art of interrogation, reading body language, even recognizing clues of suicidal behavior.

If Paige Williams was lying, he'd know it.

TWENTY-EIGHT

Black Mamba slipped down to the Kanner Lake city beach.

Ensconced upon the warm sand, lifting his face to the rays of the sun, he closed his eyes and listened to the sounds of summer. Children splashing, teenagers chattering. The call of birds and the sudden rush of breezes off the water.

Creation was such a beautiful thing.

He was part of that nature, the methodical cunning of a reptile in their midst, plotting, planning, gauging his next move. It would not be long in coming. He knew the pay phone he would use—a little way south in the town of Spirit Lake.

Something rubbery hit his right arm. Mamba opened his eyes, looked down. A ball. He glanced around the beach, his gaze snagging on a little girl, maybe four years old. She stood staring at him, one sandy finger in her mouth, blonde hair wet and matted, eyes wide with innocence. Pretty little thing, waiting for him to toss her ball back.

"Stacy, say sorry to the man." A heavyset woman in a yellow swimsuit frowned from the girl to him.

His lips widened into a slow smile. "No problem." He picked up the ball, threw it gently to the girl. "I love children."

When he reluctantly left the beach forty minutes later, he made sure to pass by the playing child and give her a wink.

TWENTY-NINE

Click. The gate to Edna San's estate began to open.

Leslie's head jerked up. Who was coming out now? Camera around her neck, she clutched her steno pad and pen, frowning at the vehicle.

Chief Edwards.

Her heart picked up speed. The immensity of her incredible opportunity gripped her by the throat. A major breaking story —and *she was still the only reporter around.*

This moment could be her one chance.

She'd known Vince Edwards since she was a little girl, attending school in the same class as Tim. She and Tim had climbed trees together as kids, grown apart during their awkward pre-adolescent years, then found one another as renewed friends in high school. Leslie had cried buckets at Tim's funeral. And her heart still bent every time she saw Chief Edwards. The grief was all over his face, drawing down the corners of his mouth, flattening his features.

The car stopped, engine chugging, waiting for the gate to swing wide.

Even as her muscles gathered, ready to spring, a split second of self-doubt flushed through Leslie's veins. These days, Chief Edwards seemed to view her with a mixture of bittersweetness and impatience. No doubt she reminded him of his son now lost, and that in itself could blend fondness and pain. But her linear focus on making it big as a reporter, with her constant probing of Kanner Lake law enforcement, obviously served as a thorn in his heel.

Les, go!

She jumped into the middle of the driveway, blocking his path.

He caught sight of her just as the gate clanked to a halt. His chin dropped in a sort of beleaguered weariness. Then he leaned over, sticking his head out the open window. "Leslie Brymes, get out of my way!"

"Just a few questions, Chief!" She flung the words with utter confidence, as Miss National Reporter covering, oh, just the hundredth crime in her illustrious career. With an assume-the-sale smile, she trotted across the gate's inviting entrance to the driver's side of the car.

Chief Edwards looked up at her and sighed. He remained leaning toward the door, right arm draped over the steering wheel. "What are you bothering *me* for, Leslie? Frank came out of here not two minutes ago."

A pout pulled at Leslie's lips. She caught it soon enough to fight it back. "He drove on by, not giving me the time of day. Imagine that. If I'm reading this situation correctly, very soon now you'll *need* the media. You'll be running to us to publish a picture, get the word out about your missing person."

The chief shrugged. "Last I heard, the *Times* only publishes once a week. You know good and well if we need someone today, it's the television folks, not you."

"So you do need dissemination!" Leslie bent toward him, trying not to out and out pant. "Please, Chief Edwards, give me a leg up, just this once. You know the media's going to come running soon—*all* of them. Just give me a scoop about what's going on."

As the words poured out, fresh guilt rose within her. Her pleading for special treatment was founded upon her friendship with his dead son, and they both knew it. At that moment she wouldn't have blamed him for pushing her off his car and driving away.

The chief lowered his head, massaged just above his nose with one finger. The breath he pulled in was long and slow. "All right, Leslie. I'll answer a few questions."

She stared at him openmouthed, then caught herself. "Okay, thanks." Her mind blanked. "Um, did the SAR team or the chopper or anybody find Edna San?"

"No."

"Did the dog pick up her scent?"

"Yes."

She waited. He said no more. "Where did it lead?"

He drummed his fingers against the steering wheel. "That I won't say."

She jotted a note. "The coroner's assistant told me he was taking away Edna San's guard dog. What happened to it?"

He looked at her straight on. Leslie could hear the gears of ambivalence grinding in his head. She willed herself to stare back without flinching.

"It was shot in the head."

Her eyes widened. "A guard dog, *shot*? So you must think there's been foul play?"

"That remains to be seen."

Leslie scribbled furiously. She couldn't let this stop, not now. Her questions came faster, popping. "When was Ms. San last seen?"

"Around nine o'clock last night. By her assistant, Francesca Galvin."

"Any forced entry, anything stolen?"

"That I won't say at this time."

"Any blood, sign of a struggle?"

"No answer to that one either."

"Do you have a suspect?"

"Not yet. We're looking into some more information."

"What information?"

"No deal, Leslie."

She raised her gaze to his face. The man who was Tim's dad, Kanner Lake policeman long before he became chief, eyed her with a strained expression. Suddenly she saw herself as he did—not as Leslie Brymes, fledgling reporter, but as Leslie Brymes, little girl and playmate of Tim, now struggling her way through adulthood while his own son's life had been unmercifully cut short. She flinched, feeling a bloom on her cheeks. She would have pushed away from the car then, perhaps even apologized for bothering the man. But the force of her dreams and the chance at hand swept aside her remorse.

"Did Ms. San's assistant hear anything?"

Something brushed across Chief Edwards's face. Recognition of who she'd grown to become, perhaps? Of her dogged determination to make something of this life she'd been afforded?

"No, she heard nothing."

"What's next in the investigation? Further searching?"

"Yes."

"Searching for a body? With cadaver dogs?"

He inclined his head. "Perhaps."

"You need volunteers?"

"Yes."

Leslie continued scribbling. Chief Edwards cleared his throat. "And now, Ms. Brymes, I really must be going."

Despite the flat tone in his voice, Leslie pushed on. She'd deal with the regret later. "Chief,"—her words softened—"give me one more thing you can part with. Just one. Some detail you won't be releasing to everyone else." She pleaded with her eyes.

He hesitated, indecision tightening his features. Then, unexpectedly, gave a small tired smile. "Leslie Brymes." He shook his head. Looked at her askance. "Here's your detail, all right? Francesca Galvin drew a bath for Edna San before retiring to her own house on the property for the night. I don't think Ms. San ever stepped into the water."

He firmed his mouth, nodded once, as if to say, *There you are.* Then motioned her away from the vehicle.

"Thank you, Chief, thank you so much!" The words spouted from her lips. "If I can do anything to help, please let me know."

Yeah, right, Leslie.

He nodded again solemnly.

Leslie wanted to say more, something about Tim, something about how bad she still felt, and how she knew tomorrow was the anniversary of his death. But the words caught in her throat. She stepped back from the car.

Chief Edwards turned back toward the steering wheel. Ace reporter Leslie Brymes raised her camera for some quick shots as he drove away.

THIRTY

From the Simple Pleasures counter, Paige anxiously watched Main Street through the store's front window.

Dragging Edna San's body into the lake.

No customers were in the store at the moment, and for that Paige was grateful. How much longer could she force the smiles, hide her trembling limbs? Moment by moment Sarah's voice played through her head like a stuck record. *A policeman called and asked your name. A policeman called—*

"Paige, you look like you're in dreamland." Sarah bustled from the back room carrying three oil lamp candles to replace those that had sold. She put them on the table, chubby hands fussing with their placement until she was satisfied, then turned toward the counter. "How about being a dear and getting me a coffee from across the street?" She gave Paige one of her blithe, nothing's-wrong-with-the-world smiles. "You could use a bit of sun, and your lunch break's still forty-five minutes away."

Dreamland. I wish. "Okay. Sure."

Sarah rested a palm against the countertop, her other hand fiddling with the gray curls at her forehead. "You remember what I like, right?"

"Um. A biggie double latte."

Java Joint had this thing about drink sizes. "You get what you ask for," was the way Bailey Truitt had explained it the first time Paige ordered. Sizes came in small, middler, and biggie. "None of this 'tall' stuff meaning the smallest drink." Bailey had tossed a look heavenward. "What kind of logic is that?"

Sarah grinned at Paige. "You got it." She moved behind the counter, pulled her wallet from her purse, and handed Paige four dollars. "Leave the extra money for Bailey."

A minute later Paige stood on the curb in the hot sun, waiting for a chance to jaywalk across the street. As she let cars pass, she glanced right and left. She saw couples walking hand in hand, friends talking, a mother and her small son. No one who looked the slightest bit like a suspect. Still, to Paige suspicions haunted every building, every square foot of the thriving and quaint downtown. The man who'd killed Edna San — if it indeed was a man — could be lurking in any shop, watching her through the window. Huddled blocks away, binoculars in his hand. Or what if the police were observing her right now from some secret perch? Noting her every facial expression, her body language? Would they see her guilt, her jumpiness at the slightest unexpected sound? What if —

Paige, no cars.

She crossed the street.

Java Joint's three tables on the sidewalk were occupied with customers. Some of them men. She hurried by, heart skimming, feeling the eyes of one middle-aged man upon her.

Was it him?

Inside the café, about a third of the tables were taken — and all four stools at the counter.

Is he here?

At the counter sat three men and one woman dressed in a business suit, talking animatedly in low tones. All locals, Paige knew that much. She didn't relish standing close to them as she ordered. Heading for the end of the counter, she made a beeline for the one person she felt inclined to trust — Bailey Truitt. The sweet and ever-smiling woman, perhaps in her midfifties, had been very friendly the three or four times Paige had ventured inside the café.

Bailey was busy wiping down the counter beyond her espresso machine. Paige waited to be noticed, tapping a thumb against the edge of the counter. She almost *felt* rather than heard the whispers to her right die away. Staring at Bailey's back, she sensed four pairs of eyes upon her.

Three men. Her ankles shook.

The man next to her looked her up and down and sniffed. She glanced at him. He was old. *Too old?* Had to be in his seventies. Milky blue eyes and a wizened, narrow face.

"Hey, Bailey." He thumped the counter with gnarled knuckles. "You got a customer."

Bailey turned, a smile on her lips. Paige thought her a pretty woman. Thick brown hair with red highlights, cut above her shoulders and tucked behind her ears. Round chestnut-colored eyes. She wore small gold hoop earrings and a little gold cross necklace. "Hi there, Paige." Her lips pulled wider.

Paige nodded briefly. "Hi." She felt like an idiot. Why couldn't she at least sound more friendly to this woman?

Bailey seemed not to notice her terseness. "What can I get for you?"

"A biggie double latte. It's for Sarah."

"Ah, of course, that's Sarah's drink." Bailey raised her eyebrows. "Anything for you?"

Paige slid her palms together, lacing her fingers, unlacing them. "No, thank you, I ... not right now."

She tried to smile and knew the gesture looked insincere. She could feel the man next to her continue to ogle.

Please just hurry up and let me get out of here.

Bailey poured milk into a metal container and began making the drink. As the machine shush-gurgled the milk into froth, the woman glanced toward her. "Have you met these folks, Paige? They're some of my regulars."

Paige shook her head in one quick movement.

For a moment Bailey focused on the machine, then shut it down and pulled the steaming drink away. She reached for a biggie cup and poured the latte into it. Slid a cardboard holder onto the cup and set it before Paige. "That's Wilbur next to you. Then Pastor Hank, and Jake. And Carla on the end. She's a real estate agent. Just returned from showing a piece of property to some folks."

The foursome chimed in tandem with various forms of "Hi, Paige, nice to meet you."

Paige's heart skipped. Why couldn't the floor just open and swallow her whole? She didn't want to meet anyone, didn't want people looking into her face, her eyes. Surely her fear and guilt were written all over her as clearly as Magic Marker on paper. Was it only yesterday she'd longed for relationships here, wanted to learn how to reach out? Now all she wanted was to run and hide. Flee this town, flee her fledgling new life. She'd find another one, somehow, somewhere. Teach herself not to need people. She didn't want friends, didn't want to be loved, didn't need anyone. Not even a sister.

She pressed her lips into another tight smile. "Hi." Her gaze fixed on the latte. "Oh. Here. And keep the change." She held the four dollars out to Bailey, shocked to see them crinkled and wadded in her hand. "Oh, sorry." She laid them on the counter, ran her hand across the bills to smooth them out.

"No problem." Bailey picked up the money and slipped it into the cash register. "Tell Sarah I said hi. And come on back for your lunch break if you can. I'll fix you a free drink. God bless you, Paige."

God bless me? If this woman only knew all the times in her life that defied blessing, especially last night. Still, something deep inside her panged at the words.

"Hey, you never offer *me* anything free." Wilbur scratched his scruffy cheek.

"That's because you don't deserve it," Carla shot back.

"And she does?" Wilbur's voice rose in protest.

"Hush, Wilbur, leave her alone." Bailey frowned at him, then shook her head with a sigh, looking to Paige. "He's harmless, really. We all are. I hope you'll come back."

Paige reached for the latte, unbearably anxious to leave. Wilbur faced her on his stool. "I am harmless, but see that guy over there?" He pointed to a thirtysomething man typing away at a computer, one leg in a white cast protruding from beneath his table. If the man heard the comment, he paid them no attention. His brows angled together in concentration, his mouth moving silently. "Watch out for him. *He's* crazy."

"Okay." The word popped from Paige's mouth sounding far too serious, as if she'd just promised to steer clear of a dangerous animal. Hank, Jake, and Carla laughed. Paige knew their good-natured chuckles were aimed more toward the man at the computer than at her. Still, she felt herself blush. She picked up the drink and turned toward the door. Spotted a man in perhaps his forties, blond and tanned, entering the café. His eyes fastened on her—and held.

Heat gushed through her chest. Was it him?

Paige, get out of here!

"Thank you," she mumbled to Bailey and, with a final glance at the counter foursome, fled from the shop.

THIRTY-ONE

His breath is hot on her neck.

Suddenly the truck, parked on a side road under cover of night, feels claustrophobic. Devon's hands paw Rachel. She pushes them off as she always does, and as always they return.

"What's the matter, Rachel? Come *on*."

She tries to take a breath, but his body is pressed so closely to hers that she can't find air. The heat, his selfishness, the darkness close in on her, and her lungs balloon with panic. Rachel smacks Devon's hands and jerks away. "I said get *off* me!"

"Hey, what—"

"Just leave me alone, okay?" She scoots back toward the door, presses against it. Tears form in her eyes and she hates that. She hates looking weak to anybody. "Isn't it clear to you I don't want to do this? Why can't you just hear *no*?"

He breathes hard, one hand hanging in the air, fingers spread. "Why do you keep saying no? I *love* you, Rachel; don't you understand?"

Her throat tightens. She wants to believe his words so badly. "Devon, if you loved me, you'd listen when I tell you to stop."

"No, no." His voice softens and he slides close to her. In the darkness Rachel can barely see the caring warmth he has painted on his face. "It's because I love you that I want you so badly. I don't mean to not listen; I just get carried away." He reaches out, gently strokes the back of her hair. "I'm sorry. Really."

149

The familiar ache throbs through Rachel. She closes her eyes, revels in his touch. What a change he has brought to her lonely life in the past six months. Last year the two girls she hung out with most moved away. *Both* of them. What kind of odds are that? What crazy parents change jobs when their daughters are juniors in high school? Now Devon is here, always Devon. Driving her to school, taking her home after she gets off work at the pizza parlor. Someone to be with, someone to talk to. Only Devon knows what she faces at home.

Rachel cannot live without him.

She lays her head on his shoulder, wipes her eyes, hoping he won't notice. He leans over her to crack open the window, then puts his arm around her. Fresh air rushes in, clearing Rachel's head.

"Forgive me?" Devon presses his fingers into her arm.

"Yeah."

She lays a palm flat against his chest, feeling his heartbeat. *What* is *wrong with me? Why don't I just say yes?* She has no clear answer, even for herself. Only a vague weariness that all her life people have taken from her instead of given. Rosa, with her warped sense of motherhood. Make that *no* sense of motherhood. And Rosa's string of boyfriends, who beat Rachel when she was little and now look at her with lust in their eyes.

It's a wonder no one has gotten to her yet.

"Come here," Devon whispers gruffly, as if she is not close enough. He raises her head to kiss her, and she knows it will start all over again. As she feels his lips on hers, for the millionth time she tells herself he really does love her. That once she graduates from high school in two months, he'll marry her like he's promised. So what if it's a civil ceremony at the courthouse? At least they'll be together — *committed* to each other. Devon is twenty and has a steady job as a construction worker. Financially they'll make it. And she'll be forever away from Rosa and her "business." Away from the remodeled house, where every wall and every new piece of furniture screams drug money. Rachel can get pregnant in a year or two. Just thinking of a baby in her arms makes her chest constrict. She will love and cherish a baby with all her soul and mind, all her being. She will never, ever treat her child with anything other than patience and love.

Devon's hand slips down from her shoulder.

Rachel pulls away, the ache in her heart swelling up her throat. "Devon, please take me home."

He doesn't argue. He doesn't swear and yell. Devon does something far worse — he turns cold. Without a word he slides across the seat to the steering wheel. Rachel barely has time to straighten her clothing before he is gunning the motor. They don't speak until he turns onto her street five minutes later.

He pulls up to the curb, casts a disinterested look at the back of a man heading up the front steps of her expanded, freshly painted porch. The man is tall and stocky, wearing a red T-shirt, the porch's dim light casting a pale sheen on his shaved head. After one o'clock in the morning and people are still coming by. Rachel knows it will be that way most of the night.

Devon turns toward her, face partially lit from a nearby streetlamp. "If you loved me, Rachel, you wouldn't put me through this every time. I just want you to know — I can't take it much longer. There are lots of girls who wouldn't do this to me."

Heat surges through her. *No, he doesn't mean it. He won't leave me.* "Devon, two months, that's all. Don't you think it will mean more when we're married?"

When you've pledged yourself to me and me alone?

His mouth firms and his gaze drifts out the windshield. Slowly he shakes his head. "I don't know if I can wait that long, Rachel. I just don't know."

The words filter through her like anesthetic. She feels her heart go numb, then her soul. A tiny voice in her head cries, *Don't get out! Drive away with him, do anything he wants, just* keep *him!*

Rachel waits for him to look at her once more, to come to his senses and take the words back. Instead he turns toward the steering wheel, puts his hand on the gearshift, waiting for her to leave.

"Devon – "

"Just go."

She reaches out to him, fingers brushing his arm. *Don't leave me, please!* The words totter on the tip of her tongue, ready to fall. But Rachel can't say them. Because if she does, if she shows her weakness, and he still makes good on his veiled threat, what will be left of her? She can only guard what broken pieces of herself life has allowed her to keep.

Devon stares straight ahead.

Rachel pulls her hand away. For a moment she stares unseeing at the dashboard. Her eyes scratch and she blinks hard.

She gets out of the truck.

As Devon drives away, she stands on the sidewalk, watching his taillights. The dull yellow of the streetlamp washes his blue vehicle a muddied green. Something about that chameleon change whispers to Rachel a warning, but she flings up a wall of denial.

He doesn't mean it. Everything will be all right. He loves me.

Her steps toward Rosa's drug haven are slow.

In the house Barry, Rosa's boyfriend of the past year, is perched on the edge of the couch, watching TV. One hand is buried in a bowl of chips; the other plays drums on his knee. Two men Rachel doesn't know are also on the couch, one dozing, the other flipping impatiently through a magazine. The TV is going, as is rap music on the stereo.

With a mere glance Rachel can tell the three men are high. Barry likes speed; apparently, so does one of his friends. The other man – who knows? He could be coming down from it.

Rachel slips by them into the kitchen for a glass of water. There Rosa is pacing, talking loudly to the man in the red T-shirt, gesticulating with both hands. The man leans against the table, muscular arms folded, cynicism twisting his hard mouth as her mother continues a diatribe about some payment.

"Hey." The man jerks his chin toward Rachel as if warning Rosa to shut up.

Rosa looks around. Rachel catches a glimpse of her mascara-smeared eyes, the overblushed cheeks. "Oh." Rosa shrugs and turns back to the man. "Don't worry about her."

Like anybody ever does.

Rachel goes to the cabinet, fetches a glass. As she turns water on at the sink, The Feeling sinks around her like a noxious cloud. That dirty, fear-tinged sense that she first experienced at age twelve, when her figure began to fill out. Without moving her head, she slides a sideways glance toward Red Shirt.

He is staring at her.

Rachel looks back toward the sink, pushes off the faucet. Her glass is too full and she splashes out some of the water. Her spine stiffens, her muscles coil, and she prays he doesn't see it. For some animalistic reason, when they sniff her fear, they only leer all the more.

She turns her back on him, hurries down the hall. In her room she locks the door, knowing how flimsy such a lock can be. Hasn't her own mother burst through it on more than one occasion? Agitation kicks up Rachel's back. She can't pinpoint why she feels more frightened of Red Shirt than the others, but something ...

Rachel, chill out. It's okay.

She sinks into her desk chair and gazes out the window, thoughts returning to Devon. What can she say to him tomorrow to whisk away the words he said tonight? She will find a way to keep him. She *has* to. Even if it means giving in to sex. Somehow she'll manage to sleep with him and not feel like a slut. Like her mother. Because she and Devon plan to get married. That makes all the difference, right? Besides, he does love her. Surely if she gives that last remaining bit of herself to someone for love, she won't be left with nothing.

Through the walls Rachel can hear the TV—someone has turned it up louder. A minute later the rap music volume increases. She hears bursts of laughter, hollow and frenetic. *How long until everyone crashes?* She has learned to sleep through the noise.

Rachel's door rattles.

She swivels toward it.

The knob moves a fraction back and forth. Once. Twice.

Rachel rises from her chair. It's probably just Rosa, wanting to borrow something. Mascara maybe.

The knob jiggles again.

Why doesn't Rosa just bang on the door?

Deep in the recesses of Rachel's mind, she knows. A tiny voice speaks that she is lucky to have escaped for so long, and now what little she has left of herself will be taken.

No. It's only Rosa.

The TV and radio battle each other. Rachel hears no more laughter, no more voices. What are they doing out there?

She swallows hard. No more sound from her door.

Then—a metallic *click*. The lock has released.

The bedroom door slowly swings open.

THIRTY-TWO

In strained silence Bailey and the others at her counter watched Paige give a wide berth to a customer just entering Java Joint, then hustle out the door. Bailey bit her cheek. Poor Paige. Something was really getting to that girl.

The customer headed straight for the counter.

"Good afternoon. What would you like?" Bailey took the man's order—an iced coffee drink and a roast beef sandwich. As she prepared his lunch, Bailey cast knowing glances at her friends. Before Paige came in, they'd been talking with grim animation about what could have happened to Edna San. They'd heard the chopper and ran out to the sidewalk to see it for themselves. But now, solemnized by Paige's nervousness and in the presence of a T, they engaged in small talk, their voices low.

The customer paid for his order, dropped a fifty-cent tip in her jar, and left. Bailey waited until he was out of earshot, then frowned at the locals, one hand on her hip. "You all ran Paige off."

"We didn't run her off. *He* did." Carla pointed a red-nailed finger at Wilbur.

The man drew back with all innocence. "I didn't—"

"We shouldn't have laughed." Pastor Hank gazed across the street toward Simple Pleasures. "I think she took it personally." He turned to Bailey. "You know her very well?"

She shook her head. "No. She's come in here maybe three times. Always seemed kind of shy, but never out and out nervous like she was today." Bailey fingered her cross necklace. "I just feel bad for her. She obviously could use a friend."

Jake rapped the counter with his palms. "That's our Bailey, always mothering."

She turned away, for some silly reason her throat tightening at the comment. Goodness, she was on edge today. John's seizure last night, Edna San missing, now this lost-looking girl. Worse, Bailey felt helpless to ease the problems of any of them.

She picked up a sponge and wiped down the espresso machine with focused intent, angling her back to her friends.

A few minutes later a group of four tourists entered the café and headed to the counter, eyes fixed on the menu written upon the wallboard above Bailey's head. Behind them, some locals filtered in. She greeted Sam Beltz from the leather goods store up the street; Henry Ikes, who worked at the gas station around the corner; and Bart Goodlet, the postal worker with the slight build of a jockey. Lunchtime was here. Bailey would soon be flying around like mad. For the hundredth time she wished she could afford to hire help. But her part-time employee had quit a few weeks ago, and Bailey had been grateful for the extra savings. That's just the way it would have to be for now.

As she hurried to take orders, Pastor Hank rose. "I've sat here like a lazy fool long enough. Time to get moving." He leaned toward Bailey. "I'll look in on John and report back to you, okay?"

Bailey's vision blurred. "Thank you so much."

Soon Carla, Jake, and Wilbur wandered off as well. Wilbur was going home for a nap. And at the end of the afternoon, when the sun was a little less hot, he aimed to go fishing.

Among the locals in the shop, only S-Man remained, tapping away at his keyboard.

By the time the flurry of customers died down, Bailey's feet ached. She dragged a chair behind the counter and sank into it, feeling sweaty and heavyhearted. How on earth was she supposed to write a post for tomorrow's blog? What to say? She didn't want to talk about Edna's disappearance, but neither could she ignore it as if she didn't care.

When the phone rang, Bailey jumped. It was Hank, calling from her house. Reporting that John looked fine, that they'd had a good visit, talking mostly about the stunning news of Edna San, and now Hank was leaving to go home. He said good-bye to Bailey, and then she heard him hand the phone to her husband.

"Hey, doll, you send him over here to check on me?" John's voice held that familiar tease, the same tone he'd used when he asked her out on their first date nearly forty years ago.

Bailey closed her eyes, love and aching for her husband welling within her. "No. But I'm glad he came. You okay?"

"'Course I'm okay; I'm terrific. Hey, that's some news about Edna San missing. What do you suppose happened?"

Bailey drew a breath. It was so like John to make light of his illness. He just didn't like people feeling sorry for him, including his own wife. Of all the people Bailey had ever known, John was the least likely to complain.

"I don't know," she said, managing a smile, "but I can tell you there are a thousand ideas floating around town at the moment, all of which have been offered at my counter within the last couple hours."

"Well, you keep me informed if you hear anything. But I probably know more than you do at this point. Hank told tell me they're done with the search at the San estate. You hear that?"

"No. He must have found that out after he left here."

"Yeah. His wife called his cell phone as he was driving over. Janet had gotten the news from somebody at church—I don't know who."

Bailey studied her glass cabinet of pastries, almost afraid to ask the obvious question. "What happened? With the search, I mean."

John exhaled into the phone. "Chief Edwards called for it. He came in from his day off. But they found big, fat nothing. No Edna, no sign of her."

Lord, what could have happened to her? Bailey fingered her necklace. "What are they going to do next?"

"Organize a bigger search. They're asking for volunteers. Sure wish I could help. And they're bringing in cadaver dogs."

Cadaver dogs. Bailey's heart clutched. "Do they really think she's dead? They must have found *something* to make them suspect that."

"I agree. But Janet didn't know any details."

Bailey's gaze cruised the café, gliding over S-Man and the other dozen or so customers. Ted pulled back from his computer and stretched his arms out wide, flexing his neck. He looked around, glaze-eyed, as if realizing with shock that he was in Java Joint, not some tower of Sauria, hiding from attacking Herians.

"Oh, John." Bailey's voice was tight. "We'd better start praying hard for Edna."

"Well, I'm with you. But in all honesty, two thirds of the town might be praying otherwise. She's not exactly adored around here."

Bailey shook her head. "But nobody would really wish her harm. Not here in Kanner Lake."

John chuckled. "Bailey, that's what I love about you. Always thinking the best of everybody."

As she hung up the phone, John's words reverberated through her. He was right; Edna was resented by so many people. Almost every local who'd come into Java Joint today had something against her, right up to the last three she'd served. Sam Beltz was married to the daughter of Wally Keller, whom Edna had supposedly cheated out of his land. Henry Ikes had talked loudly of run-ins with Edna at the gas station. And Bart Goodlet had sneered more than once at Edna's impatience when it came to receiving her mail.

Truth was, if something had really happened to Edna San, if she was in fact dead, somebody *had* wished her more than a little harm. But a murder in Kanner Lake? Bailey could not allow herself to believe such a horrible thing had happened. Not here, in this neighborly town.

A sole customer entered the shop, and Bailey pushed to her feet to serve him. Her glance brushed across the street—and fell upon a familiar figure. Vince Edwards. Walking down the sidewalk. He turned into Simple Pleasures.

Bailey stilled. The chief of police—out shopping at a time like this?

Couldn't be. He had to be entering that store for a reason. And any current reason could only have to do with Edna San.

Simple Pleasures ... Paige's nervousness.

Bailey considered the connection, then tossed the ridiculous thought into oblivion.

She looked to the customer, an automatic smile upon her face. "What can I get for you?" She heard the words from her own mouth, but her mind whirled elsewhere—on cadaver dogs and searches and Chief Edwards and Simple Pleasures.

THIRTY-THREE

A policeman walked into the store. A middle-aged officer Paige had seen around a few times. Dark hair cut short, almost military style. Not really tall, but possessing intense brown eyes and a granite-like chisel to his jaw. Tanned, strong-looking arms. Everything about him — and his uniform — screamed authority.

Paige went cold. Her eyes cut to Sarah with silent pleading, but the woman was rearranging items, her back to the door.

The policeman looked at Paige behind the counter and aimed straight for her. As he drew close, she could read his badge. *Chief Edwards.* Breath backed up in Paige's throat.

Chilly lake water hitting her ankles.

"Good day, ladies." He nodded to Paige, glanced at Sarah.

Sarah turned around, surprise on her face, a glimmering bracelet hanging from her fingers. "Chief Edwards! I thought that sounded like you." She tossed down the bracelet, hurried over to him. "What's this I hear about Edna San? It must not be true or you'd be out looking for her."

He brought a hand to the back of his neck. "If you've heard she's missing, I'm afraid that *is* true. But we're keeping an eye out for her. I wouldn't worry too much at this point."

His tone. Offhand. Light: Paige sensed it was the tone of a policeman who knew more than he wanted to tell.

160

Sarah laid her fingers at the side of her mouth. "It's hard to believe. She was in here just yesterday, do you know that? I could count on one hand the times Edna San has been in this store, and now to know she was here so shortly before she disappeared."

Shut up, Sarah, shut up!

Paige could feel the weight of her own body against the floor, as if somebody had turned up the pull of gravity. She glanced at her hand and saw it gripping the counter. Willed it to relax.

"Actually, that's why I came in to see you ladies." Chief Edwards turned to Paige. "I need to ask you a few questions about what happened yesterday when Ms. San was in the store."

"Oh, it was awful," Sarah declared. "Edna came in here when there were other customers. I was in the back and Paige was helping someone. When I came out, Edna was loudly complaining about Paige's service. Then, can you believe it, the woman turned to me and practically *demanded* that I fire her." Sarah's cheeks reddened. "As if she's got the right to tell me what to do in my own store."

Vince Edwards listened calmly, his gaze fixed on Sarah's face. His weight was on one leg, both hands low on his hips, his expression inscrutable. But Paige could practically see the video camera recording from his policeman brain, registering every nuance, every detail.

He tossed a glance at Paige, then back to Sarah. "What happened after that?"

Sarah let out a disgusted *tsk*. "She turned on her heel and stalked out. Everybody in here just watched her go, totally stunned." She waved her hand in the air. "Tell you what, I hope she never does come back in this store. Customers like her—I don't care *who* she is—I can do without."

Chief Edwards tilted his head as if in agreement. "You say you were in the back room when most of this happened?"

"Well, when it started, yes. But I sure heard the worst of it from Edna San."

"Okay." The chief turned again to Paige. "I need to talk to you about this privately, if you don't mind. It's just routine. I've got to follow up on everyone who saw Ms. San or had any kind of interaction with her in the hours before she disappeared."

Somehow Paige managed a nod. Her body had gone numb.

"Sure, go ahead." Sarah again, almost *smiling*.

The chief's eyes remained on Paige. "It's probably time for your lunch hour, isn't it? I can take you somewhere, buy you a sandwich."

"I—yes, I'm supposed to have a break now." Paige heard herself talking. Did the words sound normal? Innocent? "But I'm not very hungry."

"Then we'll just get a soda or something. It won't take long. Believe me, I've got far more important things to attend to. But I'd just like to get this out of the way."

Sarah frowned at Paige. "Go on, dear." She whisked her fingers at Paige, as if urging a dawdling child. "He's not going to bite. Chief Edwards is a very nice man. This is just part of his job."

Edna's body splashing into the lake.

Tension dug knuckles into Paige's shoulders. She was too exhausted to think clearly; she would never get through this unscathed. What if she made some slip? "Do I need my purse?"

He shrugged. "Up to you."

A moment later, clutching her purse, walking on wooden legs, Paige allowed herself to be escorted out of Simple Pleasures by the Kanner Lake chief of police.

THIRTY-FOUR

Cell phone pressed to her ear, Leslie pulled open the door to her VW. Her entire body tingled with anticipation. "Jared, with all this stuff Chief Edwards just told me, you *know* he's got to believe there's been foul play, even if he won't admit it. I mean, why else would Edna San's guard dog have been killed?"

"Yeah, I hear you." Jared sounded as pumped as she was.

Leslie slid into her car and tossed her steno pad and pen onto the passenger seat. "Listen, I'm going to run down more information, so I'll be really busy for a while. I won't be able to report in every minute, okay?"

"Go for it, girl. Just don't leave me hanging too long. Tell me everything you're up to, and I can help gather additional info."

"Sure. Absolutely." Leslie pushed sincerity into her tone, meaning not a word of it. She didn't want to share any more of this limelight than absolutely necessary. She slammed her car door and started the engine, still holding the phone to her ear. Checking Lakeshore Road both ways, she pulled a U-turn and headed toward town.

"Who're you goin' after first?" Jared asked.

"I want to find out everything I can about what was discovered on the search. There's more than Chief Edwards told me; I can feel it. I'll get in Frank West's face and see what he'll spill. Then maybe I'll tail the cops for a while, see where they go."

"What about talking to Edna San's assistant?"

Leslie braked for a curve. "No way to get to her right now. I can't sneak on the property—there are No Trespassing signs everywhere and I don't doubt they mean it. Besides, remember when I tried to interview her before, when Ms. San first moved here? Woman's lips were as tight as a drum. I don't think she's the best use of my time right now."

"Understood. I'll see what I can do with her."

"Sounds good. Talk to you soon as I can."

Leslie clicked off the line, inordinately pleased with herself. She'd handled the call perfectly. Leslie Brymes, reporter on her way to fame, had a few plans up her sleeve, and the last thing she'd do was give her boss a chance to shoot them down. Okay, so her plans were kind of wackball. But under the circumstances they could majorly rock. That adage about being safer to ask for forgiveness than permission was definitely in play here.

And no doubt before the day was out, she'd be begging forgiveness. *"Jared, I know I should have checked with you first. But I just got caught up in the moment, you know? And suddenly there I was, making the calls ..."*

Downtown Kanner Lake was about ten minutes away. Leslie hadn't a moment to lose. Quickly she dialed the number of the place she used to work as a high school student.

"IGA." Store owner Ralph Bednershack sounded irritated.

"Mr. Bednershack, Leslie Brymes here. I need to speak to Marge O'Reilly."

"Yeah, you and everybody else. How're we supposed to get any work done around here with the whole town calling?"

"I'm not 'the whole town,' I'm Leslie, and this is my *job*. Come on now, be nice and let me talk to her."

"Okay, okay, hang on. Marge!" He seemed to holler right into Leslie's ear. She could imagine the bulldog-faced old man turning every head in the store. "It's Leslie Brymes, and you know what she's gonna want!"

Leslie clenched her teeth in frustration. "Do you have to inform the entire world?"

"Yeah, well, I got her for you, didn't I." Ralph breathed into the phone like Mr. Snuffleupagus. "Okay. Here she is."

Leslie heard muffled noises, the sound of a receiver being passed.

"Hi, this is Marge."

Her tone was guarded. Marge O'Reilly's husband had been involved in hundreds of searches in Washington and Idaho, and no doubt she knew all about reporters. Leslie needed to win her over in a hurry.

"Hi, Marge, it's me." Clipped and businesslike. "Have you heard from Lester yet? I just got through talking to Chief Edwards and he told me the search is done."

"Oh. No, I haven't heard a word."

Drat.

"Have *you* heard something?"

Leslie thought fast. "Yes. They did not find Edna San. I can't say the other details I know—they'll come out soon enough. I just wanted you to know that your husband's fine, the dog's fine. But it looks like there's going to be a bigger search. Volunteers are being called."

"Goodness." Marge inhaled a quick breath. "Doesn't sound good. Thanks for letting me know, Leslie."

"You're welcome." Leslie rushed on. "Will you take down my cell number and call me if you hear any further particulars? I promise to keep you informed too." She held her breath.

"Okay, fine."

Leslie rattled off her number. Marge repeated it as though writing it down. Still, Leslie had to wonder as she ended the call. Oh, well. Some leads panned out, some didn't.

On to the next—Frank West.

Dynamite-looking cop that he was. Plus he had a sultry voice. As Leslie dialed the police station, she allowed herself a fleeting daydream of being up close and personal with the man. She sensed he was attracted to her, but he also seemed intimidated. Maybe he just didn't want to mix it up with a reporter. Well, they'd just see about *that*.

The phone rang once, twice. "Come on, Frank," Leslie whispered. "Be there."

The voice she'd hoped to hear answered the phone. *Yes!* She plunged ahead.

"Hi, Frank, it's Leslie Brymes. I've been talking with Chief Edwards out at the San estate. From what he told me about calling out cadaver dogs and volunteers, I understand you all suspect foul play. How can I help? Can I call volunteers for you?"

A pause. "I don't think so, but thanks. I'm already getting that coordinated."

Aha. Note—already coordinated.

"What time do you expect to have people back out there? Especially the cadaver dogs?"

"Soon as possible. Probably in about another half hour."

Another new tidbit.

"What about the timing of Ms. San's disappearance? Sounds like it must have happened just before she stepped into that bath."

"Uh, yeah." He sounded surprised that she knew this. "That's what we surmise."

"Which would make it . . ." She pushed out a quick breath. "I can't consult my notes while I'm driving. What time did Chief tell me she was supposed to take the bath?"

"Nine o'clock. That's her schedule every night."

Leslie grinned. "Oh yeah, nine o'clock. Right."

"Look, Leslie, I gotta go." Frank's tone turned brisk.

"Okay, just a final question. Who's your main suspect?"

"I cannot divulge that information at this time."

Oh, great. Cop-speak.

"So you do have one."

"I didn't say that."

"What about her son and daughter? Former husbands? You call them?"

"Leslie, I need to go."

"Any of them have any idea who could have done this?"

He sighed. "Huh-uh. No can do."

"Come on, Frank." Her voice softened. "Do it for me. You know I can call her son and daughter myself. Jared and I talked to them for our articles when Edna San first moved here, and they liked us."

"So go call them. I'm hanging up now."

"Frank—"

The line clicked in her ear.

"Oooh!" She made a face at the phone and threw it on the passenger seat.

After another mile Leslie hit town. She planned to pull over on the first block of Main Street, out of sight of Jared in the *Times* office. She'd need both hands free to write down the numbers from Information. *Let's see.* She calculated the various contacts she should make. FOX News—home of her fave reporter, Milt Waking, so that one was a no-brainer. CNN. MSNBC. CNBC. That ought to do it.

The rest of the media were going to come running soon anyway, national included. What she needed was to position herself as liaison for the all-news channels right up front. With any luck, one or two of them would interview her for information. Sure, reporters liked to break their own stories, but if she made herself indispensable, just maybe ... She'd seen it a million times on the cable news networks—a local reporter with on-site information being filmed. All those perfectly coifed, slick television reporters from Spokane would salivate over the chance at a national segment. Leslie had to beat 'em out.

Leslie turned right on Main Street and spotted a parking place just down from Java Joint. She pulled in and put the car in park, leaving the engine running and the air-conditioning blasting.

Here goes, girl. Sound professional, not like your heart's in your throat.

The first part was easy—getting the numbers from Information. That done, she took a deep breath and forged ahead.

Each network bounced her from person to person. It took her a while to reach Someone Who Mattered. And she never did speak with anyone whose name she recognized. Still, she persisted, and hung up from each phone call believing she'd made a contact. She told them enough details to hook them (which didn't take much more than Edna San's name and the word *disappeared*), then let them know she had exclusive information. Each network took her cell phone number and said they'd look into sending out a camera crew and reporter. Leslie winced at the *r* word. As for the camera crew part, she knew renting a satellite truck from Seattle and getting it to Kanner Lake would take the afternoon at the very least. They'd probably try renting the smaller microwave trucks from Spokane, since it was so much closer. But the Spokane stations would be needing those trucks for their own coverage at Kanner Lake.

Last call made and her mouth totally dry, Leslie lowered the phone to her lap with relief.

Now. Until those fancy national reporters showed up, she needed all the inside scoop she could get. A quick trip into Java Joint for an iced mocha and any new leads she could muster, and she'd be on the road again.

Leslie switched off her engine and withdrew the keys. Her hand was on the door latch when she spotted a familiar figure across the street and up one block, turning into Simple Pleasures.

Chief Edwards.

Leslie froze, her reporter's antennae waving furiously. At a time like this, no way the man was shopping. Why wasn't he at the station, setting up his command post for the missing person case?

Oookay. Maybe she didn't need that iced mocha after all.

The car was already getting hot. She restarted the engine. Then perched in her seat, muscles twitching, eyes laser focused on the door of the shop. A few minutes later Chief Edwards materialized. With him was a twentysomething woman. Short, spiky black hair. Prominent cheekbones, model pretty. Leslie had seen her around a few times.

Whoa. One-on-onesies with the chief of police, so soon after he left Edna San's place? This girl knew something.

Leslie watched them walk up the street one block and cross. She opened her car door, stuck one foot out on the pavement, half-rising. Craning her neck to see where they went.

Into the chief's police car, that's where.

Double whoa.

When the car pulled out of its parking space, Leslie followed.

THIRTY-FIVE

Well now, look at that.

Black Mamba stood in the doorway of Savors, a restaurant on the third block of Main open for dinners only. With its long white awning, recessed entrance, and current closed state, Savors afforded him the perfect place to wait and watch. Shadowed in the tiled and arched threshold, he wore a baseball cap and new T-shirt he'd bought over in Spirit Lake.

With great satisfaction he watched the Kanner Lake chief of police escort a young woman up the street to his car. Paige Williams.

For this, Mamba had returned from Spirit Lake before making his phone call. Standing at the pay phone in that town, he'd *felt* something. A primal instinct coiling within, the sense that events in Kanner Lake were slipping along like a serpent through swamp. In his work over the years, he'd felt the same prescience many a time and knew to heed it. Mamba had stilled, the phone in his palm. In such a moment an apprised snake would pull up, flicker its tongue, seeking the source of vibration. He fancied himself doing the same, in tune with the primordial fibrillation ...

After a moment he'd replaced the receiver.

Now he would wait no longer in the Savors doorway. Passersby who happened to spot him would think little of someone stepping out of the sun for a cooling moment but might wonder if he lurked too long. He would cruise the shops idly, watching the entrance of Simple Pleasures. Would the police bring Paige Williams back? Or had they already linked the earring to her?

Little matter. His phone call would seal her fate.

THIRTY-SIX

Rachel is caught. Trapped in her own bedroom.

Red Shirt fills her threshold, the spread fingers of his huge left hand lingering against the door. From his right hand dangles a pocketknife — the tool that so easily popped her lock. Music and TV noise swell from down the hall.

Rachel can't move. Her mind zings, frantically searching for some weapon she can snatch up to defend herself.

He steps inside, closes the door. His eyes don't leave her face.

Rachel tries to convince herself not to panic, but it's no use. His calculating expression screams his intent. Her legs shake. She slips a hand over the back of the chair and holds on.

Red Shirt raises his chin, looks at her down his wide nose. "We can do this quietly or you can get stupid and fight — the choice is yours. Either way I win." He speaks with perfect calm, as if talking about the weather. Then shrugs. "Just trying to save you some bruises."

Rachel's limbs go numb. "Where's Rosa?" The words squeak from her throat.

"Drugged out, like the rest of them. They probably think I walked out the front door."

She swallows. "I'll scream. They'll be here in no time."

He lunges.

Before Rachel can move, he clamps her body and arms against himself in a vise, the other hand around her throat. He shoves his big face into hers, snarling. "You scream, you pay. Got it?"

Rachel struggles to breathe. Her nostrils flare, her jaw hinges open. His fingers press harder and black dots crowd her vision. Choking sounds gurgle from her mouth. Somehow she manages a nod.

"Good girl." He releases her throat and she slumps against him, furiously rattling in air.

He massages her shoulder like some longtime lover. "I prefer a relaxed ambiance myself."

The feigned warmth of his tone chills her soul.

He pushes her onto the bed. A voice within Rachel accuses that she deserves this, that the remaining part of herself she should have given Devon will now be trampled in the dust. *Devon won't want you now, you know. He won't want you at all.*

She closes her ears to the words.

Red Shirt puts his hands on her. Cold. Grasping. Stripping away her dignity. Her very *self.* Rachel endures the violation — until its black treachery will swallow her alive.

She clamps down all emotion then. Every little piece of it. Just like when she was a kid and Rosa beat her.

I am not here.

Her defeated spirit draws away, up, up, and out of her. Helpless, hovering in the far top corner of the room, Rachel turns away from her own degradation.

THIRTY-SEVEN

Questions ran through Vince Edwards's head like ticker tape as he opened the passenger door of his vehicle for Paige Williams to get in. And every one of them made him uneasy.

This should be a routine interview. Although he was obligated to follow up on the lead, he hadn't expected it to get him very far. How could a twentysomething gal with no priors be savvy enough to shoot a guard dog in the head, enter a protected house without setting off the alarm, and force testy Edna San all the way through the woods to a waiting car?

And yet the girl next to him was scared to death.

She'd been frightened the moment he walked into the shop. Oh, he'd pretended not to notice, chatting with Sarah, keeping it all friendly. But the young woman's pulse practically beat through her neck, and her body looked stiff as a board. Her anxiety had only increased when he escorted her out of the store and up the street. Now her taut spine barely touched the back of the seat.

He headed for Kanner Lake Road, which ran west over to Highway 41. He couldn't think of one place in town where he could take Paige with any amount of privacy. The streets were already buzzing with the news of Edna San's disappearance. During the few minutes he spent at the station equipping himself with the hidden tape recorder, they'd received nearly a dozen phone calls from the curious, wanting to know if the rumors were true.

Out a few miles on Kanner Lake Road sat a small diner called Lakeside. A misnomer, since it was nowhere near the water. Owner Bud Brankser, a retired California policeman, no doubt had been dreaming big when he opened the place over ten years ago. Dreaming either of the lake overflowing its banks all the way up to his doorstep or of making enough money to move to a building at water's edge. Either way, his dream hadn't come to fruition. But his diner was quiet, with checkered plastic table-cloths and decent sandwiches, and one particular table removed from the rest in a small raised alcove. "Lovers' Ledge," Bud called it, due to the privacy it afforded occupants. Vince had used the table numerous times. As for Bud—once a cop, always a cop. When Vince asked for that table, Bud knew the drill.

Vince glanced at Paige as he drove. She was staring blankly out her window. "You all right? Air-conditioning cool enough for you?"

"It's fine." Her head did not move.

He spotted a familiar car some distance behind them. *Wonderful.* Leslie Brymes, reporter extraordinaire. How had she heard about this so quickly? He cast another look at Paige, hoping she remained unaware of the blaringly painted VW behind them and who was at the wheel. Knowing a reporter was on her tail might spook Paige even more, cause her to clam up. That he didn't need.

"We'll be there in just a few more minutes," he told her.

No reply. They drove the rest of the way in silence, save for the squawks on his radio, which he turned as low as he could.

Vince's mind drifted to Tim. Then Nancy. If this investigation stretched into fateful tomorrow—which was likely—he couldn't take the day off. As much as he'd promised his wife to stay by her side on the anniversary of Tim's death, duty would call. And Nancy would not understand, not this time. She needed him far too much. He should be with her. Holding and soothing her.

Fact was, Vince had no energy for that. Even worse, a part of him was glad for the excuse to be away. For work to keep his mind occupied. If he could blitz through the day, distracted by responsibilities, how much easier would that be?

Vince, you are pathetic. What kind of a husband have you turned into?

He rounded a curve and Lakeside diner came into view. "There's a place to stop up ahead." He spoke the words with a smile in his tone. "They make a great chicken salad sandwich."

Paige nodded.

So fearful. Guarded. Why?

Maybe it was nothing more than being questioned by an officer during an investigation. But his gut told him it was more than that.

He'd soon find out.

Before getting out of the car, he slipped a hand under his shirt and switched on the hidden tape recorder.

THIRTY-EIGHT

Sometimes it didn't pay to drive a yellow VW bug with pink daisies on the side. Like now, as Leslie tried her best to tail Chief Edwards without being noticed, like some clandestine CIA operative. Worse, this wasn't exactly San Francisco, where she could hide in traffic. Chief was tootling down Kanner Lake Road—with no one but Leslie behind him. The best she could do was hang back, waaay back, keeping her focus glued on his sun-soaked, gleaming silver bumper, hoping he didn't maneuver some sudden turn that left her in the proverbial dust.

Where was he going?

Energy revved through Leslie like gasoline through a racing engine. She was onto something, no ifs, ands, or buts—and she wasn't about to lose it. Whatever *it* was.

The chief's car disappeared around a curve. Leslie resisted the urge to punch the accelerator. "Okay, Chief, just don't do a beam-me-up-Scotty while you're outta view."

She rounded the curve and caught sight of him once more.

Yo, girl, go.

Driving with her left hand, not daring to take her eyes from the road, Leslie fumbled for her phone on the passenger seat. Clutching it in her palm, she used her thumb to dial 411 for a connection to Simple Pleasures.

Sarah Wray answered on the first ring.

"Sarah, hi! Leslie Brymes here."

VIOLET DAWN

"Oh yes. Hello, Leslie." Sarah sounded worried.

Ah, I can use that.

"Listen, Sarah, I'm on this Edna San case, as you've probably guessed." Leslie spoke rapidly before the woman could cut her off. "I've been out at the estate and talked to Chief Edwards and know quite a few things that haven't been made public yet. Now I see the chief taking your employee off in his police car. That can't be good on a day like this. What's going on?"

"Oh, Leslie, you're not going to print anything about this, are you?" Sarah's voice pinched. "Paige hasn't done anything wrong. Chief told us this was just a routine interview. Besides, what happened yesterday was Edna San's fault, *all* of it."

Paige. Leslie made a mental note of the name.

"Sure, Sarah, I can believe that, knowing Edna. But I want to get my story exactly right so there's no unnecessary dirt thrown on Paige. Hit me with the details, would you? I won't quote you if you don't want me to. But I will help straighten things out about your employee."

As Leslie drove, keeping an eye on the chief's car, the story tumbled from Sarah. *Whoa.* A run-in with Edna San the day before she disappeared. Rotten timing for this Paige person. Leslie yearned for a third hand to write down everything. But best she could do was file the information away in her ninety-mile-an-hour brain.

When Sarah finished, Leslie pumped her for a few extra details. What was Paige's last name? Who else was in the store when the unfortunate event took place? Why should the chief believe Paige had something to do with Edna's disappearance just because the actress had behaved like a complete toad?

"I have no *idea*," Sarah huffed. "No way Paige could be involved with this. She is one of the sweetest girls I've ever met. She's just quiet. Keeps to herself, but then I don't think she's had the easiest life. You should call Paige sometime, Leslie. She needs

178

a friend. Doesn't have any family of her own, can you imagine that? *No* one."

No one? Leslie narrowed her eyes. Everybody had someone. Maybe it just wasn't a someone Paige Williams wanted anything to do with …

Leslie added that piece of information to the tickler file in her head. This definitely needed a follow-up.

The chief's car vanished around another curve. When Leslie spotted it again, the vehicle was pulling into the small gravel parking lot of Lakeside diner.

Ah. He was taking Paige to lunch. A friendly little chat over a meal. How nice.

Leslie slowed down. No way to avoid being spotted now. As she passed the diner, the chief was opening the passenger door of his car. She caught a quick glimpse of Paige as the girl slid out. Chief Edwards glanced in Leslie's direction and gave a small wave.

Drat. Leslie thumped the steering wheel with her palm. He'd probably known she was behind him all along.

Head held high, even though she was now out of Chief Edwards's sight, Leslie drove on, telling herself her cheeks were not flaming and she was still a knock-'em-dead sleuth. That she'd been spotted was totally the VW's fault.

Besides, she shouldn't let it get to her. She was just doing her job.

Leslie slowed further, seeking a place to turn around. For a moment she considered pulling off and waiting for the chief and Paige to emerge from the diner, then nixed the idea. Nothing more to be gained by following them back to town. Her time would be better spent checking out the latest happenings at the San estate.

And sometime very soon she'd start working on that friendship with Paige Williams.

THIRTY-NINE

Hard wooden slats on the chair pushed against Paige's back. The cramped alcove made her claustrophobic, the window on her left with cheery red curtains doing little to reduce the pressure in her chest. The knotty wall to her right sported various hunting pictures—a dog with a bird in his mouth, a man sighting down the barrel of a rifle, three men in a duck blind. Hunting—an apropos theme. She may just get shot out of the water herself.

You'd better get a grip, Paige.

Chief Edwards settled across from her, elbows on the table, hands loosely clasped. He regarded her with an open expression and kept his tone neutral, almost light. Paige wasn't buying his demeanor for a minute. If this little lunch was so routine, why was it happening *now*, with the news of Edna San's disappearance so fresh upon the streets? This leader of law enforcement should have better things to do. His focus upon her smelled of priority as surely as Edna San's body had smelled last night.

Paige repressed a shiver.

"Hey there, folks." A balding man, about sixty, approached their table, all smiles, two plastic-coated menus in hand. These he lay before them, his brown eyes flicking from the chief to Paige. No question in that expression, no hint of surprise. He folded his arms, stood with feet apart. "What can I get you to drink while you're deciding?"

Paige ordered a Coke, and the chief, a 7-Up. The waiter spread his hands as if to say *Whatever I have is yours* and left them.

For a moment they perused their menus in silence, Paige huddled over and frowning as if choosing the last meal of her life. She hid her hands in her lap, afraid the chief would notice the scrapes on her palms.

The chief put down his menu. "Because we're talking, I need to tell you your rights. Just a formality, you understand." Before she could respond, he launched into Miranda. Her right to remain silent, her right to a lawyer, and so on. Paige's nerves tingled. This was sounding less and less like a friendly little chat. Why had she agreed to this?

"Do you understand your rights?" he asked.

"Yeah, sure." Paige's throat felt tight.

"Good." He leaned back in his chair. "So tell me, when did you move here?"

Paige pushed her menu aside, struggling to gather her wits. "A month ago." Did her voice sound okay?

He nodded. "How long have you worked at Simple Pleasures?"

"Almost that long. I was lucky to find the job right away."

"Do you like it here?"

"Yes, very much. The area's beautiful and I like Kanner Lake. I hope to stay a long time."

"Where do you live? In town?"

"No. Out on Lakeshore Road just a little down on the west side, about ten minutes from town. It's a rented house kind of up on a hill, with a view of the water. I can look at an angle across the top of the lake and see the lights of town at night."

"Must be very pretty."

"It is."

He rubbed his temple. "What's the street number of your place?"

"Thirty-six ninety-two."

"And your landlord?"

"Clinton Ryskie." *Edna's chained body yanking her down, down in the water.* "You know him?"

The chief nodded. "Yeah. He's lived here all his life, like me. I used to mow his lawn when I was a kid."

She managed a little smile.

The chief asked her a string of innocuous questions, then abruptly turned a corner. "Do you have any idea what happened to Edna San?"

Struggling for the surface, aching to breathe.

Paige widened her eyes. "Not at all. I don't even know the woman."

He regarded her for a moment. She forced herself not to look away.

He drew a breath. "So tell me about yourself and what made you come to Kanner Lake."

Of course, Paige knew it would come to this. Rather ironic, after all her efforts last night to protect her anonymity. On the drive here she had dug deep into her soul, seeking strength to do what must be done, when she felt none at all. Just like last night. How many times in her life had she been faced with the same Sisyphean task? At this table, sitting with this cop, Paige Williams knew she was on her own once again, with neither God nor man to care. She'd been on her own since birth.

God bless you, Paige. Bailey Truitt's words popped into her head. Not likely, after all she had done.

Paige swallowed. "No taking notes?"

Chief Edwards gave her a little smile. "You've watched too much TV."

She nodded briefly. Under the table her fingers sank into her legs. " 'Tell me about yourself' is kind of a broad question. What exactly do you want to know?"

He shrugged. "First tell me where you were born, where you grew up."

The waiter returned with two cans on a small round tray, lowering it with a flourish, Paige's soda on her side and the chief's on his side. "Here you go." They picked up their cans, set them down. The man looked satisfied. "Okay now, what can I get you for lunch?"

Chief Edwards ordered the chicken salad sandwich on croissant. Paige stared into the waiter's face, her mind a blank. "Uh, same for me, thanks."

"Coming right up." The man withdrew, leaving Paige to her fate.

"Okay. So." Chief Edwards spread his hands. "I'm listening."

A strange, static-filled calm settled over Paige, like the sudden stilling of an electrical storm. She raised her eyes to the chief's. "I don't want any trouble, okay? I understand you have to ask me questions, and I'll answer them. But I don't like to talk about my past, because I'm trying to leave it behind me. Not everybody has a childhood worth talking about, you know?"

He nodded. "Yeah, I hear you."

She licked her lips. "I was born in Kansas on April 12, 1981. My parents' names were Betty and Justin. They were killed in a car accident when I was three. They'd left me with a babysitter while they went out to dinner. So I've been told, anyway."

"Where in Kansas?"

"Whitsung. You probably never heard of it. It's a small farming town a little north of Wichita."

"I see. So who did you live with after you lost your parents?"

Paige sighed. "I had no brothers or sisters. No aunts or uncles who wanted to take me in. Evidently, my parents weren't close with their families." Paige watched a bead of moisture run down her soda can. "So I had to go live with a foster family."

"What were their names?"

"I don't remember. I didn't stay with them long. Well, maybe two years. I really don't remember much of anything about that time. Except that their house burned down and they lost everything. After that, they figured taking care of their own three kids was enough, so they ... gave me back." Paige affected a little shrug. "You know, kind of like a dog you don't want anymore."

Chief Edwards pulled in air, let it out slowly. "I'm sorry to hear that. The foster system can be so tough on kids."

Their waiter returned, in each hand a plate with a croissant sandwich, cut in half, and chips. He laid the lunches down, asked if he could get them anything else. They shook their heads and he retreated.

The chief picked up a piece of his sandwich. "Then where did you go?"

Paige eyed her plate. Her stomach grumbled with unexpected hunger at the sight, yet the thought of eating made her queasy. She picked up a potato chip, took a small bite. "Another foster home. But don't ask me their names, because I don't remember them either. See, I ended up in"—she narrowed her eyes at the hunting pictures on the wall—"six altogether. Some of the homes were okay. But most were awful. I was neglected, abused—in more ways than one—and put to work like Cinderella. The last home I was in had two teenage sons who were into drugs. The police must have gotten a tip from somebody, because they came to search the house. The oldest son found out they were on their way and stuffed the drugs under the mattress in my room. I wasn't home at the time. The police found the stuff. The boys insisted it was mine. I was afraid they were going to arrest me so I ran away."

The chief chewed his sandwich, frowning. "You must remember the name of this family?"

Paige hesitated. "Johnson was their last name."

"First names?"

She shook her head. "I don't remember. I just called them Mom and Dad Johnson."

"How old were you at this time?"

"Fourteen."

"Pretty young." The chief sounded empathetic. "Where'd you go?"

Paige dropped her gaze. A potato chip had fallen from her plate onto the table, and she pushed it around with one finger. "I left the state, I was so scared. Ended up in South Dakota. I lived on the street for a while—at least it was summer, so I didn't freeze to death." Her voice tightened. "Then I found a boyfriend—a man in his twenties. And I moved in with him." She pushed at the crumb. "It didn't turn out to be a good thing, but I didn't have anywhere else to go, you know?"

"I understand." The chief's voice was low. "He mistreat you?"

Paige closed her eyes and nodded.

A moment of silence passed.

He cleared his throat. "I'm sorry, Ms. Williams. I truly am."

She lowered her head in a gesture of thanks. "The good part about it was, I had a decent job as a checker in a grocery store. I stuck it out a long time so I could save enough money to buy my used Ford Explorer." She gave a wan smile. "With wheels and a little extra cash, I was able to get out of there."

Chief Edwards gave her a minute to relax while he ate two more bites of his sandwich. With reluctant hands Paige picked up her own sandwich and took a small bite. It was surprisingly good.

"Looks like you scraped your palms a little there. What happened?" The question fell with such casualness that Paige wondered how long ago he'd noticed. Her mouth stopped chewing. "Oh." She swallowed the food, suddenly tasting like sawdust. "I slipped yesterday on my gravel driveway. Caught myself with my hands."

He nodded as if accepting her explanation. For a moment they ate in silence. Paige did her best to down a few bites.

The chief wiped at his mouth with a paper napkin. "So how did you end up in Kanner Lake?"

Memories of her lonely and fright-filled trip filled Paige's mind. "I took to the interstate, not really knowing where I was going. Only that I needed to get away before Ronnie—the man I lived with—came looking for me. I went north and then headed west. I'd always liked the idea of being around forest and mountains, so Idaho sounded good to me. I could have ended up in Montana, but I wanted more space between me and the past. Guess I might have gone on to Washington, but Montana was so long that when I reached Idaho, I figured I'd gone far enough."

"You came across on 90, then, into Coeur d'Alene?"

"Yes. I could have stayed there. I did for a day—it's so beautiful. But I didn't want anyone from the past to find me—ever—and Coeur d'Alene was a bigger town, with their resort bringing tourists from all over. I decided to look for a smaller place—somewhere near a lake. When I first saw Kanner Lake, I knew." She shrugged a shoulder. "And then it seemed like fate when I saw the Employee Wanted sign in Simple Pleasures. Sarah said she'd just posted it and expected to find someone within a day. It's like the job was waiting for me, you know? So here I am."

Paige took a long drink of her soda. The chief finished his sandwich and started in on his potato chips. She attempted another bite.

"Well, I thank you for that story." Chief Edwards looked straight into her eyes. For a moment Paige wondered at his choice of word. "Okay. Let's get the necessary questions out of the way so I can take you back to work. Can you tell me where you were last night?"

Paige forced herself to look Chief Edwards in the eye. "At home."

"All evening?"

"Yes."

"By yourself?"

"Yes."

He eyed her inquisitively. "Is that what you usually do, just go home from work and stay there?"

She dropped her eyes, feeling the sting of his question for more reasons than one. "I don't really know anybody here yet. I mean, that I would hang around with. I hope to make friends, but that takes a while, you know? I'm not all that good at it yet."

"I'm sure you'll make friends, Paige." His voice was gentle. "This is a great town, with good people."

For a moment they were silent. Chief Edwards ate some more potato chips. "What did you do all evening?"

Paige sighed inwardly. "Read mostly. I didn't used to read much, but it's something I started doing since I came here. I get novels from the library. I like to sit out on my deck with a book. The view is beautiful."

"What time did you go to bed?"

Paige focused on a truck driving by outside. "I don't know. Eleven thirty, maybe. Twelve." She looked back to him, her heart pumping. *Please don't ask if I stayed there.*

"Okay. So. Now if you'll just tell me what happened when Edna San came into your store."

The memory surged through Paige. "Not a very nice story, but if you want it ..."

She began with the two teenage girls—apparently sisters—who'd entered Simple Pleasures. How she'd started to approach them but stopped halfway, watching as they oohed and aahed over the glittery jewelry and picture frames. "I was thinking how much I'd like a sister. Someone who'd really understand and accept me, you know?" Paige glanced at the chief. This dream of her heart wasn't easy to relate. But if he saw her sincerity here, he might be less inclined to question other parts of her story.

He nodded.

Paige turned her gaze out the window again, the heat of yesterday's humiliation stealing through her veins.

One of the girls had turned and caught her staring. Paige looked away, embarrassed, pretended to straighten a few items. "Excuse me?" The girl said, holding up a blue-rhinestone-studded address book. "Do you have one like this in pink?"

Paige apologized that she didn't, then thrashed about for something to say, just to keep the girl talking. Suddenly the girl's eyes rounded, focusing on something behind Paige. Paige turned to find herself face-to-face with a woman she knew from old movies—Edna San.

"Good afternoon, Ms. San," she stuttered. "May I help you?"

The actress's lips were pink and outlined in fuchsia; bleached blonde hair hung straight to her shoulders. She waved a bejeweled hand at Paige. "No, no, just looking." Her whiny drawl sounded just as it did from the movie screen. She wandered a few feet to inspect a silk flower garland.

Paige looked back toward the girls. They busied themselves at the display of address books, furtively watching every move Edna San made. Paige faded toward the counter, eyeing her as well. The woman dropped the garland upon its table as if it failed to measure up. She moved on to a vase and bouquet, feeling one petal before turning to Paige with an impatient frown. Her long-nailed fingers sought the sides of her head, massaged the temples. "Is this *all* you have in silk flowers?"

Paige flushed with self-consciousness, aware that the two girls watched. Edna San's scowl seemed directed at her personally, as if her employment at this disappointing shop devalued her worth. She pushed away from the counter. "We have some other arrangements farther back. Would you like me to show you?"

Another dismissive wave. "Don't bother. I can see for myself."

Paige could do nothing but return to her stool behind the counter as Edna moved from one display area to another, mere glances apparently enough to tell her that what she sought could not be found. Just as Paige thought the woman would give up, Edna slowed before a soft pink cashmere blanket draped over a chair. She felt the fabric, then picked up the blanket and unfolded it, checking its length. She turned toward the cash register, item in hand.

Near the address book table, the two girls still took in the scene. By now other customers in the store had noticed the actress, casting sidelong glances at her as they feigned nonchalant shopping.

"I'll take this." Edna heaped the blanket, still unfolded, upon the counter and rubbed her forehead. She plopped down her purse, pulled out a pair of expensive-looking sunglasses, then a wallet, and set them both beside her purchase.

"Do you have a headache, Ms. San?" Paige reached for the pink fabric, seeking the price tag.

Edna closed her eyes, flicking a hand in the air as if sending an annoying servant from the room. "Yes, yes. Just ring it up quickly."

The coldness in her tone rattled Paige further. The last thing she needed was to upset this woman in front of the whole store. Hurriedly Paige pushed the edges of the blanket around, looking for the small white tag.

"Hey." Edna's hand shot toward her sunglasses. "Watch—"

They slid off the counter and clattered to the wooden floor.

"Oh!" Paige froze. "I'm so sorry!" She moved to go pick up the glasses. "Here, let me—"

"Never mind," Edna spat. She bent over to retrieve them, then straightened, withering Paige with a look. In one hand she held the glasses, in the other, a single lens that had popped out. "See what you've done."

Paige's cheeks burned. "I'm really sorry, Ms. San. I'll pay to have them fixed. Or if I have to, I'll buy you another—"

"You couldn't afford these with a month's salary." Edna's sharp tone reverberated through the store. She blinked her eyes and winced, as if the sound of her own voice heightened the pain in her head.

The noise brought Sarah Wray hustling from her rear office.

"Just forget the blanket." Edna threw the broken glasses into her purse and grabbed her wallet. "With this headache, I don't know why I came in this place anyway." She glared at Paige. "As for you, learn to pay attention to what you're doing. You were so gaga-eyed, watching those two girls, you could hardly focus."

The perfectly fired poison arrow buried itself in Paige's heart. Behind Edna, the two girls stared at her, wide-eyed and pitying. It was the pity she couldn't stand.

"What's going on here?" Sarah reached the counter, blinking with dismay from Paige to Edna. "Ms. San, what can I do for you?"

Edna pulled her head back, heavily mascaraed eyes flaming. "You can hire some better help, that's what." She pointed a shaking finger at Paige. "If I ever come in here again, I expect *her* not to be here." Snatching up her purse, the actress swiveled on her heel and sailed out the door, chin held high.

In the store, shoppers remained locked in stunned postures. Paige felt cemented to the floor. Sarah pressed her lips, her indignant face flushing. A man near the entrance broke the spell, slipping outside. He spoke a few words to Edna, which only seemed to anger her more. A moment later her car appeared and picked her up.

Paige's one solace was the disgust shared between the two young sisters. "Nasty old bat," whispered the girl Paige had spoken to. The sister rolled her eyes. "No kidding."

Across the table from Chief Edwards, Paige stared at her plate. She gave a little shrug. "And that's what happened."

The chief made a sound in his throat. "Didn't exactly make a good impression on you, did she."

Paige shook her head.

He pushed his plate away. "You remember who all was in the store?"

She looked at her half-eaten sandwich. "Those girls and two or three other women, each by themselves, I think. And the man who talked to Ms. San outside. I think he was trying to calm her down, but it obviously didn't work." Paige took a slow drink of her Coke.

Chief Edwards pursed his lips, as if confused. "You sure you told me everything? After Ms. San left the shop, you didn't say anything else, do anything else?"

Paige thought a moment. "No. I don't think so."

He gave one slow nod—a nod that sent prickles darting down her back. Some suspicion in his law enforcement brain was pushing through his friendly facade, some *aha* that her last words had birthed.

"That's not quite what I'm hearing," he said.

Paige stilled, her fingers lingering upon her can of soda. "What do you mean?"

He leaned forward, his eyes probing. "I heard you threatened to kill Ms. San."

FORTY

The house is huge.

Rachel turns off the engine of her ten-year-old Honda and gawks at Rosa's new home. The stucco walls are perfectly white, windows trimmed in blue. A graceful porch extends the length of the first story, creating a deck, bordered by sculpted posts, for the upstairs front rooms. Wicker furniture on the porch, a green lawn, even flowers.

And nothing but dirt living inside.

Rachel gets out of her car and stares some more. Myriad reactions hit her, then bounce off. This house is like the ones in her childhood dreams — where she was loved and nurtured, and friends came over to play and spend the night. Now she is twenty. Two years on her own since high school, living in a tiny dump of an apartment — and *Rosa* lives here?

So what, Rachel? You know how they bought it.

Why had she come here? She should have ignored her mother's invitation.

Rachel walks slowly up the perfectly edged sidewalk, smelling honeysuckle. A breeze plays with her hair. At the first porch step she falters, searching within herself for any hint of weakness. Though she lives only ten miles away, she has not seen Rosa for over a year. Rachel vows to display nothing of herself here, not one emotion. No resentment, no bitterness. No if onlys. Her life is fine. She has a steady job as a receptionist in a large office, even has

192

a few friends. Many men want her. She just doesn't want them. She does not need Rosa, and certainly doesn't need anything the woman might try to give her.

As if her mother could make up for all those black years. For all the neglect and abuse, and failing to protect her when she needed it most —

Rachel, don't.

She steadies herself. Almost turns around. Suddenly she is not feeling strong, not at all, and this she cannot afford. Why does she fear seeing Rosa yet long to see her? Why does she both hate and love the woman? Rachel has a life to live. She *will* belong some-day — to someone. To a husband who needs her, and children. She *does not need* her mother —

The fancy wide door with etched panes of glass swings open.

"Hi, hon! Welcome to my humble abode!"

Hon?

Rosa poses with one hand on her hip, the other on the edge of the heavy door. Her head angles with supreme satisfaction, her bright red lips wide in a proud smile. Her bleached hair lies dry and spiky on her bare shoulders. She wears a short leather skirt, reveal-ing skinny tanned legs, and a beaded white halter top. Around her neck hangs a tasteless chunky gold chain.

"Well, come in, and hug your mother. I haven't seen you for so long!" Rosa tosses out the words, so blithe, so cavalier, as if they are long-lost buddies with nothing but happy memories between them.

"Hello, Rosa." Rachel keeps her voice even as she steps inside. She doesn't want to give Rosa even a cursory embrace, but Rosa reaches out both arms theatrically and pulls her near. Musky per-fume fills Rachel's nostrils and she holds her breath. She doesn't bother to hide her own stiffness, but if Rosa notices, she doesn't let on.

"Okay, come on." Rosa bounces like an excited child. "Let me show you the house. Eddie's not here right now, so it's just us two chicks." She titters.

Eddie — the big drug man. The latest boyfriend who helps Rosa afford all this.

Reluctantly Rachel follows, keeping her chin high, holding on to her heart. Rosa's heeled sandals *clap-clap* against the polished hardwood floor of the entryway, the large kitchen. Everything is immaculate. Someone other than Rosa clearly keeps up the place.

"We have a maid," Rosa explains as if reading her mind. Her hands make circles in the air, gold bracelets tinkling. "I drop something, she picks it up. She's the *best*, Rachel. You really should have one." She seems to forget that Rachel could ill afford such a luxury.

Rosa chatters her way through the formal dining and living rooms, pointing out designer furniture, the fine stitching of throw pillows, the marble fireplace. Rachel murmurs through it all, "Yes, it's beautiful" and "Oh, how nice." Rosa flits through the den with a huge plasma TV, the rec room with a pool table, then scoots up the stairs. As Rachel reaches the plush white carpet of the first step, the irony of it all hits her again. Such loveliness — built on filth. On selling illegal, dangerous drugs that lead to addiction and death. Any day now, Rosa's fairy-tale world could come tumbling down. She could sleep in these fine surroundings one night, on a thin mattress behind cold iron bars the next. And Rachel marvels anew at Rosa's never-ending self-centeredness. The more the woman shows off her new belongings, the less she seems aware of Rachel's wooden responses, until she doesn't even wait for one at all.

"We have four bedrooms up here, including the master suite, which you won't believe." Rosa hums as she sails through the open door of the first bedroom. "Look at this one, Rachel. I decorated it just for you. Remember when you were little how you wanted a bedroom in baby blue with a four-poster bed? Well, here it is!"

Rachel halts at the threshold. She takes in the double bed with lacy coverlet and matching canopy. Lined curtains of the same material at the two large windows. Freshly painted light-blue walls, plush blue carpet. It's everything a little girl could hope for.

Pain stabs her like a hot-bladed knife. In that moment, amid Rosa's happy chatter and the pristine bedroom, everything Rachel has lacked in her life, everything she has ever dreamed of, swirls together in a dust storm that batters her very soul. The force is so strong, so stinging, that it leaves Rachel reeling. She reaches out and hangs on to the doorframe for support.

Rosa sweeps past her back out into the hall. "And in this bedroom over here—"

"*Rosa!*" The name jumps from Rachel's mouth. She whirls to face her mother, heartbeat surging.

The woman jerks in surprise, red-nailed hands hanging in the air. "Huh?"

"Are you still doing *business* with Blake?"

Rosa blinks at the harsh tone. Her animated expression fades. "Why do you ask that?"

"Because I want to know."

Rosa's head draws back and her lips tighten. She looks like a spoiled child whose party was just disrupted. "Okay, yes. Not that it's any of your business."

Indignation and fury stiffen Rachel's back. "It is my business. It was always my business. Because I'm your daughter. Because I lived in the same house with you, and whoever came in and out of our front door affected *my* life. Don't you get that?"

Rosa's eyes widen. One hand finds its way to her throat. "Well, I always tried to do what was—"

"You always did what *you* wanted, Rosa. Never what I needed!" The sudden tornado blows harder in Rachel's chest and there is no stopping it now. It is wailing and moaning, sucking up every brick in her carefully constructed wall and spitting it out.

"Wait just a minute." Rosa's expression turns hard. She leans toward Rachel, shaking a finger in her face. "Don't you tell me how to be a mother until you're one yourself. You have no idea how hard it is—"

"He raped me, you know." The ugly truth spurts from her. "Blake. Your business contact. That first night he saw me. He raped me in my own bed. In your house. And where were you, *Mother*?" The word bludgeons. "High on speed in the den, that's where. You and your latest boyfriend and the sorry, stinking lot of you!"

Tears fill Rachel's eyes. She despises her weakness, but she despises the woman in front of her more. She grips the doorframe, waiting for a response from Rosa's twisted mouth, wanting … *something*. Some word of apology, a sense of horror and shame.

Rosa draws herself up, nostrils flaring. Her eyes narrow. "You little liar. You're just jealous of what I have. Can't stand to see me happy. You have to come in here and spoil it for me, don't you?"

Even coming from her mother, this is unbelievable. Rachel's throat burns. "You know what? I think you knew what happened. You were just too drugged out of your mind to care. Then if you acknowledged what he did, you wouldn't have been able to let him come around anymore, would you? You'd have been out your supplier."

Bright red circles dot Rosa's cheeks. "Oh, really. If it's true, why didn't *you* do something about it?"

"Who would I go to, Rosa? The cops in our area were on the take, remember? Who'd have believed me over protecting you? And if they did listen about the rape and the drugs, where would I be then? You'd have gone to jail and I'd have been out on the street, and goodness knows if they would've caught up to Blake. He'd have come after me in a heartbeat."

196

Rosa flings her arm toward the stairs. "Get out! I don't know why I had you come here. I don't want to see you here ever again!"

Rachel's body goes cold. "No, I suppose not." She pushes out of the doorway. "My presence — and the glaring truth — might taint your sterling white walls."

The world blurs as she stalks down the stairs, clinging to the polished rail for support. Rosa hurls caustic words at her back.

"I was a good parent! I did all I could do for you. You've been a *brat* since the day you were born!"

At the bottom of the staircase Rachel turns and looks up at her. Rosa huddles at the top step, knuckles white against the banister, cords standing out on her splotchy neck. At forty-two she looks at once ragged and old, and the petulant, stubborn child.

The storm within Rachel abruptly dies, leaving her with the aching emptiness she brought to this horrible place. "Rosa." She is amazed at how calm her voice is. Dead calm. "*No* baby is a brat. Babies are meant to be loved."

She turns toward the expensive front door, away from the woman fate gave her as a mother. Her steps clatter hollowly across the floor and down the perfect porch steps.

FORTY-ONE

Vince had watched Paige carefully as they talked. He was no lie detector machine. As a human he was far more, and far less, than electrodes and recording graphs. He came with his own emotions, lacking the cold objectivity of science. Sometimes those emotions could be a hindrance, sometimes a help.

At the moment Vince couldn't decide which was true.

Paige Williams's childhood represented everything wrong with this evil-tainted world. Neglect, abuse, a life riddled with disappointment and hurt. She was only a few years older than his own son would have been. All that Tim had enjoyed as a child—love and happiness and a stable household—Paige had never known. As Vince Edwards the father heard Paige's story, felt her miasma of weariness and despair, he couldn't help but grieve with her. No doubt the emotions he sensed from her were genuine.

Unlike pieces of her story.

As with Francesca Galvin, he'd watched where Paige's gaze roamed as she spoke. Her body language and expression. He couldn't decipher every true detail from the false ones. Rather, they fell into general patterns. For example, her story of why she fled Kansas, he didn't buy. Her road trip to Kanner Lake, he did. She seemed to be telling the truth about being home the previous evening, although lacking an alibi certainly didn't help her.

The question was, were any lies she may have told significant to this case?

A lie detector machine would objectively decry the lies themselves but lack the ability to understand any foundation of emotional truth. So while the policeman in him detected some falsehood, his human side wondered if the lies mattered. People had lots of different reasons to be less than forthcoming with the police. For Paige it could be shame, guilt, the desire for her past to remain as anonymous as possible as she built her new life.

Now came the moment of significance—Paige's reaction to the accusation that she had made a death threat toward Edna San. Vince cataloged her every move.

The young woman's eyes grew wide and her head jerked back just the slightest. Her breathing lulled. Color drained away from her face like whitewash running down a window. "That's not true!" The denial sounded cinched, shocked. "I never said *anything* like that."

He held her gaze, saying nothing, knowing she'd fill the silence.

"Who told you that? Why would anybody say that?"

He shrugged. "Maybe they're wrong. That's why I needed to check with you."

Paige's color rushed back, ruddy and blotched. Her mouth hardened. "I'll say they're wrong. You can ask anybody in that store. Ask Sarah; she was right there."

"All right, okay." Vince held up both hands. "I'll do that."

Her eyes darted around the table. "I wish I could tell you who else to ask. It's just that, like I said, I don't know the name of anybody else in the store. I'd recognize those girls if I saw them, but who knows if they're still around. I can't even remember what the other people looked like. Believe me, if I did, I'd send you right to them, because *any* of them would tell you—" She cut off her words, some new realization seizing her features. Her gaze sought Vince's face and hung there. "But that's just it, right? One of those people told you that. Why would any of them do such a thing? I didn't say anything even remotely like a threat." Her words tightened further, brightness in her eyes. For a moment Vince thought she might cry. She leaned toward him, a hand at her throat. "Tell me it wasn't one of the girls. *Please.*"

The pain in her tone cut Vince to the core, where his own grief weighed like hot steel. Vince the police chief faded while Vince the father of a dead son reeled. With one plea this girl had laid herself bare. Amid all her anxiety about the accusation, Paige Williams seized upon the one possibility with the power to shake her world even more—that these sisters, who had buoyed her soul by showing indignation on her behalf, might turn on her, reinforce the harsh reality that she was unloved and unlovable.

Paige's pain was not far from Vince's own. He grieved for love taken. She grieved for love never known.

"Paige." He shook his head, voice low. "It wasn't one of those girls."

She drew back, swallowing hard. For a moment she said nothing, relief soothing the lines in her forehead. "Okay. Well, I don't know who else it would have been either. All I *do* know is, it isn't true." She looked into his eyes. "Ask Sarah. She'll tell you."

He nodded. "I believe you, Paige. And I'm sorry I put you through this, but ... you understand why I had to."

She regarded her plate as if the thought of food made her sick. "Can we go back now?"

"Yeah. We're done." He gestured toward her sandwich. "You want to take that with you?"

"No. Thanks." Her shoulders remained stiff.

Vince leaned toward the window until he caught sight of Bud at an angle through the alcove doorway, and waved. Bud hustled over with their check and removed their plates.

On the way out, Vince ducked into the bathroom and switched off the tape recorder.

He and Paige did not speak as they exited the restaurant. She opened the passenger door of his vehicle and slid inside, turned her face toward the window. They drove back to Simple Pleasures in silence. Vince did not spot Leslie Brymes tailing them this time. The girl was probably long gone and talking a blue streak with Sarah Wray.

Vince's gut told him to believe Paige's denial. Yet Edna San had claimed Paige threatened to kill her. Why?

Paige had not told the truth about the reason she fled Kansas. Why?

Vince parked close to the store and escorted Paige back inside. While she took over manning the counter, Vince asked Sarah Wray to step inside her office, where the woman confirmed in no uncertain terms that Paige Williams had said no such thing, and that the girl was far too sweet to even think such a thought.

By the time Vince returned to his car, he was convinced Paige had not threatened Edna San. Which, as far as he could see, left two possibilities — either Edna had embellished the Simple Pleasures incident as a way to legitimize her roiling anger, or Francesca had done so to divert attention away from herself. Knowing Edna, Vince considered the former a possibility. As for the latter, it would definitely cast further suspicion on Francesca.

Vince started the engine, pondering the second scenario. If Francesca was involved in Edna San's disappearance, lying about Paige Williams seemed like such a stupid thing to do. The woman manages to pull off a crime leaving little clues — and then spins a tale so easily unraveled? One involving a young woman with no former ties to Edna and without substantial reason to harm her? It didn't make sense.

Nonetheless, Vince would need to question Francesca again about the alleged threat.

Heading out of town, Vince used his cell phone to check in with the station. Frank told him his men had been busy. The San estate had now been sealed off as a crime scene, with Roger Waitman posted at the gate. A forensics team was at the house, searching for evidence. Vince regretted not being there with them but knew they were capable of handling the task. He made a mental note to catch up with them as soon as possible. Two cadaver dogs and their handlers were now searching the woods and road near the San estate, starting at the point where Lester's hound had lost the scent. And Jim had assembled a team of volunteers—mostly folks from the city council and chamber of commerce, plus the town's volunteer firemen—to comb the outlying woods as well.

"Okay, Frank. Thanks."

Vince clicked off the line and headed back to Lakeside diner. There, he knew, Bud would have a present waiting for him—Paige Williams's can of soda, carefully emptied of its contents and placed in a paper bag. He and Bud had worked out their system some time ago. Whereas Lakeside typically poured sodas into glasses, Bud knew when Vince showed up with one person and asked for seating in the alcove, he needed to bring the cans instead.

Vince would see that Paige's soda can was taken to the lab for lifting of prints. Her fingerprint would then be scanned into AFIS, the Automated Fingerprint Identification System, to look for a match. Using powerful configurations to create unique mathematical maps of fingerprints, AFIS was capable of checking Paige Williams's print against millions of others in a matter of seconds.

However, the process wasn't quite as simple as determining that one perfect match. Rather the system would provide a candidate list of the closest matches. A fingerprint examiner would then review the potentials to determine an exact match. It was a blend of machine and human working together, human making the ultimate call.

Meanwhile techs at Edna San's house would be looking for fingerprints as well. Any discoveries they made would also go through AFIS. The handles on the french doors leading into Edna San's kitchen would be a good place for them to start. Their possible discoveries were another reason Vince had wanted Paige's prints.

By evening Vince would know if Paige Williams's prints matched any found at the crime scene or on the earring he'd already sent to the lab. And he would know if they matched any within AFIS. Since Frank West's earlier check of Paige's name had come up clean, Vince didn't expect her print to be found in the existing arrest records, although he'd make sure that was checked. But if her print was determined a match to one in the unsolved crime database, the lies he believed she'd told about her past would take on new meaning.

Paige Williams wasn't in the clear yet.

FORTY-TWO

Paige's hands wouldn't stop trembling.

Sarah had offered to let her go home early. The woman had emerged from the office, Chief Edwards in tow, her cheeks spotted red. As soon as he left, she started spouting to Paige and didn't stop until a customer entered the store. "How could anybody have told the chief such a story!" She stuck her hands in her hair and paced. "As if you'd really stand there and threaten to kill Edna San in front of perfect strangers. The whole idea is insane. I *know* you'd never be capable of any kind of underhandedness, much less something like that! I'd sure like to get my hands on the person who made up that story. I might do a little strangling myself."

When she offered to let Paige off—with pay—for the rest of the day, Paige faltered. How she wanted to say yes. She longed to go home and sleep. Maybe when she woke up, she'd discover that the last twelve hours had been a bad dream. But despite her weariness, she couldn't take the offer. What if Chief Edwards somehow heard she'd gone home early? Wouldn't he view that as a sign of fear? She had to appear strong, nonchalant, as if she had nothing to be afraid of, nothing to hide.

"Thanks, Sarah," she said, clasping her hands behind her back, "but I'll be fine. It's Saturday. I can't leave you all alone with customers."

"You sure?"

"Positive." Paige tried to smile.

Sarah shook her head. "You sure are a brave gal, Paige Williams. If I were in your shoes, I'd be shaking like a leaf."

Paige gave a little shrug and looked away. If Sarah only knew.

FORTY-THREE

Black Mamba's eyes flicked right and left, checking the street in Spirit Lake. He'd parked his car a block away and walked down, baseball hat pulled low over his brow. The pay phone sat outside and to the left of a small convenience store on the other side of the road. Two cars dotted the parking lot, a couple shoppers visible through the windows of the store. Other vehicles passed by, but it seemed unlikely that any drivers would pay attention to someone at the phone.

His call was supposed to be anonymous. But in the likelihood the Kanner Lake Police Station had special caller ID, he didn't want any possible witnesses as to who used the phone at the designated time. For the same reason he would use gloves when making the call. No need to leave fingerprints for snoopy police.

He hurried across the street, head down, anticipating the call that would further link Paige Williams to the unfortunate demise of Edna San. From here things would happen quickly.

The number for the police station was tucked away in his memory. He pulled on the thin cotton gloves, dropped the coins, punched the buttons. One ring.

"Kanner Lake Police." A male voice.

"Hi." He kept his tone low, feigning hesitancy. "I have some information about Edna San. But I don't want to get involved, know what I mean?"

"That's fine; you're welcome to leave an anonymous tip. What do you have?"

"Okay. Well, it's going to sound kind of weird. But I think you should check the backyard of the young woman who lives at thirty-six ninety-two Lakeshore. I—this is kind of embarrassing. I was camping in the woods and had binoculars. I couldn't sleep and saw lights go on at some house around two in the morning. I looked through the binoculars and saw this woman—she looked young—tugging at something on her deck. Like a body. Well, I didn't really think it was a body at the time, but now that this has happened . . . I don't know, maybe it's nothing. The light over the deck wasn't real bright. But I think you should check it out."

"All right." A pause. "You said thirty-six ninety-two Lakeshore. How do you know it's this address?"

"Uh, this morning I packed up and came out of the woods. When I heard the news about Ms. San, I drove around Lakeshore looking for the house I thought I'd seen. I think it's thirty-six ninety-two Lakeshore. I walked through the woods near the house until I could see the backyard and deck. I'm pretty sure I recognized them."

"All right, thanks. Anything else?"

"No, don't think so. Except I hope you find Ms. San safe."

"We do too. Thanks again."

Black Mamba hung up the phone.

A few minutes later he was back in his car, starting the engine. He pulled out onto the road, imagining the haunted look in Paige Williams's eyes when she was arrested for the murder of Edna San.

PART THREE

Trapped

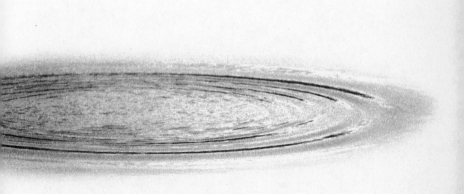

FORTY-FOUR

On his way to the police station after picking up Paige's Coke can, Vince's thoughts bounced from her interview to Tim to tomorrow's anniversary like Ping-Pong balls. With a sigh he glanced at his vehicle's digital clock: 1:55.

Edna San had been missing for seventeen hours.

In law enforcement the first seventy-two hours after a crime were considered crucial. With each hour that passed, the trail of the perpetrator grew colder. Fifty-five hours remained within that key time frame. Would he find his answers before that time expired?

Fifty-five hours. By then the anniversary of Tim's death would be long over, ushering out the first numbing year of grief. Ushering in the second.

Where would he and Nancy be a year from now?

A keen, cruel image of his wife alone tomorrow, curled up and sobbing on their bed, cut through Vince. He *had* to be with her. If he was any kind of man at all, any kind of decent husband, he would be at her side.

Vince pulled into the small parking area outside the station.

Inside he handed Paige's soda can, in its brown paper bag, over to a ready and waiting Frank West. The kid still looked as charged up as he had that morning. "Make sure this gets to the lab as soon as possible." Vince gestured toward the bag. "And get right on AFIS, as we discussed. I want that information by tonight."

"Will do, Chief." Frank's words were clipped and serious, like some actor in an old cop film.

Vince suppressed a smile and nodded. "Thanks." He turned to leave. "I'm on my way back to the San estate. The techs should still be there and I want to see what they've got. I also want to question Francesca Galvin about—"

"Hey, Chief, glad you're back." Al Newman, one of the officers pulled in from his day off, stuck his head out of a nearby office. Al was in his late forties, with a chunky build and a round balding head that had earned him the nickname C. B., for Charlie Brown. "I just ran down a whale of a tip about fifteen minutes ago. Frank and I've been getting 'em by the dozens, but I think you oughtta hear this one."

His head disappeared. A moment later he returned, white piece of paper in hand. Briefly he told Vince about an anonymous male caller who claimed to have seen some odd behavior at a house in the wee hours of the morning. The station's caller ID, which automatically logged the numbers from pay phones, told them the call had been made from one at the convenience store in Spirit Lake. "The man said he thinks the address of the house is thirty-six ninety-two Lakeshore."

Vince blinked. C. B. went on, explaining that he'd checked county records and found the owner to be Clinton Ryskie. Vince held up a hand to stop him. "I know—it's rented to Paige Williams."

"Whoa." Frank's eyebrows rose.

C. B. locked eyes with Vince. "The same gal you just questioned, right?"

Two conflicting thoughts spun through Vince's head. First, suspicion of the name that kept surfacing in this investigation. Second, a notion that this tip was just a little too tidy, particularly coming on the heels of a claimed threat that he believed never happened. And from a pay phone, no less.

Was someone trying to set Paige Williams up?

But if so, why her? Someone new to town, with no apparent connection—other than yesterday's incident—to Edna San. Didn't make sense.

He pictured Paige in Lakeside diner—the way her eyes roved to her right as she talked about her reasons for leaving Kansas. Her overall nervousness, her rapid pulse. Had this girl gotten tied up with the wrong people back in the Midwest? Someone who wanted Edna San dead?

Vince drew a deep breath and let it out. "Okay." He thought a moment. "Guess the techs will just have to continue without me for a while. C. B., get somebody over to that pay phone pronto to dust for prints. I'll drive over to this Lakeshore property and eyeball the backyard, see if anything catches my attention."

Frank buffed the top of his head with his hand, leaving a shock of hair standing up. "Want me to go with you?"

Vince turned toward the door with a surge of energy. "No, you're more needed by the phones for now. I'll let you know if I notice anything out there."

Within sixty seconds he was driving out of the parking lot onto Main Street.

Nine minutes later on Lakeshore Road he slowed, checking a mailbox. Rathum, read the name painted on the side in large white letters. The street number was 3374. Vince knew he was close. Addresses on Lakeshore followed country road logic—the numbers were spread far apart. A mile farther and two houses down, he found the address he was looking for. Number 3692 Lakeshore sat back from the road about fifty feet, connected by a gravel driveway. It was a small wooden house, painted beige with dark-green trim at the windows. A tiny front porch supported by square posts led back to a recessed front door. Fairly sizable one-car garage on the north side. On each side of the house was about twenty feet of patchy lawn, with woods beyond.

Vince passed the driveway, pulled onto the shoulder of the road's opposite side, and parked.

As he clicked his car door shut, he heard the mournful cry of an osprey overhead. He slowed and searched the sky until he spotted it. The bird circled above him, then headed toward the water. He watched it disappear with the irrational sense that it was sent from Tim as some kind of message.

He shook the thought away.

His gaze returned to the house. Without a warrant he couldn't simply walk upon the property and look around. But the "penumbra of privacy" rule didn't keep him from checking out the place from a distance.

Vince crossed the road and entered the forest on the north side of the house.

The trees weren't too thick, and he was able to pick his way over fallen branches and bushes, keeping the house in sight. By the time he drew even with the backyard, he could feel a bead of sweat trickling down his forehead. Veering right, he skirted an area of young trees and denser undergrowth until he reached the clearing.

Vince wiped the sweat from his face, gazing intently at the property. The house was built on a knoll, allowing a beautiful view down the wooded hill and to the lake. He could see why Paige enjoyed the place so much. But how could she afford it? According to Paige's story, she was hardly rolling in money. This house was small, but lake views were worth bucks. Where she might pay five hundred dollars for a one-bedroom apartment in town, this house could fetch closer to eight or nine hundred. That was a huge difference in price for someone whose income couldn't be much more than eight dollars an hour.

Vince focused on the deck. It stretched half the length of the house, beginning just past the garage. Two side steps led to the lawn. In the corner of the deck closest to him was a large sunken hot tub, sticking up about a foot and covered with a brown vinyl top. Vince narrowed his eyes at the tub, wishing he could see underneath its cover. Next he stared at the deck, trying to discern anything unusual upon it. He saw no pattern of footprints. He shaded his eyes and squinted, looking for the slightest sign of a trail that could have been caused by something dragged across it. Nothing. In fact, the wood looked amazingly clean, almost as if it had been swept recently.

Interesting.

He perused the sliding door to the rear of the house. With the brightness of the day, he couldn't see beyond the glass into the home. He checked the threshold for any possible signs of something—or someone—being pulled from the house onto the deck. Again nothing.

Vince sighed and took another swipe at his forehead. What to think about that phone call? No way was it coincidence that Paige Williams lived here. Yet this house sat near the top west side of the lake, while Edna San's estate lay about equal distance from town on the east side. If Paige or someone she was in league with had managed to force Edna San off her property, why bring her all the way over here? And one other thing. The bloodhound had traced Ms. San's scent three miles farther down Lakeshore Road, headed away from town. If someone wanted to transport Ms. San from her place to here in the quickest time, they'd head back toward the north end of the lake and around, not south.

Also, the anonymous caller had said nothing about seeing *two* people drag something on this deck—only one. Which meant Paige Williams would have accomplished all this by herself.

Vince's gaze traveled across the deck toward the steps and down to the lawn, then bounced up to a door leading to the rear of the garage.

Wait.

His eyes returned to the grass near the deck's lower step. His chin came up and he leaned forward, frowning. The grass looked a little lighter in that spot, as if it had been slicked down. He stared at the surrounding area. The lightness narrowed into a trail perhaps a foot wide. Slowly his eyes followed that trail—right up to the rear garage door.

Was he imagining things?

He shifted on his feet, turned his head a slight angle and stared some more. Still he saw the subtle difference in color. Very subtle. Almost as if someone had tried to fluff up the grass to erase the trail . . .

Vince looked at that area of grass a long time. Then raised his eyes again to stare at the clean deck.

As he headed with renewed purpose back to his car, he was sure of one thing. Paige Williams would soon have a lot more explaining to do.

FORTY-FIVE

The tub is full of hot water. Rachel is about to undress and get into it when the phone rings.

She hesitates. Should she answer? It's ten o'clock on a Wednesday night and she is tired from the day's work. Michael, a salesman at the office, has asked her out for the third time, and for the third time she has turned him down. Her stated reason is understandable enough — she doesn't want to date anyone at work. But Michael doesn't buy it. A darkness crossed his face, and he turned on his heel with a "Fine, then, *Princess*, if that's the way you want to be" and stalked away. This scares Rachel. What exactly might Michael do to her come tomorrow? Will he tell lies on her, try to get her fired?

Surely this isn't him calling. Her number's unlisted.

The phone rings again.

Rachel sighs. She tells herself to let it ring, but something compels her to walk into the bedroom and pick up the phone.

"Hello?"

"Rachel, it's me."

Rosa.

Rachel freezes. She hasn't talked to her mother since that summer day over a year and a half ago. Now Rosa's voice is clipped, tight. Instinctively Rachel knows the woman wants something. Or she would never bother to call.

"Hey, are you there?"

217

Rachel's muscles harden. Mentally she slams the door on any wayward emotions. "What do you want, Rosa?"

"I need you to come over here right now."

Oh, right.

"Rachel?"

"What for?"

"Because I need you, that's why. I can't talk on the phone now. Just come. *Please.*"

Please? Since when does Rosa ever plead with her for anything? Maybe she really does need help.

Fine, let Eddie help her, or Blake, or one of the cops she knows so well.

"Rosa, seems to me the last time I was over there, you said you never wanted to see me again."

"I didn't mean it, Rachel, you know that! I was just mad, and—okay, I believe everything you said that day, does that help? It's all true, so will you please just come over, because I really need to see you right now and I promise you won't be sorry."

Conflicting emotions battle within Rachel. This is the first time her mother has ever sounded so desperate for *her.* The ancient longing for the bond-that-never-was surfaces. If there really is something she can do, maybe …

"I was about to go to bed." Rachel forces coldness into her tone. "I'm not coming over there until you tell me what you need. Besides, where's Eddie?"

"Eddie's here, but he can't help. Just—there's not much time; you gotta leave *now.* Some people I work with are trying to cut me off, and one of them's coming over here, and he's gonna *steal* from me, Rachel, so I want to just give you something to keep for me so he won't take it, because I know you're the only one I can trust with it, so please come right away!"

One of them's coming. Rachel grips the phone. "You mean *Blake*? You want me to come over there, knowing Blake is on his way?"

"No, no, it's not him!"

Can she believe that? "Rosa, whoever's coming, I'm not holding drugs for you."

"It isn't drugs!" Rosa is crying now. "It's my own property, so please, please come. I will make it up to you; I will make *everything* up to you, just ... Rachel, *please*."

Rachel's eyes close. Her chest grows heavy with empathy, even as her feet root to the floor. She so wants to trust Rosa. But she knows she shouldn't go.

"Look, Rachel, when you come, park around the corner, okay? All you have to do is walk to the door; I'll give you the stuff and you can leave. In a few days I'll take it back. Please come right now; I'm waiting."

The phone clatters in Rachel's ear. The line goes dead.

A minute passes as she stands in her bedroom, staring at the receiver in her hand, as if it will tell her what to do. Then she throws it down, grabs her purse and keys, and hurries from the apartment.

FORTY-SIX

Leslie paced just outside Edna San's gate, eyes throwing daggers at the cop on the other side. Of all officers the Kanner Lake police had to station here, it had to be Roger Waitman. The man was in his forties and cantankerous as any two-year-old. He hated the press and made no beans about it, and particularly hated Jared Moore, although Leslie had no idea why. Waitman hadn't given her one lousy new piece of information—surprise, surprise. Not *one*. All he'd done was intone "No comment" like some brainless robot, which as far as Leslie was concerned just about summed up his lowly existence.

Her cell phone rang—Jared's ID. She whipped it open and stuck it to her ear. "Jared. What you got?"

"What do *you* have?"

She bared her teeth in a silent growl. "Nothing since I told you about Paige Williams, thanks to the *very* unhelpful policeman doing his best to ignore me."

"Well, girl, save your energy; that's what cops do."

Yeah, but not to *her*. She was supposed to be able to charm anybody.

"Fine, Jared." She couldn't keep the petulance from her voice. "Anyway, I called Sarah Wray. Paige is back at Simple Pleasures. Apparently, the whole thing had to do with someone claiming that Paige threatened to kill Edna San. Which Sarah insists never happened—and she was right there."

Jared made a sound in his throat. "Who do you suppose could have told the police that?"

"No idea. Maybe someone in the store at the time of the argument."

"Does Sarah remember who was there at the time?"

"Nope. No one she knew. But I'm going to rattle Frank West's cage again, see if he'll give me some details." A honeybee cruised by. Leslie ducked from its path "So what have *you* got?"

"Well, a few things. First, I got through to both Edna San's son and daughter, and they were willing to talk. Neither has any idea what could have happened to their mother. Both have been talking to Francesca Galvin, who's told them about the search going on at the property. Got some good quotes and a few interesting details. Did you know that this morning the sliding door that leads from the kitchen onto a rear patio was unlocked?"

From the corner of her eye Leslie caught movement in the woods. She peered into the trees, wondering if it was someone searching the property. A large wild turkey cocked his head and stared at her. She glared back. "Really."

"Yeah. So the SAR team started their search off that patio."

The turkey watched Leslie, unmoving. She turned away. "Where'd the scent take them?"

"Through the woods; that was all Francesca knew. Apparently, the police aren't telling her anything they find."

Leslie frowned. "Think she's a suspect?"

"She was the last person to see the woman, Leslie." Jared's voice carried a *well-duh* tone. "Of course they're gonna look at her real close."

Leslie huffed a sigh. She hated it when Jared treated her like a know-nothing. *Just wait till I get myself on TV, Jared Moore.*

"You think Edna's son and daughter will talk to other reporters as easily as they talked to you, Jared? This inside scoop may not last too long."

"Well, I like to think not. We do have a history with 'em."

A *click* sounded in Leslie's ear. "Hey, Jared, gotta go. Someone's trying to call." She lowered the phone and punched a button. "Leslie Brymes."

"Hi, it's Bailey." The woman sounded hurried. "I just have a quick minute. Wanted you to know I just saw a news van for KREM head up the street, probably toward the police station."

Leslie's shoulders slumped. *Drat it.* She checked her watch. Almost two thirty. If the CBS station in Spokane was already here, folks from the other major networks couldn't be far behind. They'd all be doing stories for their evening news shows.

"You there?"

"Yeah, Bailey. Thanks for the info. Would you call me if you see any other reporters?"

"Absolutely." Bailey paused. "Do you know anything more, Les? I'm so worried about Edna."

"They haven't found anything, I'm sorry to say. And you know, with each passing hour . . ."

"Yeah." Bailey took an audible breath. "I'll just keep praying."

Leslie clicked off the line, the words resonating in her head. Bailey was always praying. Leslie went to the same church she did, listened to the same sermons from Pastor Hank every Sunday. But she sure wasn't as close to God as Bailey seemed to be.

She turned toward her car, shaking the thought away. She wasn't getting anywhere out here. Might as well return to town, hit up the police station again. Maybe she could wheedle some juicy new tidbit out of Frank West—

Her phone rang a third time. She pulled up short and checked the ID. Somebody long distance. Hope surged through her.

"Leslie Brymes," she answered in her most professional of tones.

"Ms. Brymes, this is Alison Votle, reporter with FOX News. I'm in a microwave truck from Seattle, headed to Kanner Lake. We should be there in about three hours. I understand you called us at FOX about this story, and I want to thank you for that. Wanted to check with you now and see if you've got any updates for us."

Leslie made a face. *Updates, yeah, right.* Like she was going to give her story away to this gal.

On the other hand, she didn't exactly want to tick off the reporter.

"Yes, I'm on the story and do know some people on the inside." Leslie clipped her words. "I'm on the run with a development at the moment but will be happy to talk to you when you get here."

Leslie pulled open her car door and slid inside. She slammed the door shut, hoping the woman would hear.

Dear Alison would have none of it. The woman did her best to extract information as Leslie gunned her engine and pulled a U-turn on the road toward town.

Huh-uh, babe, no way.

"Tell you what," Leslie said, cutting her off. "Call me when you're about thirty minutes away from Kanner Lake. By that time I'll know plenty more. I grew up here; I can get people to talk to me who'll never talk to you. Besides, I'll have a good six hours' lead on you with this story. I'm sure we can work something out."

Alison Votle capitulated—but then, what choice did she have? Leslie could have sworn she heard a grudging respect in the reporter's tone as they said their good-byes. At least she wanted to believe that's what it was.

She threw the phone onto the passenger seat with a grim smile. *Leslie, you go, girl!*

Just outside town she passed a news van with KXLY on the side, driving in the opposite direction. ABC News was headed toward Edna San's estate.

Great. She'd better find some more inside information on this story soon. Like now.

FORTY-SEVEN

As Vince drove toward town, feeling the rev in his gut of an investigation about to turn, an idea formulated in his head. By the time he hit Main Street, he knew he should follow it up right away. It was a shot in the dark but it wouldn't take long, and who knew what the payoff might be.

He passed Simple Pleasures on his left, driving farther up to the station. In the parking lot he hurriedly shut off the engine and climbed out of his car.

Inside the station he informed Frank and C. B. of what he'd seen. "I'm going to make a phone call. Then I'm picking up Miss Williams again to go back out to her house for a cursive sweep. Frank, I'll want you to meet us out there, as long as she allows our visit."

C. B. shook his head. "You think that young gal could pull this thing off by herself? She must've had help."

"Probably did," Frank said. "We really don't know that much about her, just that she's new to town, no relatives here."

"Yeah, well, maybe we can remedy that." Vince headed for his office.

"Hey, Chief," Frank called after him, "CBS was here. Followed by ABC. I think they've headed out to the San estate."

Vince slowed at the threshold, assimilating the news. Not that it was unexpected. Once information had been released to the media, he knew they'd be sending out crews. He just hoped none of them would spot him coming out of Simple Pleasures with Paige. Leslie Brymes already knew too much.

"Okay. Thanks."

He eased into his office and closed the door. Seated at his desk, he pulled a pad of paper near him and reached for the phone. Before he could pick it up, his cell phone rang. He pulled it from its holder and checked the ID. His own home number displayed.

Nancy, home from work. Guilt pierced him. He hadn't thought to call her.

He flipped open the phone. "Hi, Nance."

"Vince." She sounded worn. "I heard about Edna San at the grocery store. Do you know anything new?"

"We're working on some things, but it doesn't look good." He closed his eyes, rubbed the area between them. His headache was coming back. "Nancy ..." The words he needed to say stuck in his throat.

"I know. You're going to tell me you can't stop working on this case, aren't you? That you're not going to be able to stay home tomorrow, the day I've been dreading for weeks."

"Nance, I'll do everything I can to be with you. But I just don't know what's going to hap—"

"Oh, *I* do. You won't be with me, that's what." Her tone turned off-key. "I'll go through the day alone, the night too. You'll give everything you have to your job, and I'll get nothing."

The pain in her voice tightened Vince's throat. He dreaded tomorrow too, but he couldn't fault her for focusing on herself. Such was the insidiousness of grief—slicing between a weakened couple like an ax through shriveling wood. His eyes roamed to the photo of Nancy and Tim on his desk, taken on Tim's nineteenth birthday. Good-looking, tall Tim with an arm draped around his mother, Nancy's head inclined toward him, almost touching his chin. Her blue eyes clear, unpainted by sadness.

"Nancy, I promise you, I'll do everything I can to come home —soon. And stay with you tomorrow. I'm following leads the minute I get them. I haven't stopped all day."

She gave a slow exhale. "I know. I'm sorry." The words pinched. "I'm just ... I need you, Vince. And it doesn't feel like I have you anymore."

His shoulders slumped. "You have me, Nancy. You do." *What's left of me.*

The sound of their breathing intermingled over the line. Vince thought of Paige Williams and the loneliness in her eyes. How could he not take care of the family he had?

"Okay, Vince." Nancy's voice fell to a whisper. "Thanks. I'll see you ... when you get here."

Vince closed the cell phone and lowered his aching head into his hands. Minutes passed before he could pull his thoughts back to his work.

Slowly he straightened, resolve flowing through him. He had more reasons than one to break his case quickly. Vince picked up the receiver on his desk. Through Information, he learned the number of the police station in Whitsung, Kansas, where Paige had grown up.

In a large sense law enforcement officers were family. If anyone in Paige's hometown might be willing to spend a little time running down information on the Williams family, it would be a fellow officer. Williams was a common name, but it shouldn't be too difficult to track down the right family in a small town.

He dialed the number and was connected to a young-sounding officer named Daryl Brumley. Vince jotted the name down on his pad of paper as he launched into an explanation of why he was calling.

"Sure, I'll do what I can," Brumley replied. "I'm pushing a lot of paperwork right now on a burglary; you know how that goes.

But when I get this done, and if I'm not called out on something else, I'll start looking into things for you."

"Okay. Here's what I know about Paige Williams. Twenty-five years old; date of birth April 12, 1981. Parents' names were Betty and Justin. Paige told us they were killed in a car accident when she was three. From there she entered the foster care system. We've run her name and she comes up clean. But I'm suspicious of how truthful she's been about her past. She says she ran away from a foster family named Johnson at age fourteen and left the state. I wonder if you might call a few Williamses in the phone book there, see if you can locate any relatives. I'd be grateful for anything you could find out."

"Okay, will do."

"Thanks much. I really appreciate it." Vince gave Officer Brumley numbers for the station and his cell phone. "Look forward to hearing from you."

Five minutes later Vince was parking his vehicle on Second Street, around the corner from Simple Pleasures.

There would be no need to Mirandize Paige Williams again. The Miranda he'd given her was good for twenty-four hours. To cover his own backside, he'd like to be presenting her with a search warrant. Problem was, warrants had to be item-specific, and he had no idea what he was looking for. He couldn't exactly carry away a patch of flattened grass from her backyard. If this little expedition yielded anything suspicious, he'd work on a search warrant pronto so he could return to Paige's property and take possession of the item. Meanwhile he'd be just friendly enough to persuade her to sign a consent for the sweep. Once he was inside that house, his trained eyes would take over.

He would soon know if Paige Williams had been up to no good last night.

FORTY-EIGHT

Paige looked up from the counter to see Chief Edwards reentering the store—and knew she was doomed. Electricity singed her nerves from head to toe. More horror scenes from the previous night flashed through her mind. How would she ever explain? Who would believe her?

"Miss Williams." He nodded to her, unsmiling. No feigned casualness, no light tone. A thin manila folder was in his hand.

Sarah hustled over from a shelf she was rearranging toward the rear of the store, her face full of concern. "Chief! What's wrong now? Why are you back? Have you found Edna San?"

The chief rested a hand upon the counter. "Afraid not. I need to talk to your employee again, if you don't mind. Just a little follow-up from our lunch."

She regarded him for a moment, then glanced at Paige. "Sure. You can use my office if you'd like."

On shaky legs Paige followed him into the little room. Begging prayers filtered through her head. *Please, God, I can't go to jail. Please help me!*

Chief Edwards closed the door and faced her. "Sorry to bother you again at your work."

Paige managed a shrug. "It's okay."

"What I need from you now is a quick look around your house. I just want to put some closure on our conversation today. If you'll sign this form, we'll get right to it, and I'll have you back

229

here as soon as possible." He pulled a piece of paper from the folder and laid it on Sarah's desk.

Paige stared at the form. "Why? I mean, what could be there that has anything to do with ... anything?"

The chief spread his hands. "Like I said, I'm not really expecting anything. I'd just like a quick look."

Paige's thoughts flung in all directions. He'd seemed satisfied after their conversation. What happened? Did he know something?

And what could he find if he searched her place?

She pictured herself that morning, sweeping, vacuuming the car, raking the grass. She'd thrown her clothes in the wash, along with the sheet and gloves. Exhaustion had gripped her, but she'd remembered everything. Hadn't she?

"Miss Williams?" The chief watched her intently.

Maybe she could put him off until after work. Then she could fly home, look over the place one more time—

But what will he think if I say no? What if this really was routine, but her denial made him suspicious?

She felt her mouth open, form words. "Okay. I mean, I have nothing to hide." She forced a smile.

"Good." He slid a pen from his shirt pocket and held it out to her.

Her heart flopping into double time, Paige signed her name.

Back at the store counter, she picked up her purse as the chief explained to Sarah that Paige needed to go with him again. Sarah's eyes jumped from him to Paige, one hand pulling at a strand of hair. "Sure everything's okay, Chief?"

"Everything's fine. I'll have her back quick as I can."

As they stepped out into the July heat, Paige's gaze fell upon Bailey Truitt across the street, wiping one of the tables on the sidewalk in front of Java Joint. The woman straightened up from her task—and their eyes met. Her head pulled back in surprise, one hand clutching the wet rag. Slowly her left fingers rose in a brief wave.

Paige turned up the street, warmth flushing her cheeks.

As she slid into the chief's car, the awful realization hit her. During her cleaning last night, she'd never checked the hot tub.

FORTY-NINE

The February night is unusually warm as Rachel drives to Rosa's house. She turns up the air conditioner. Suspicions pop in her mind, but she forces herself to put her cynicism on hold. She will simply do what Rosa asked. It will take three, maybe four, minutes to pick up Rosa's precious belongings – probably jewelry – and return to her car. All will be well. And Rosa will be so grateful. Maybe they can build on that gratefulness … somehow.

Rachel passes Rosa's house. The porch is dark, but lights shine from various windows. No cars are parked at the curb. Apparently, she has arrived in time.

At the next corner she turns left, drives halfway down the block, and parks. She pushes her purse underneath the seat, gets out, and locks the door. The key slips into her jeans pocket.

The briny smell of the ocean, three blocks away, wafts around her as she walks briskly toward her mother's house. Briefly she wonders if some of the cops who've protected Rosa's "business" have now turned against her.

Sudden fear pierces Rachel. What is she doing? If she gets in the way of rogue policemen, who will ever help her in this town?

She slows, almost turns back. Then she pictures Rosa, desperately waiting for her, and forges ahead.

The upscale residential streets are quiet on this Wednesday night at 10:20. Not one vehicle passes Rachel. She pictures the other homeowners already in bed, preparing to wake early for their jobs as lawyers and doctors and business executives.

She reaches Rosa's house.

Hurrying up the steps, Rachel is aware of how vulnerable she is should anyone drive up. She jabs the bell twice, her heart picking up speed. The door swings open and Rosa pulls her inside before she can protest.

"Whatever it is, give it to me. I want to get out of here." The words blurt from Rachel as she takes in the scene — Eddie slouched in the living room doorway, sizing her up; Rosa, pale and trembling, eyes wide and mascara smeared. Rosa clutches a small box-style purse, an art-deco design painted with pink poodles. She thrusts it into Rachel's hands.

"Here. Go now, out the back door. Did you pass us and turn left to park?"

"Yes."

"Good. Cut across our neighbors' yard to hit that street. Come on, I'll take you through the kitchen."

She grasps Rachel's arm, pulling her along as if they are being pursued by some mad monster.

"Better not dip into that!" Eddie throws at Rachel's back.

Huh?

They reach the kitchen, skitter around the large cooking island. Rachel can hardly keep up. Rosa's fear swirls like fog, setting her own heart banging. She has no time to ask what or who or when —

"Rosa!" Eddie's voice bursts from the living room. "He's here, getting out of his car!"

"Oh!" Rosa slides to a halt, arms waving. Rachel knocks into her and they both totter for footing. "What do we do?" Rosa's face etches with panic. "If he has someone with him, watching the house, they might see —" She whirls in Eddie's direction and calls,

"Anybody with him?" Her nails sink into Rachel's forearm as they await an answer.

Eddie appears around the corner. "I don't see anybody. *Go*, Rachel; he's on the porch."

Before Rachel can say a word, Rosa yanks back the sliding kitchen door and shoves her outside. The front doorbell rings. "Eddie, don't answer yet!" Rosa hisses, then leans over the open threshold, her face taut with fear. "Listen, Rachel." Her words spill over themselves. "If anything happens to us, remember these names: Ron Hardinger, Bill Veretsky, Roland Newell. Got it?" She repeats them. "They're the cops who know what's going on. They'll be wanting that purse and will probably come to you looking for it. Don't hold out on them; it's not worth your life. Just hand it over."

The doorbell sounds again, followed by pounding.

"Rosa, come on!" Eddie pulls her away and slides the door shut. Rachel hears final words from her mother before it closes completely.

"Rachel, I loved you as much as I could!"

Rachel wheels away, clutching the purse, terror of the unknown driving her across the deck and onto the grass. She has no time to think or question; she simply does what must be done. She hunches over as she reaches the edge of her mother's lawn, quickly checking the neighbors' house. No lights. Maybe they're gone. Her heart clambers up her throat as she ventures across the soft grass, diffused light from a distant streetlamp barely piercing the darkness. She prays that if the neighbors are home, they won't glance out their windows and spot her shadowed figure in flight.

Pop. A sound from Rosa's house tumbles through the night. *Pop-poppoppop.*

Gunshots.

The knowledge streaks through Rachel. She jerks to a halt, muscles rigid. For a moment all reasoning flees, her brain flashing white. Questions and terror follow, swelling her thoughts.

"If something happens to us ..."

Rosa! She has to go back.

No, Rachel, you want to die?

She turns toward her mother's house, blood pounding in her ears, then hesitates, telling herself those sounds weren't gunshots. *Just go, get out of here!* Her gaze darts to the neighbors' windows, expecting a light to come on. All is quiet now. She freezes, listening for the sound of a front door closing, a car driving away.

Silence.

She peers toward Rosa's kitchen window, seeking movement.

Nothing.

With a strangled cry Rachel stumbles back to her mother's house.

FIFTY

From the corner of his eye Black Mamba watched the chief escort Paige Williams up the sidewalk across the street. His lips curled with impatience. Certainly took these small-town cops long enough. What had they been doing since his phone call?

Mamba stood near the window of Read Ones, a campy little used bookstore decorated in the color that punned its name. Red walls, red-lettered signs upon the shelves. An ancient cash register in gilded gold and red. A charming place to browse as he waited for the next tile in his mosaic to fall into place.

And fall it had.

Of course Paige Williams had allowed the police's request, never guessing the choice morsel to be discovered in her hot tub. Oh, the sudden bustle that would soon occur at her house.

He must hurry to witness it.

Mamba ran a finger over the book in his hand, calculating. He'd spent too much time in this place to leave without a purchase. The owner would not be happy. He didn't mind. He found this *Biography of Vlad the Impaler* quite fascinating.

At the counter he paid for the book and complimented the proprietor on his delightful shop.

Two minutes later he was headed west out of town in his car, making sure the police vehicle somewhere ahead of him was nowhere in sight.

FIFTY-ONE

Bailey stepped back inside Java Joint, feeling sick to her stomach. Something was very, very wrong. She'd been relieved to see Paige Williams return to Simple Pleasures over an hour ago. Whatever the chief had wanted with her, it must not have proved that important. Now the girl was being escorted out of Simple Pleasures *again*. She and the chief walked up the street and disappeared around the corner. Where were they going?

Oh, Lord, please help her. She looks so scared.

Bailey sank onto a stool at the counter, focusing without seeing on the walls of her café. Suddenly the place didn't seem so cheery. It was empty of customers except for S-Man, who still typed away on his laptop. Hours ago he'd plugged the computer into an outlet when the battery began to die. Bailey wondered how he could sit in one position for so long.

S-Man glanced up, his eyebrows knit with intense concentration. He caught her staring and his features relaxed. He sat back from the keyboard. "Shak."

Hi in Saurian. She managed a smile. "Shak."

He inhaled deeply, looking around as if he'd just stepped from a time machine. "Man, it's quiet in here. What happened to everybody?"

"They left a while ago, Ted. It's three thirty, that lull time of day."

"Oh." He scratched his head, then looked at her askance. "What's wrong?"

What's wrong. This guy was amazing. "Edna's still missing. And Paige Williams—you know the gal who came in here before lunch? Works at Simple Pleasures?"

Ted regarded her blankly, then shrugged.

Bailey gestured toward the window. "Chief Edwards has been over there twice to talk to her. He just took her out of the store for the second time."

S-Man's eyebrows rose as he mulled over the information. "Doesn't sound good for her. Not good at all."

He pushed back from the table and struggled to his feet, his casted leg sticking out at an angle. "Oh." He winced, moving his neck from side to side. "Been sitting too long."

Bailey watched him stretch. "You never had lunch. Want your sandwich now?"

"Yeah. The regular." Ted clumped his way toward the end of the counter and pulled the bathroom key from its mug. "You call Leslie? She probably knows what's going on with that Paige person. If she doesn't, she'll want to." He turned and headed with awkward gait toward the bathroom.

Leslie. Not wanting to gossip, Bailey hadn't mentioned anything about Paige when she'd talked to Leslie earlier. Especially since she'd seen the young woman return to Simple Pleasures with the chief. But now curiosity—and some indefinable, unsettled feeling—sunk its claws into her. Something—maybe God?—was prompting her to make the call.

But duty first. Bailey returned to her place behind the counter and began pulling out the ingredients for Ted's sandwich. Sourdough roll. Roast beef and ham—a strange combination, but that was S-Man's choice. Jack cheese, mayonnaise, mustard, and pickles. No onion. She made the sandwich on automatic, her mind elsewhere. Ted returned with the bathroom key and paid for his lunch. The minute he turned away and thumped back to the table with his food, Bailey picked up the phone and dialed Leslie's cell number.

FIFTY-TWO

Parked outside the police station, Leslie tapped a long pink nail on her steering wheel, cell phone in her left hand. Her brain spun thoughts like a lottery wheel. Paige Williams with the chief—again. Apparently, the police weren't so sure after all that the death threat never happened.

Or maybe they'd found something else.

Drat. Leslie made a face at the station. If only she'd gotten Bailey's call before she sailed in there to pump Frank for more information. The guy had been zip, zero, zilch help just five minutes ago. If she went back in now, he'd probably bar the door. Have her arrested for trespassing.

Well. Where there was a will, there was a way.

Tossing down her cell phone, Leslie put her VW in gear and backed out of her spot.

She saw no parking places on Main near Simple Pleasures. At the top of the block she turned right onto Second Street, looking until she found one yet another block up. She parked the car, then picked up her cell phone and flung herself out on the sidewalk, pushing the phone into her jeans pocket. Trotting around the corner, she prayed the store would be empty of customers.

She found Sarah Wray by herself, hovering behind her counter, tugging furiously at her hair.

"Sarah!" Leslie had no time for preamble. "Why is Paige back with Chief Edwards?"

240

The woman brought a hand to her cheek, her roaming gaze seeking a place to land. Leslie had never seen her look so perturbed. "I don't know what to make of it, Leslie. He wanted to look around her house."

Leslie's chin dropped. "Her *house*? Sarah, that's not good. They're looking for something."

"Well,"—Sarah's eyes found Leslie's face—"I wondered. But what could they possibly be looking for? I told them Paige never threatened to kill Edna San."

Leslie bit her cheek, thinking. "It has to be something tangible. Like maybe they think she wrote something or has an item that belongs to Edna."

"She doesn't *know* Edna!" Sarah hugged her arms to her chest. Her eyes glistened. "What's happening in this town? Whatever is going on?"

Leslie put a hand on her arm. Poor Sarah. She could be so naïve sometimes. "It'll be okay. The chief's a fair man; you know that."

Her mouth said the words, but her thoughts flew elsewhere. Paige Williams, snookered into letting the police into her house without a warrant. And talking to them all they wanted. Probably answering every question—*without a lawyer.*

"Sarah, did the chief take her in his own vehicle?"

"I don't know. I think so." She put both palms to her cheeks. "Do you—"

"Wait." Leslie held up a hand. "Let me think a minute."

Leslie wandered over to a table of bracelets and rings, absentmindedly fingered stones of sparkling blue. Sarah's earlier words replayed in her head: *You should call Paige sometime, Leslie. She needs a friend.*

What if she called Arthur Gretz? If the defense attorney heard he had the chance of picking up a client caught in the Edna San case, he'd come running like a coyote on speed. Gretz knew publicity when he saw it.

And Leslie's helpful gesture would jump-start that friendship with Paige. A friendship that could reap a harvest of inside information ...

She drew back from the bracelet table. On the other hand, if Chief Edwards ever heard about what she'd done, he'd be royally ticked. Forget wheedling information out of him ever again.

Leslie narrowed her eyes at the floor, thinking. Weighing the choices.

She drew a deep breath and turned back to Sarah. "I'm going to help Paige big-time. But you have to promise not to tell a soul. Okay?"

Sarah nodded.

"Good." She whipped her cell from her pocket. "While I make this call, go write down Paige's phone number for me."

FIFTY-THREE

Déjà vu, thought Vince. Paige Williams in the passenger seat of his car, staring out the window.

They drove without speaking. Vince had asked for directions to her house, not wanting her to know he'd already been there. Then he tried to make small talk, remarking on the weather, the number of folks at the beach. Paige's one-syllable responses hardly made for easy conversation. With his own whirling thoughts and aching head, Vince soon gave up.

Three miles from Paige's house his cell phone rang. He flipped it open without checking the ID, shoved it to his ear. "Chief Edwards."

"Hi, it's C. B. Just talked to Frank. He's at your destination, waiting for you. And I got another piece of information on Paige Williams."

From Whitsung? Vince could only hope. "Okay, shoot."

"Apparently, various folks on Main have seen you taking Miss Williams out of Simple Pleasures, and you know how news travels in this town. Just received a tip from Rex Walloughby, who lives at 3766 Lakeshore. You know him?"

Rex—twenty-eight years old and single, a hard-partying guy. Managed a liquor store down in Spirit Lake. "Yeah."

"Walloughby says he was driving home late last night from some shindig at a friend's house at the south end of the lake. Best he remembers, he got home a little before four a.m. Says he passed a car—a dark-colored SUV—going around a hair-pin turn on Lakeshore a few miles from his house. He thinks it could've been Paige Williams."

Vince resisted a glance at Paige. The gal may be sitting like stone, but no doubt she registered his every word. "Why?"

"His headlights shone into the car as he came to the turn. Said he saw a flash of a woman with short, dark hair. He doesn't know Paige Williams but heard her described that way, and he heard she lives not far from him on Lakeshore. So it's somewhat conjecture. But I checked what kind of car she drives. It's a dark-blue Ford Explorer."

A dark-colored SUV. A little too much coincidence for Vince, given how many times this gal's name had already popped up. "Right." He kept his voice neutral. "Thanks."

He closed the phone, wishing he could have a good look at Paige's car. But they'd left it back in town.

"Miss Williams, let me know when we get near your house, okay?"

"Okay." Her voice was flat.

A minute later she told him her driveway was up ahead on the left.

"All right. I've asked another officer to meet us there. He's a young guy; you'll like him. Name's Frank West." Officer policy—Vince would not enter a house alone with a woman if he could help it. Especially not when she was a suspect in a possible homicide.

He glanced at Paige. Her gaze cut to his eyes and hung there, registering recognition at Frank's name.

Vince turned into the driveway and eased up behind Frank's vehicle. Frank stepped out of the doorway to the edge of the porch and raised a hand in greeting. Paige climbed from Vince's car, house keys in hand, as if she wanted to get this over with as quickly as possible. Vince introduced her to Frank. Paige's green-blue eyes barely met the young officer's, but Frank's gaze lingered upon her face. When he pulled his eyes from her, he caught Vince watching him. Frank gave a little sniff and looked away.

Paige unlocked the door. Stood back stiffly, allowing them to enter.

They walked into a small linoleumed entry. Straight ahead lay the kitchen. Vince could see the sliding glass door that led onto the back deck. A living room was to their left, a hall, evidently to bedrooms, to their right.

Paige closed the door and leaned against it. Vince caught a mixture of emotions on her face—fear, suspicion, and a vague defiance. She gazed back at him and swallowed, looking like a trapped animal. Vince had the clear impression that the presence of two men alone with her in the house frightened her as much as the fact that they were police officers.

He gestured toward the living room. "Mind if we look in here?"

She tipped her head.

Vince entered the living room, Frank behind him. The most striking feature was the fireplace. Small but surrounded by river rock up to the ceiling. Furniture was sparse and in neutral colors. Brown couch with a couple of throw pillows, one matching armchair. An end table with reading lamp. An eighteen-inch TV. Inexpensive white curtains at the front window. No knick-knacks, no plants. The place looked as sterile as a motel room.

No pictures.

The realization struck Vince. No photos of family, no prints or posters on the wall. Nothing that spoke of memories, a life lived and cherished. His thoughts flashed to his own living room, decorated by Nancy—to its cheeriness of blue and yellow, scattered family photos spanning the years.

I need you, Vince. And it doesn't feel like I have you anymore ...

Vince pushed his wife's words away.

From the living room he and Frank wandered into the kitchen. Paige followed at a distance. Vince's gaze made a quick scope of the room. Beige walls. A wooden table with four chairs. Clean. No dishes in the sink. He studied the linoleum floor, looking for dirty footprints or any sign that something had been dragged across it, but saw neither.

"Wow, great view." Frank skirted the kitchen table to stand before the sliding glass door, arms folded. "Must be pretty at night too, with the lights from town." He turned toward Paige, a small smile on his face.

She nodded briefly. "It is."

He looked back toward the deck, gesturing with his chin. "You use the hot tub a lot?"

Something coiled through Paige. Vince *felt* it. Her shoulders straightened, head pulling back ever so slightly. She stared at Frank as if gauging hidden meaning behind the words. "Sometimes."

Vince stood still, watching her. Paige's gaze moved from Frank to him, then bounced away. She pushed off from the counter. "Want to see the rest of the house?"

Vince nodded. He and Frank followed her from the kitchen into the hall.

The first bedroom, on their right at the front of the house, was completely bare. Paige shrugged. "I haven't had any reason to fill it yet. When I save the money, I was thinking of getting a computer, putting it in here."

Vince's eyes roamed the light-brown carpet, stopping at the base of a door. "That a closet?"

"Yes. It's empty too." She walked over and slid back the door as proof.

In the bath next to the empty bedroom, Vince peeked at the drains in the tub and sink. Aware of Paige's watchful eye, he couldn't check them as much as he would have liked. She could stop their search at any time.

Across the hall, between the kitchen and the master bedroom, was a laundry area. Vince stepped in for a cursory look. Not much more than a washer and dryer, side by side, with one built-in shelf on the wall above them.

His gaze snagged on the top of the washer. Spilled white speckles of detergent. Everything else in the house had been so tidy. Had Paige been in a hurry to wash something?

He pointed to the lid of the washer. "Mind if I look in here?"

Paige licked her lips. He could see her body tensing. "Okay."

He lifted the lid and peered inside.

A small load, both dark and light colors, washed and compressed together from the spin cycle. Vince frowned at it, trying to decipher the various items. Frank eased up beside him, his weight on one leg as he leaned in for a look.

Vince looked to Paige. "You run these this morning?"

"Oh. Yeah. I forgot. I did that just before I went to work."

Vince regarded her. No way had she forgotten. He kept his voice light. "What's in there?"

She glanced from him to Frank. "Some clothes. And, um, I think a sheet."

A warning bell went off in Vince's head. Bedding was usually washed together—top and bottom sheets, pillowcase. "Just one sheet?"

Paige shifted on her feet. "Yeah. I spilled something on it."

He nodded. Scratched his cheek. Frank stuck a hand in the washer and pulled out a black glove. Held it up. "You need this in the summertime?"

Paige stared at it. Vince could see the rise and fall of her chest as she breathed. "No. That pair's been dirty for a long time, and I finally remembered to wash them."

"Makes sense." Frank shrugged and set the glove back in the washer. Paige watched him, her jaw set.

Vince put his hand on the dryer, sensing the need to move on. As much as he wanted to take the gloves as possible evidence, and the sheet, he didn't dare without a warrant. Some indignant defense attorney prancing about in a suppression hearing would persuade a judge to throw out the stuff in a heartbeat. Twenty years ago things had been more lenient for cops, but those days were gone. Now, seeing that a search warrant was needed, Vince couldn't let on how much the items interested him. Paige was growing more concerned by the minute, and he couldn't risk her stopping their sweep. He wanted to take an unsuspecting Paige back to Simple Pleasures and obtain the warrant before she could return here after work and make things disappear.

"Anything in here?" He tapped the dryer.

"No. Have a look if you like."

Vince bent down to open the machine. Empty. He clicked the door shut and straightened, giving Paige a brief smile. "We're almost through, Miss Williams. We really appreciate your cooperation."

In silence they walked the few steps over to Paige's bedroom, Vince's mind spitting out data to include on the paperwork for the search warrant. *Argument with missing person. Small abrasions on the palms of her hands. Possibly seen at night in car. Possibly dragged something on deck. Grass bent. Sheet, dark clothes, and gloves washed.*

Too many pieces for mere coincidence. If Vince hadn't quite believed it before, he did now. Paige Williams was involved in whatever happened to Edna San.

The growing realization weighted his chest. He wanted to solve this case—quickly. But the loneliness in Paige Williams's eyes had touched the core of his own pain. He would not relish the hard questioning he would have to put her through, nor the potential results.

Vince entered Paige's bedroom.

With windows looking out to the lake, it was fairly large, but like the rest of the house, sparsely furnished. A small bedside table held four stacked library books. Here, in the most intimate of areas, Vince found the barrenness even more bleak. Again no photos. No knickknacks or memorabilia. Vince envisioned his daughter's room before she moved out at twenty. Concert tickets stuck into the corner of her mirror. Pictures of friends on shelves and her dresser, pinned to fancy-framed bulletin boards. Figurines of fairies and butterflies, fluffy pillows and throw blankets. The room of a twenty-five-year-old may not display such ambient girl-brightness, but Vince couldn't believe a mere five years would have reduced Heather to this.

He focused on the bed. It was made but the coverlet was rumpled, as though someone had lain on top of it.

Bed not slept in last night? Sheet and dark clothes washed early this morning . . .

Paige hung back in the hallway, clearly uncomfortable being in her bedroom with Vince. Or perhaps her anxiety still fizzled over his discovery in the washing machine. Frank stayed near Paige in the hall, merely poking his head in the bedroom door, as if seeking to ease her disquiet.

"Okay. Thanks for letting us have a look around." Vince smiled at Paige as if he'd seen nothing suspicious. "We'll just check your garage quickly, okay?"

She stilled. Looked to Frank. "There's not much to see in there."

"Yeah." Frank gave her an empathetic look—*I know this is crazy.*

With a sigh she led them back down the hall and to a door on the far side of the kitchen. They stepped through it into a roomy single-car garage with an open rafter ceiling.

The first thing Vince noticed was the cleanliness of the floor. No dust, no dirt. Not even tracks where the car would drive in. Place must have been swept very recently. This morning?

He walked to the center, where Paige's car would be parked, his eyes roaming. In the back corner of the garage, left of the door, stood a monster of an old metal cabinet, supported by thick two-inch legs. He pointed toward it. "What's in there?"

Paige leaned against the wall, hands clasped behind her. "Garden tools and stuff. They belong to my landlord, Mr. Ryskie."

"Mind if we look inside?"

She shrugged. "Go ahead."

Frank walked over and opened the cabinet's double doors, Vince on his heels. Not much to see. To the left stood a rake and broom. Two shelves on the right held garden scissors, a hand trowel, a hammer, a coil of rope, a flashlight, and a small assortment of screwdrivers. Thinking of the flattened grass, Vince examined the teeth on the rake, looking for obvious signs that it had been recently used. He couldn't tell.

They closed the cabinet. Vince took a moment to walk to the other side of the garage and open the door to a crawl space. He bent down, peering into the area, dimly lit by a window along the back wall. His gaze moved over hard-packed dirt, pipes running along the ceiling, but he couldn't see very far. Some of the pink insulation on nearby pipes lay scattered in little pieces.

"Looks like you have rats."

"Had." Paige's voice was tense. "I heard them at night. I set traps."

Vince closed the crawl space door and latched it. "Catch any?"

"Three."

"Wow." Frank pressed his lips in a *Way to go* expression. "Good for you."

Paige's mouth tightened into what might've been an attempted smile.

"Okay," Vince said, "just a quick look around the backyard, then we're done." He saw fear trail across Paige's face. She started to say something, then closed her mouth. He headed for the rear door before she could stop him.

As his hand fell on the doorknob, a phone rang inside the house. Paige jerked toward the sound, her eyes widening. A second ring. She hesitated, then looked at Frank. Relief at the serendipitous interruption wafted from her shoulders. "Could you wait a minute while I answer that?"

They had no choice but to agree.

FIFTY-FOUR

Paige hurried through the kitchen door, more anxious for a moment away from the cops than to know who was calling. But who could it be? Probably either a salesman or Sarah, wanting to know what was taking so long.

She reached the counter and picked up the cordless receiver. "Hello?"

"Hi, Leslie Brymes here. Is this Paige?"

Leslie Brymes. Where had she seen that name? The voice sounded young but edged, as if the matter were of utmost importance. "Yes."

"Oh, good. You don't know me, but I'm a friend of Sarah Wray's, and I want to help you out. I heard Chief Edwards went to the store to talk to you, so I came over to Simple Pleasures to ask Sarah about it. She told me what's going on. I take it the chief's still at your house?"

Paige gripped the phone, reactions oscillating through her head. People in town were hearing that the police were questioning her? The thought made her stomach churn. Everyone would start to talk. The media might hear. The anonymity she'd taken such chances to protect would dissolve ...

Should she even answer the question?

I want to help you out.

Paige focused through the window at the hot tub, her thoughts mercurial.

"Yes, they're here."

"Who's *they*?"

"Chief Edwards and another officer. Frank West."

"Oh." Leslie's tone turned wry. "I know Frank too. Listen to me, Paige; we don't have much time. You've got to get those cops out of your house—*now*. You don't have to let them be there, understand? Anything they see, anything you say, they can use against you. Although I'm sure you've got nothing to do with Edna San's disappearance, for some reason they're targeting you. They wouldn't *be* at your house if they weren't looking for something specific. Plus, I know they've already talked to you once. You need a lawyer, *right now*."

Lawyer? The very word froze Paige's muscles. Guilty people needed a lawyer. People who were arrested, who had to go to trial. People in jail.

Bubbles pinging her face. Edna's weighted body pulling her down, down in the frigid water.

The truth wrapped ghostly fingers around Paige's neck. She *was* guilty. And she would not get away with her deed. Even if by some miracle she could convince the police she hadn't killed Edna San, she would still go to jail. She'd hidden evidence, lied in her interview, hindered a criminal investigation. The all-encompassing scope of the law no doubt harbored a string of felonies she could be charged with. She could spend *years* in jail.

"Paige, are you there?"

"I—yes."

"I've called a lawyer for you, a friend of mine. Name's Arthur Gretz. He's ready to meet with you right now, for free. All you have to do is let him."

Paige's eyes squeezed shut, exhaustion and disbelief snaking through her gut. The advice sounded right. She never should have let the police in her house. But what would they think if she stopped them now?

"Paige, do what she says." Sarah's distant voice filtered over the line. "Leslie knows what she's talking about."

"Did you hear that?" Leslie asked.

"Yeah, I heard." Paige rubbed a hand across her forehead. She could barely think straight. "Leslie Brymes." Her voice had fallen to a whisper. "Who are you?"

"Your friend, Paige, that's who. Like I said, I'm doing this to help. But you can't tell *anyone* about this conversation, okay? Sarah's already promised to keep it quiet. Really, it could mean my job."

"I won't tell." A question about the nature of that job floated across Paige's thoughts like blown milkweed, then was gone.

"Thanks. Listen, did the chief drive you out there in his car?"

"Yes."

"I was afraid of that." Leslie sighed. "Okay, here's what we'll do. You have a piece of paper and pen? I'm going to give you my cell phone number."

"Wait a minute." Paige scurried to her miscellaneous drawer and pulled it open. Rummaged through its contents, searching for a pen. *There.* She snatched it up, then sidestepped to the table for one of the napkins stacked upon it. "Ready."

Leslie rattled off the digits. "Whatever you do, *don't* let them see that number. And remember, as of this minute Gretz is your lawyer. So you march over to those cops right now and tell them so. Tell them Gretz says to leave your property immediately. They'll have to go; it's the law. But you stay behind. I'll come pick you up and bring you into town to Gretz's office. He'll want to advise you right away." Leslie paused. "Got all that?"

Paige felt the gathering of a cataclysmic storm. What could she do but follow Leslie's advice? She moved to the drawer and dropped the napkin inside. "Yes, I have it."

"Okay, girl. Now *go*."

The line clicked in Paige's ear.

FIFTY-FIVE

"You're sure you don't want one of us to take you back to town?" Vince stopped in the entryway of Paige's house, working to keep his expression neutral. Frank's hand was already on the front door.

"Thank you. I'm sure." Paige's voice was curt, her gaze not quite meeting his. That telephone call had lit the fire of her resolve, but Vince could see the lingering dampness of fear. If he were a lesser cop, he might play on that emotion, convince her to change her mind. But he wouldn't bend the law. Art Gretz would have his hide in court.

"All right then. Appreciate your time."

Frank gave a final, tight-smiled nod to Paige and they stepped out onto the porch. The door closed firmly behind them. Vince heard the bolt click into place.

Exchanging grim looks, they walked around to the driver's side of Vince's vehicle.

"Arthur Gretz, huh." Frank's voice was low.

Vince shrugged. "Surprise, surprise. Shows how quick word gets around the streets. Whole town probably knows we've been talking to her by now." He rubbed his jaw. "I've got to get back and start on a search warrant. I saw enough in there to convince me she's involved."

"Yeah, me too." Frank studied the ground, ambivalence creasing his forehead. "That deck sure was clean."

"Yeah, I noticed that when I was looking at the backyard."

"And the garage too. Not to mention that sheet and those gloves in the washer." Frank shook his head.

Impatience surged through Vince. He opened his car door. "We need to get moving on the warrant. Let's hope we can rustle up a judge on a summer weekend. I'll check in with the search teams and techs on the way back to town. They should be done with the scene by now, and someone should have dusted that Spirit Lake pay phone for prints. Maybe we'll have some further information."

"Okay." Frank took two steps around Vince toward his own car, then stopped. Turned back. "I just can't believe..." He raked a hand through his hair. "She doesn't look like the type, know what I mean? Something about her." His eyes roamed the house as if looking for answers to the mysterious young woman inside. "She seems so...I don't know...vulnerable. But in a way, strong at the same time. And she's obviously scared to death."

Vince studied him, remembering the flicker of interest in his eyes when he met Paige, the reassuring looks he'd given her. "Frank." His voice was low. "Don't go there."

Frank pulled in a breath and let it out. Flexed his shoulders. "Yeah." He turned with resolve and headed for his car.

Vince slid into his own vehicle, thoughts flitting from Frank ... to Tim ... to Nancy. With a sigh he pulled out his cell phone and began making calls.

FIFTY-SIX

Black Mamba peered from behind the tree in the forest, binoculars trained on the front of Paige Williams's house. He'd found the perfect spot for lurking, thick with vegetation, but beyond it a narrow, clear line of vision. Farther down Lakeshore, parked out of sight on an old logging road, sat his car.

He'd arrived at this spot to see two police vehicles gracing Paige's driveway. Anytime now one of those cops ought to be bringing the little lady out in cuffs. Mamba sighed. Too bad he couldn't watch the back of the house as easily. How luminous a sight their discovery of Edna San would be.

Paige's front door opened. Mamba leaned forward, anticipation curling through his veins.

One cop walked out. A young one. Followed by the chief of police.

The door shut behind them.

Mamba stilled.

The policemen walked together toward the rear car, frustration in their gaits, on their faces. They stood talking for a moment, the chief's hands on his hips, the younger one shaking his head.

What was going on?

They split up, both climbing into their vehicles. Mamba heard their engines start. They backed out one after the other—and drove away.

Slowly Mamba lowered the binoculars. His tongue flicked out, touched his lips. His brain thrashed through possibilities, explanations. Was this a ruse? Were they somehow onto him?

Impossible. The police never trapped Mamba.

Were these small-town cops just too *stupid* to look in the hot tub?

He couldn't imagine that either, not with the clues he'd given them through his anonymous tip. Besides, by this time, in all this heat, wouldn't the smell alone lead them once they stepped out on the deck?

What then?

Paige was obviously still in the house. *Without* her car. At least he assumed she'd been driven here by the chief. Were the police leaving her here, without a vehicle, intent on returning to arrest her?

No way. One of them would have stayed to keep an eye on her.

Mamba pressed his fingers against the binoculars, anger coiling up his spine. He was not accustomed to altering his plans. Paige would pay for this.

Face hard, muscles tense, he slunk through the woods at a northerly diagonal toward the road, aiming well beyond Paige's house. As he neared the road, he laid the binoculars on the ground. He would retrieve them later. Checking right and left, he crossed Lakeshore and slid into the forest on the other side, snaking around trees, hurrying for a position from which to view Paige's backyard. At the first glimpse of her deck in the distance, he pulled to a halt, breathing hard.

He crouched low and eased his way toward the house. At the edge of the clearing he saw no one. What was Paige doing inside those walls?

Little matter. She would not be doing it for long.

Bent over, he ran for the side of the garage. Flattened himself against its wall and peered into the window.

No car.

His lip curled.

He slid toward the back corner, peeked around it. Still clear. His eyes snapped to the deck. The hot tub lay covered. He sniffed the air. Nothing.

An insane thought hit him. He pulled back, mind reeling. Surely this young woman, this stupid *nobody*, hadn't outwitted him. No one did that to Mamba.

Propelled by the mere idea, he darted around the corner and toward the deck, uncaring now if he was seen. At the edge of the steps, he leaned over to reach with both hands for the thick brown cover of the hot tub. He lifted it and peered underneath.

Empty.

Rage shot through him. Mamba hissed through his teeth. As the realization settled over him, taunting irony stared him in the face. He'd conjured an anonymous tip about a body being dragged—and apparently it had *happened*.

Seething, he dropped the cover. Did this young woman really believe she could outsmart him? How utterly laughable. She'd succeeded in nothing but cutting her worthless life even shorter. Never mind his original plans to slither through darkness into the Kanner Lake jail. Guilt-ridden Paige Williams need not take her own life tonight in a holding cell. She could die right here, right now, just as well.

Mamba slipped up the two stairs and across the deck.

FIFTY-SEVEN

Not a sound from the house.

Rachel bends low, making her way through Rosa's dark back-yard. Her fingers grip the boxy purse so hard, they ache. She will not let go of it now, not for anything. Whatever lies inside it has cost her, will somehow keep costing her. She doesn't even know how yet, or why. All she knows is the pounding of her heart, and the gut-churning silence.

She reaches the deck. Shuffles toward the sliding door. Press-ing herself against the side of the house, she slowly leans forward, peering into the kitchen.

No movement.

She leans further, her eyes traveling over the table, the cooking island, to a door leading to the hallway.

She sees no one.

Her hand grasps the metal door handle. Holding her breath, she eases back the door a few inches. Cocks her head, listening.

All is quiet.

The silence is so thick, so *loud*, it fills her head. The urge to run shrieks, and she snatches her hand from the door only to grasp it again, push back a few more inches. Another and another, until there is room to squeeze through.

She sticks her left fist through the short purse handle, pushes it up her arm to leave both hands free. Steps fully in front of the door. If anyone is watching from inside, he will surely see her now.

Breathing a prayer, she eases into the house.

Rachel freezes, listening. Hearing nothing but the faint tick of Rosa's grandfather clock in the living room.

Pulse grinding, she manages two cautious steps, halts, then two more.

If only she could see through a front room window. Is the man's car – whoever he may be – still out on the street? She tells herself it is long gone, driven away as she hesitated in the neighbors' yard. She simply couldn't hear it over the banging of her heart.

She reaches the cooking island. Grips the cool tile for support. Quietly shuffles around it. She fastens her eyes upon the threshold of the hallway, watching the hardwood floor slide into view. Still no sound, no movement.

Where's Rosa?

From deep within Rachel a voice whispers that her mother is dead. The mother she never had, and helplessly hoped someday to have, and now never will.

Rachel can't listen. She can't bear to.

At the hall she presses her palm against the doorway, steadying her trembling limbs. Six feet ahead on the right is the wide entrance to Rosa's formal living room. Rachel can't yet see the front door, around the corner of the stairwell to the left.

She forces herself forward, hugging the wall.

Her lips part, seeking oxygen. Her mouth has gone so dry that each breath snags on the walls of her throat. She covers about two feet, stops, pricks her ears for the tiniest whisper of sound.

The clock ticks.

Rachel holds her left arm against her stomach, pressing the purse against her so it won't dangle and knock against something. Whatever is inside does not rattle.

She is two feet from the living room entrance. Fear clutches her with strangling hands. Not a second longer can she wait to see the fate that has found her mother. Her feet cross the distance. She strains her neck to search around the corner.

On the floor crumpled legs stick out from the end of the couch. Rosa's. One foot is missing a shoe.

Rachel's chest ices over. She flings herself across the white carpet.

In front of the sofa Rosa lies on her side. Eddie is close by, one of his arms thrown across her shoulders. His eyes are wide open, two red-black holes in his forehead. A handgun lies inches from his right hand. Across the room, near the front window, lies a third body. A man on his back, arms twisted, a gun trapped in his motionless fingers. Blood oozes from a wound in his chest. Rachel stares at him.

Blake.

"You want me to come over there, knowing Blake is on his way?"

"No, no, it's not him!"

Like melting wax, Rachel's limbs shrivel her down to the floor. Freeing her arm from the purse handle, she crawls toward her mother's head. Rosa's face is covered by her strawlike hair. Rachel sweeps it back, seeking her mother's eyes. *Just look at me one more time, Mom; don't die. Just see me.*

Rosa's eyes are closed. Her mouth sags open. Rachel feels for breath with her palm.

Nothing.

Why did this happen, Mom? Why did you lie to me when you knew Blake was coming?

The questions pinch off. The answers don't matter; all that matters is her mother is dead, shot mere minutes after Rachel slunk away in the night. Didn't she know something like this would happen? What if she had stayed? Could she have saved Rosa?

No. Even Eddie couldn't save Rosa. He and Blake must have shot each other in the same second …

Rachel kneels by her mother and time melts away. She finds herself rocking, rocking, head in her hands. Grief floods her brain, pools behind her eyes, but she can't remember how to cry, because tears were beat out of her long ago. She thinks of her mother over all the years, and suddenly the only memories that surface are the few good ones. Rosa's laugh – before it turned raucous. Rosa's blue eyes – before they grew cold. A hug when Rachel was a child, many years ago …

How long Rachel lingers, she doesn't know. She can't even think what to do, who to call, how to explain her presence in a house with three dead bodies. She raises her head, looking toward the heavens for some answer, for *Someone* to help –

Headlights sweep the street outside. Rachel stills, her eyes piercing the sheer curtains of the window.

The sound of a car driving up.

Instinct rockets Rachel into action. Before her brain can register her choice, she has snatched up the purse and is dragging it across the carpet, scuttling on all fours toward the entryway. On some distant plane knowledge screams in her head that whoever is coming will kill her, take the purse. Whatever lies inside is valuable enough to have caused the deaths of three people. Rachel will let no one else have it – ever. Whatever it may be, it is the *one and only* thing Rosa entrusted to her, the one remaining piece she has of her mother.

Rachel hits the hardwood floor and slips around the corner, bruising her knees in her escape. Fear drags her into the kitchen, around the cooking island. She tumbles through the open sliding glass door onto the deck, pressing the purse against her chest. With controlled force she pulls shut the door, thrusts to her feet, bends low.

Rachel runs.

Having covered this ground twice before, she no longer needs to pick her way. She flies through the dark, propelling herself across the neighbors' property, onto the sidewalk. She sprints across the street, skids to her car, and yanks open the door. Throws herself inside. The purse thumps to the passenger floor. Stretching out her legs, she leans back, fumbling in her pocket for the key. Three times her shaking hand shoves the key toward the ignition and misses. When the car finally starts, she rolls away in the lamp-lit street, turning on her headlights only when she has turned left at the corner.

On impulse at the next corner she turns left again. When she reaches the next block, she peers down the street toward her mother's house. A police car is parked out front.

Rachel veers right.

She drives by rote for a mile until she remembers Rosa's words. *"They'll want the purse and will come looking for you ..."*

The bizarre truth punches her in the stomach.

She can't go home.

FIFTY-EIGHT

The minute she hung up from talking to Paige, Leslie called Arthur Gretz back, telling him all was set. If he'd come downtown and open up his office, Leslie would have Paige there in about half an hour. He agreed to meet them. "And, Leslie," he added, "she's my client now. Thanks for the referral, but you know I'll be advising her not to talk to you or any other reporter."

Fine, Gretz, all I need's the drive back to town. "Sure, Arthur, sure. I'm just helping her out. See you soon."

She flipped her cell phone closed, sparking with energy. Swept a strand of hair from her eyes and spun to point a finger at Sarah. "I need your car keys."

"Huh?" Sarah stood flummoxed, one hand on the counter, her brain obviously miles behind Leslie's.

"I have to drive out to Paige's house and pick her up." Leslie waved her hand toward the door. "I can't go in my car because I'm likely to pass the chief on Lakeshore as he's headed back. If he sees my VW, he'll put the pieces together. I *can't* let him know I'm the one who called Paige."

"Oh. Okay." Sarah pushed away from the counter and bent down—far too slowly for Leslie's taste.

"Sarah, hurry!"

"Okay, okay, just getting my purse."

A minute later Leslie trotted up the sun-drenched sidewalk, cell phone stuffed in her pocket. For some insane reason Sarah had parked her blue Honda Accord around the corner and up two blocks on Second Street, not far from Leslie's VW. Surely closer parking spaces had existed when Sarah opened the store that morning. But no matter. Leslie could hardly believe she'd struck such a major coup. Now if she could just get Paige Williams to talk on the drive back to town. Her mind spun, figuring the best approach. What if Paige asked about her job? As much as she wanted to make use of this situation, she couldn't bring herself to out and out lie. But Paige would probably freak to hear she was a reporter. Somehow she'd have to extract juicy tidbits while convincing Paige that she was just looking out for her.

Guilt twinged Leslie's stomach as she turned the corner. Paige had sounded so scared on the phone. And Sarah had made a big deal about her not having any friends. How would Paige feel when she heard everything she'd told Leslie reported in the news?

Yeah, but she *had* told Paige to get a lawyer, hadn't she? And that was a big help. Where would Paige be right now without that advice?

Still, her remorse refused to dissipate. Leslie forced her thoughts to safer ground. What on earth did the chief have on Paige Williams?

Leslie reached Sarah's Accord and whipped the cell phone from her pocket. Inside the car she tossed the phone onto the passenger seat. *Whew*, it was hot. She could feel a sheen of sweat under her shirt. *Doggone July weather.* If she did make it on national news tonight, she'd look like a wilted tulip.

She gunned the engine and took off up the street. Her brain hummed. No time to lose here; she had calls to make. She snatched up the cell phone and hit 03 to automatically dial Jared at the office. He answered on the first ring. "You won't believe where I'm headed," she blurted. She spilled her story, saying she'd report in as soon as possible. Jared tried to tell her how to pull information from Paige Williams on those precious ten minutes back to town, but Leslie's thoughts were already on the next call. "Okay, Jared, okay. Talk to you soon."

She closed the phone with one hand and opened it again. Punched in the next number.

"Hello, Java Joint," Bailey's ever-friendly voice sounded in her ear.

"Bailey, Leslie here." She couldn't keep the excitement from her tone. "I'm in a real hurry; can you talk for a minute?"

"Sure."

"Tell me what you know about Paige Williams."

A pause. "Well, I doubt I know much more than you do." Bailey's tone became guarded.

Leslie frowned. Since when did Bailey protect some newcomer over helping her get a story? "Bailey, come on, what's the deal? You called me about her, remember? I'm not asking anything about this case; I just wonder what you know about Paige personally."

"That's just it; I don't know much. She's only come into Java Joint a few times. But she has this … aura about her. Like she's really lonely and wants friends but is afraid to reach out. I don't know, something about her makes me want to hug her and tell her everything will be okay."

Leslie tossed a look heavenward. What else was new? Bailey wanted to hug everybody. Still, Sarah seemed to feel the same protectiveness toward Paige. What was it about this girl? "Anything else?"

"Not really. Except, like I told you before, she was scared to death when she came in here today. Very, very nervous."

"Okay, thanks. See ya later." Leslie snapped the phone shut.

She followed Lakeshore as it curved around the top of the lake and headed south. No sign of Chief Edwards on the road yet.

Leslie drove straight-backed, practicing her pitch, trying to ignore the skein of guilt in her belly. So she was taking advantage of some friendless person to get a story. It wasn't *her* fault Paige Williams had attracted the attention of the police. The girl obviously had done something. Leslie adjusted a vent, aiming the air-conditioning directly on her face. Did famous reporters like Milt Waking have to use people like this? She flipped through her mental catalog of his major stories. Of course he did. But in the end he helped solve the crimes—and wasn't that a good thing?

Up ahead, driving toward her, came a black-and-white police car. Leslie drew in her shoulders, wishing for an invisible cloak. The car whizzed by, followed by a second. She sighed with relief. The coast was clear.

Story, here I come.

FIFTY-NINE

Paige lay trembling on top of her bed, curled into a fetal position, fears and memories fissuring her head.

She couldn't believe it had come to this.

The reaction of those cops when she'd told them to leave! As much as they'd tried to appear passive, their frustration and suspicion could not be contained. She could only imagine the cataloging of all they'd seen. Why hadn't she remembered the gloves in that load of laundry? And the attention they'd paid to her swept floors, her rumpled bed. Suddenly everything she'd done that morning to hide her crime seemed a blaring mistake.

Paige closed her eyes. An oily ball of wax rolled through her stomach. She was going to jail, even with an attorney's help. If she stayed in Kanner Lake, they would catch her in her crimes. Why hadn't she called the police last night? Anything would be better than what she faced now.

She would have to flee. Tonight. Dig up the metal box buried in her backyard and hit the road. Again.

But how could she? They'd be looking for her car. Her picture would splash across the news. Then *everyone* would be searching for her. Where would she go? When could she ever settle in and start a life? A *real* life?

Tears stung Paige's eyes. For the first time in years she let them fall. To think that just over twelve hours ago she'd been dumb enough to believe the promise that she'd meet her long-awaited sister today. That a girl somewhere out there, with a past as rough as her own, would show up on her doorstep—just like that—and spill all the secrets of her miserable childhood. How stupid. How utterly, ridiculously *naïve*. Paige Williams was a loner now and always.

Any pieces of hope she'd swept together in Kansas should have been left there.

Paige wiped her tears. Enough. She had to pull herself together. Soon Leslie would arrive. Paige couldn't let on that she was beaten down, that she had anything to hide. She couldn't even imagine telling the truth to this attorney. *No one* here knew the truth about her. Who would accept her if they knew?

Paige, who's going to care about your past when they find out what you did last night?

A sound from the other end of the house. The *click* of metal.

Paige halted her breath, listening.

A muffled rolling sound.

The sliding glass door?

She sat up. Leaned forward, head cocked. Had she imagined it?

No more sound. But her heart drummed like the rataplan of rain on a roof.

Paige pushed to her feet. Stood still, shoulders drawn in. An inexplicable sense of evil stole over her, blanketing her limbs. She bit her lip, trying to discern what was happening.

A man materialized in her doorway.

SIXTY

Rachel drives through the dark streets, a woman on the run with no place to go. Her spine is stiff, her fingers glued to the steering wheel.

Questions sear her mind.

How long will the dirty cops look for the purse at her mother's house? Police have radios. They'll know her license plate. What if they find signs of her being there? A hair, a shoeprint? Will they try to pin the murders on her?

Surely some detective could tell the two men shot each other.

Yes, but can he be trusted? These are *cops*. They stick together. How can she trust any of them?

Rachel passes the street she would turn on to head home. She needs to get out of Pensacola. Maybe even out of Florida. Headed where, she doesn't know. She just has to get somewhere safe long enough to figure out what to do ...

She heads toward Interstate 10.

What are those cops' names Rosa told her? Rachel curls her fingers around the steering wheel, forcing herself to remember ...

Roland Newell, that's one.

And Ron something. Starts with an H.

Come on, come on. Ha ... Ha ... Hardinger!

The third? Last name is Veretsky. Bob?

No. Bill.

271

Roland Newell, Ron Hardinger, Bill Veretsky. Rachel whispers the names over and over until she knows she won't forget.

At the freeway she turns west. She does not allow herself to think. Just drives.

Rachel doesn't stop until she hits Mobile. There she takes an exit, finds an all-night grocery store, and pulls into the parking lot. Locks her doors.

With trembling fingers she draws the purse off the floor of the passenger seat. Sets it firmly in her lap and opens the latch.

The painted box yawns open.

She peers inside.

Money. Rachel gasps.

By the light of the parking lot she can make out a thick stack of bills, bound with a slender rubber band and lying on its side. She looks around her car, making sure no one is near, and withdraws the money from the purse.

Beneath the stack lies a second.

Breath stalling in her throat, Rachel pulls it out as well. She blinks in wonder at them both, turns them face up. A one-hundred-dollar bill lies on top of each. She checks the bottom bills. Also one hundred. Rachel sets one stack on her lap, flips through the other. All hundred-dollar bills. Same with the other one.

How much money *is* this?

Heart racing, she sets the stacks side by side on the console. They're of equal height — about two inches each. She takes the rubber band off one of them and counts.

One hundred ... two hundred ... on and on Rachel counts. Three hundred ... four. And sixty-five more. Four hundred and sixty-five bills. Times one hundred.

Rachel's mouth sags. She is holding $46,500 in her hand.

And that's only one stack.

Ninety-three thousand dollars. Rosa gave her a purse contain-ing *ninety-three thousand dollars.*

Air seeps from Rachel's throat. A dozen thoughts bounce through her head. For this much money, those cops will search the state for her. Surrounding states too. People will *kill* for this much money.

People already have.

Now what? What can she do?

She can't go back. She can't turn over this money. No doubt it's from drugs. There would be questions, long interrogations, while the tainted cops watched in feigned innocence. How could she explain?

Whom can she trust?

Terror rises in Rachel, ice-cold and stinging. She has to get out of here *now.* She has to go … somewhere, anywhere. Just get away. Far, far away. And never come back.

Limbs shaking, she stuffs the money into the purse and shoves it all far underneath the passenger seat. Heads out of the grocery store parking lot, back toward I-10. There she turns west again.

She drives all night, frozen to the wheel, thoughts sinking into a glacial lake of numbness. She does not stop to sleep until she hits Houston.

SIXTY-ONE

Leslie slowed the Accord and leaned to her right, frowning at the white letters on a black mailbox. Childress, they read. Number 2751.

Not far to go. She hit the accelerator.

Her phone rang and she jumped. Leslie scooped the cell off her lap and glanced at the ID. It looked familiar. She sucked in a breath. FOX News.

She flipped open the phone. "Leslie Brymes."

A tight curve loomed ahead. Leslie braked, gripping the steering wheel with one hand.

"Ms. Brymes, this is Alison Votle. We're just outside the Kanner Lake area. I've been making phone calls along the way and am already formulating a story, but if you've got some things you think we ought to know, we'd still like to talk to you."

Trying not to sound too needy, are we? Leslie gauged the curve, taking it as fast as she could. Time to cut to the chase with Ms. National. "Ms. Votle, I have information that no one else has, I can guarantee you that. Perhaps even more than the police. And I'm just about to learn more. When you're setting up your truck here, do call me. If you're willing to interview me on camera, I'll help you break this story. Otherwise, no deal."

"I see." Alison's tone was cool. "Well, if we need you, we'll get back to you."

A mailbox up ahead. Leslie strained her eyes to read the numbers. "Fine. I gotta be going now." She clicked off the line, hoping to heaven she'd win the dicey gamble. She glanced back and forth from the mailbox to the road. The numbers grew readable—3142.

Almost there.

SIXTY-TWO

Numbness gripped Paige. She stared at the man, her heart stalling.

"And so we meet, Paige." He spoke the name with sarcasm, one corner of his mouth curling. He leaned casually against the doorjamb, one glove-covered palm up and spread across the opposite side. Beneath his facade, Paige sensed a venomous anger, one that could strike at any moment. "Although not quite as I had planned."

Paige's lips parted but no words came. Deep in her brain a faint memory stirred. Medium height, slim. Brown hair and eyes, a pasty, angular face . . .

"Ah, I detect a filament of memory." He smiled and it chilled her to the bone. "I was in your store yesterday. You know—when you threatened to kill Edna San?"

Air backed up in Paige's throat. In a flash she pictured the scene—red-faced Edna, the two sisters. A male customer who followed Edna out to the sidewalk.

The man's hand fell from the doorway. With a sigh he moved toward her. "I just had to tell her what you said." His smile faded. "Such fast thinking on my part, don't you think? Although she wasn't very happy to hear it." He stopped two feet away, studying her, drinking in her terrified understanding.

Paige's tongue lay dead in her mouth. "Wh–what do you want?"

His face blackened. "*I'll* ask the questions. What did you do with the body?"

Her ankles shook, the tremors traveling up her legs, her torso. This man had lied about the death threat. This man had killed Edna San. Was he here to kill her too?

He sprang.

In an instant he'd whipped her around and to his chest, her arms pinned between her back and his body. The crook of his elbow jammed against her throat. "When I ask you a question, you answer, hear?" The words oozed venom.

Paige's jaw dropped open as she fought to breathe.

The elbow tightened. "Talk to me."

Choking sounds spilled from her mouth. "I — Sh – she's in the lake."

The man spun around and threw her onto the bed. She landed on her side with a cry, head bouncing against the wall. He hulked above her, arms stiff and eyes slitted. "How did you know she was here?"

Paige flinched from him, drew her knees up to her chest. "I found her in the hot tub. In the night."

Slowly he straightened, his chin lifting. He drew a deep breath, regarding her with utter, cold contempt. "How very clever of you."

Paige pulled her arms around herself. "Why?" Her voice was flat, dead. "Why did you pick me to blame it on?"

Dark amusement creased his face. "Can't you see the brilliance of one death covering for another? Now your outrageous actions last night will only convince everyone of your guilt." He gave a mock bow. "I thank you for your help, although truly it was not needed. You may not know I was here yesterday, while you were at work. Picking up your earring."

Earring?

His mouth flattened into a cruel smile. "And now, Miss Williams, the time has come. Your despairing, murdering conscience is about to catch up with you."

SIXTY-THREE

On the drive into town, Vince's adrenaline rose like a swelling river. Given Paige's lack of personal ties to the town, she was too much of a flight risk. He needed something, *anything* solid, to give him reason to arrest her. With Paige detained for a few days, he'd have a little more time to pull evidence together. Besides, he had a hunch that the taciturn Miss Williams would break pretty quickly behind bars.

He opened his cell phone, mind pinging from one detail to another. First he checked with the crime scene techs—they were finished and back at the lab. Among other things, they'd lifted fingerprints and vacuumed Edna San's bedroom carpet. Now to see if anything they'd picked up was foreign to the house. Prints from the earring and the Spirit Lake pay phone also would be examined. Next Vince made a call to Officer Jim Tentley, out with the search crews. Jim told him they'd found no trace of Edna San. Third he phoned Officer Waitman, still standing guard at the gate to the estate, who informed Vince that news vans were gathering like vultures. Finally Vince called C. B. at the station. C. B. complained phones were ringing off the hook, with calls coming in from the media as well as townsfolk. News about Paige Williams had spread like wildfire.

Vince sighed. "All right, I need something from you right away. Ignore everything else for now and focus on tracking down a judge. I'm coming in to write up a search warrant. Let's just hope every judge in Bonner County isn't out on the water somewhere."

C. B. promised to get right on it.

Stopping at the first light in town, Vince rubbed his temple, thoughts flitting to Nancy and tomorrow's fast approach. *Please, God, let me get a break in this case—for Nancy's sake.*

At the station he gunned into a parking space, Frank pulling up beside him. Inside the small building Vince aimed straight for his office, spewing orders to Frank over his shoulder. "Hop on the phones too. Help C. B. round up that judge. I'd like to be able to head out as soon as I'm done with the paperwork."

He heaved himself into his chair and punched on the computer, thrumming his fingers against the desk, mind already composing the warrant. As the machine booted up, Vince's eyes fell upon the photo of Tim and Nancy on his desk. He focused on it, the wounds in his heart seeping.

The opening screen on his computer appeared. He clicked to create a new document in Word and began to type.

With careful attention he laid out the mounting evidence against Paige. Her argument with Edna San. Her apparent lies during questioning. Her scraped palms. The tips about her dragging something across the deck and perhaps driving her car in the middle of the night. A distant view of the grass in her backyard, apparently flattened. Their cursive sweep (with signed consent) of her home, and what they'd found. He listed the items they would be looking to seize in the search. Some he knew about specifically, such as the gloves and sheet in the washer. Perhaps all evidence on them had been scrubbed away, but he had to be sure. Just in case, he also described the earring that could be a match to the one found at the crime scene. Beyond that he'd search for hair, a piece of lint, anything that might be traced back to Edna San—

"Hey, Chief."

C. B.'s voice made him jump. Vince turned to see the officer in his doorway.

"Sorry to bother you." C. B. bounced his knuckles against the wood. "But I just got a call from someone who says you'd want to talk to him. Name's Officer Daryl Brumley. From somewhere in Kansas?"

Vince sat back in his chair. "Put him through."

C. B. disappeared. Vince waited, his gaze pulling back to the picture of his wife and son.

His phone jingled and he snatched it up. "Officer Brumley. Thanks for calling me back so soon."

"No problem." Brumley's voice held a note of intrigue. "Actually, the information you wanted wasn't too difficult to find, once I had the chance to get to your request. I discovered some interesting answers for you."

Vince pulled a pad of paper close and picked up a pen. "Shoot."

"Okay, I located the parents, Justin and Betty Williams. Had to trace them through a relative who still resides in Whitsung."

"The parents are *alive*?"

A chuckle. "Very much so. They were quite surprised by my phone call, I can tell you."

Vince stared at his desk, assimilating the news. "Go on."

"They moved away from Whitsung in 1987. They now live in Roanoke, Virginia. However, on April 12, 1981, when they still resided in Whitsung, Betty Williams gave birth to a baby girl—Paige Beth Williams. So I have no doubt we've got the right people."

"Yeah, sounds right. What did they tell you about Paige? Despite her clean record, she must have done something."

"Oh, she did something, all right." A pause. "Probably not quite what you're expecting."

SIXTY-FOUR

One death covering for another?

Paige's eyes widened, her mind flailing to make connections. Dark scenes from her past sooted her brain. Had she survived all that—to die for an act she hadn't even committed?

She swallowed. "Who are you?"

Hooded eyes measured her. "Black Mamba."

He lowered himself to sit on the edge of the bed, angling toward her, a calculating satisfaction twisting his mouth. He reached out a hand, ran a finger down her cheek. Paige shrank from his touch.

"Like it or not, in my work I've occasionally had to kill." Mamba's voice was low, dripping poison. "I shot a detective in his bed in Ohio. Drowned a Vermont judge in his bathtub. Cut up a woman and her pregnant daughter in California." He stroked Paige's skin. "Now you—for your insolence in breaking the rules—will die slowly. But with no marks except those on your lovely neck." He trailed his fingertip down to the pulse in her throat. "I don't need a weapon to make you obey. I can make you writhe in pain with my bare hands. If you run, I will catch you in an instant. Do you understand?"

Her head nodded.

"Good." He cupped her chin in his palm and smiled. Then eased to his feet. "Now get up. We have work to do. First you will write for me."

Write?

Paige wasn't sure her legs could hold her up. Without taking her eyes from Black Mamba, she pushed off the bed and onto feet of jelly. Her thoughts wouldn't focus. She searched inside herself for some semblance of strength, some cunning move toward escape. But where would she go? She didn't even have a car to run to.

Leslie.

The realization sizzled through her. Leslie was coming.

No matter. He would kill her too.

"Into the kitchen we go." Mamba slipped behind her, one hand massaging her back.

Paige obeyed.

At the kitchen table he pulled out a chair, nudged her into it. He spotted the pen she'd used to write down Leslie's number and picked it up. "You keep paper in here?"

For a moment her mind went blank. *Paper* ... She shook her head.

He exhaled, then spotted the napkins on the table. Reached for one and laid it before her. "This will suffice." He held out the pen. "Now write what I tell you."

Paige felt herself reach for the pen, avoiding his touch. But her body suspended on some other plane, watching in shocked detachment. Her heart fibrillated; her head turned light.

Mamba moved close, rested a heavy hand on her shoulder. "I'm sorry I killed Edna San."

Paige looked up at him, staring numbly. "What?"

His fingers dug into her flesh. "*Write* it."

She looked at the napkin until its white texture blurred. Like some goblin's hand, her own touched down the pen point and wrote:

I'm sorry I killed Edna San.

"Very nice." Mamba drew the second word into a hiss. "Now explain where you put the body."

Paige's arm trembled. This couldn't be happening. She pressed her wrist against the table for steadiness. How to tell where Edna was? Her brain wouldn't work.

"Come on."

The pen touched paper.

> Her body is in the lake at the old swimming hole where the drop-off is.

"Good, good. Now sign your name."

> Paige Williams

He chuckled. "You still don't understand, do you? You think Edna San's death was about her? No, no. This has always been about you. Lying, scheming, thieving *you*." He caressed her shoulder. "Sign your *real* name."

Like a locomotive rushing out of darkness, the truth hit. Paige's body seemed to break into a thousand pieces. This man was from her past. Of course. Why had she been so stupid to believe she could simply disappear? Her mother's final warning echoed in her head.

Paige's eyelids slipped shut. If only she'd left the purse behind. If only.

"*Sign* it." Mamba pressed his knuckles against her neck.

Worn, exhausted, and defeated, she wrote her name on the napkin.

> Rachel Brandt

SIXTY-FIVE

Finally—the mailbox Leslie had been looking for. Number 3692. She slowed Sarah's Accord and turned left into the gravel driveway. *Please, please, Paige, talk to me.*

Leslie pulled up and stopped about fifteen feet from the garage. As she turned off the engine, her cell phone rang. Impatiently she checked the ID. Some long-distance number—Atlanta? Her heart performed a double beat as she shoved the phone to her ear. "Leslie Brymes."

"Ms. Brymes, this is Gretchen Versloos from CNN. We're working on getting some camera equipment out there to Kanner Lake to cover the Edna San case, and we'd like to talk to you about being interviewed for a news show tomorrow."

Excitement ping-ponged through Leslie. She flapped a hand to expel some of her energy, then struggled to keep her voice level. "That's certainly a possibility. What would be involved?"

Gretchen Ver—whatever her name was—yakked away, detailing time, setup, possibilities for cancellations, yada, yada. Leslie drank in the words, even as her antsiness grew. What if Paige was watching through a window, wondering who on earth she was talking to so long?

The car interior was roasting. Leslie opened the door.

Gretchen V. wanted her to take some information down. Leslie scrambled for her steno pad and pen on the passenger seat. "Okay, I'm ready."

Names and phone numbers followed. Leslie scratched ink across the paper. "All right. Fine. Thanks so much." She tossed an anxious look toward the little house. Paige must have heard her drive up. She would have some explaining to do. "Is that all?"

She shouldn't have asked. Questions followed. What did she know about the case? Any new developments? Like they were going to milk her for all she was worth right here and now. What would be left for tomorrow?

As with the Alison person at FOX, Leslie turned aside the queries. She knew she had them hooked. "Look," she finally said, "I'm onto something big here and I really need to go. Can we talk later?"

By the time she snapped the phone shut, she was doubly sweaty from sitting for ten minutes in the hot car. She tossed the cell on the passenger seat with a huff. "Reporters," she grumbled as her feet hit the driveway with a *crunch*.

SIXTY-SIX

Paige huddled in the far corner of the backyard, just before the drop-off down the hill. Black Mamba pressed close, gripping her arm. In his other hand was the trowel—the same one she'd used the night before to pry loose the anchor. "It's here." She pointed to a patch of grass.

He narrowed his eyes at it, tracking the barely visible lines where she had cut through the lawn and lifted the grass away like a piece of sod. He sniffed. Thrust the trowel into her hand. "Dig it up."

Paige got down on her knees, aware of him behind her. Wondering if a killing blow would land upon her head at any moment. *But then, that wouldn't be a slow death, would it?*

Her arms shook as she used the edge of the trowel to pierce the grass. The smell of dirt assailed her nostrils, slamming her thoughts back to the shivery crawl space. As she worked, her fingers turned brown, earth lodging underneath her fingernails. The grass broke away. Paige dug through the soil.

Black Mamba yanked her hair. Pain shot through her scalp and she gasped.

"How much is in there? You couldn't have spent it all, from the looks of this place."

Paige longed to press a palm against her scalp, rub away the tenderness. Instead she hurried her digging, dirt chunks flying. "Seventy thousand."

He pulled, keeping the pressure on her hair. Hot needles pricked her flesh. "What did you do with the rest of it?"

Paige's eyes watered. She blinked hard. "I spent it coming across the country. And I bought a used car. And some furniture and clothes."

He made a sound in his throat. "This all of it?"

Her mind flashed to the extra five thousand hidden under her mattress—budgeted help with rent for one year. "Yes. I buried it so I wouldn't use it easily."

Mamba laughed. "I applaud your frugality."

Clunk. The trowel hit metal. Paige hadn't buried her treasure very deep. She dug in silence, teeth gritted against the pain in her head. An eternity later she set down the trowel and sank her hands into the square hole. She wrapped her fingers around the waterproof box, lifted it, and laid it upon the grass.

"Look at this mess you've made." Mamba eyed the hole with disdain. "Now fix it."

As Paige pieced the ground back together, he picked up the metal container, opened it. Withdrew a dingy purse, boxy and painted with pink poodles. He opened it and pulled out a bundle of hundred-dollar bills, flipping through them with a smirk.

"Good." He stuffed the money back into the purse. Reached down and hauled Paige to her feet. "Let's go."

He pushed her across the yard, Paige stumbling on legs of water. Up the deck and into the kitchen. "Pick up a chair and bring it with you." He shoved Paige toward the table. Her thoughts tumbled and twirled, even now looking for a chance to run. Some way to save herself.

"You hear me?" Mamba threw the purse on the counter. In one fluid motion he jerked her to his chest again, shoved a hand against her voice box. Pain gripped her, deep and throbbing. She struggled for air, guttural sounds spitting from her mouth.

Abruptly he let go. Paige slumped toward the floor, heaving in oxygen. He grabbed her by the hair. "That was a sneak preview. Now pick up the chair."

Weak and shuddering, Paige lifted it.

Mamba opened the door to the garage, gestured with his chin. "Take it out there. Put it down in the middle of the floor."

She did as she was told.

He stepped into the garage and closed the door. "Sit down."

Paige fell into the chair, tears filling her eyes. She bent over, hugging herself against the terror. "Please don't hurt me. I'll go away from here and no one will ever find me. You can have your money."

He moved out of sight. She heard the sound of the metal cabinet opening. Items being moved. What was he going to *do* to her?

Panic surged up her spine.

Paige sprang to her feet and raced for the back door.

Mamba caught her with superhuman quickness. His arms locked her in a vise and picked her off the floor. She struggled and kicked, desperate to hurt him, to free herself, to *live*. He hauled her toward a wall, forced her down to the cement, onto her stomach. Straddled her legs and grasped both arms, twisting them up and back until her shoulders wrenched against their sockets.

Paige screamed.

Mamba pulled harder. "You going to do what I say?"

Tears blinded her eyes. She could hardly breathe. "Y–*yes*!"

He let her arms go.

Paige's hands smacked to the cement. Sobbing, she scooted away from him and rolled to her side, curling into a ball.

"Fine. You just lie there." He returned to the cabinet.

She brought both fists to her mouth, groaning at the throb of her shoulders. Her eyes clenched shut. She didn't want to see, didn't want to know. What could she do to save herself anyway?

Mamba slithered about for what seemed an eternity, barely making a sound. Paige cringed on the hard, cool floor and prayed.

"All right. Get up."

Quivering, Paige forced her eyes open. Carefully turned her head and looked up.

A slipknotted noose hung low from one of the rafters, brushing the back of the kitchen chair.

SIXTY-SEVEN

Leslie reached out to slam the Accord's door shut—and heard a scream.

She froze.

Her frightened glances flew in all directions. What was that? Where had it come from? The garage?

She cocked her head, listening.

More sounds. Vague, muffled. The quiet drone of a man's voice, so low she wasn't sure she heard it at all.

Should she investigate? Leslie glanced at her feet. The gravel driveway wasn't exactly made for sneaking around.

She bit the inside of her cheek, thinking. Then leaned inside the car to retrieve her phone. She slid it into her jeans pocket. Leaving the car door open, she crept toward the garage, carefully placing each foot.

As she drew near, she heard nothing more. Maybe she'd imagined the whole thing. Leslie looked toward a front window. If Paige Williams saw her skulking around like this, the girl just might find her own ride back to town.

She reached the garage door, barely daring to breathe. Listed to one side, pressing her ear against the wood.

Noises. Faint ones. Somebody moving around.

Well, so? Maybe Paige was cleaning in the garage and a mouse ran over her foot.

But Paige Williams had just sent two nosey policemen out the door. She was supposedly scared to death and waiting to be picked up to see her defense attorney. What would she be doing in the garage when her car wasn't even there?

Leslie's mind raced over possibilities. Removing evidence … Hiding something …

This had to be checked out. She pulled in a silent breath. Maybe the garage had a side window.

With furtive steps she moved toward the corner.

"All right. Get up."

Leslie tensed. A man's voice, cutting and cruel. No way had she imagined that.

Something was happening here. Something … not good.

Random thoughts spritzed through her brain. She was a reporter; she had to get the story … The man inside—where had he come from? … S-Man's crazy warning—*"Be very careful …"* Her camera—it lay in the car.

Leslie's pulse shifted into overdrive. She hit the edge of the gravel, heart pummeling her ribs, and stepped off into quieting grass.

Toward the rear of the garage she spotted a window. Dampened sounds of movement and voices emanated from the wall. Leslie drew a staccato breath and ventured down the side of the house.

SIXTY-EIGHT

Paige's disbelieving eyes fixated on the rope.

Above the noose, tied perpendicular to the rope, was the broom she'd used to clean away evidence that morning. It hung like an uneven balance, weighted toward its bristle end. The free end of the rope ran across two ceiling rafters, then down to the floor. It was tied off to a leg of the metal cabinet in the corner.

Black Mamba approached, looking down on her with glittering eyes. He held out his hand.

"Please," Paige whispered.

He smiled. "I like it when they beg."

Paige's limbs flushed with weakness, nausea swelling in her stomach. Something in the very pit of her being crumbled and scattered away like dry leaves in the wind. Why did her life have to end like this? After the abuse and longing. The struggling and will to survive against the odds. All for nothing.

Mamba leaned over, both palms out. "There is nowhere for you to go." His voice was bitingly calm. "Nothing you can do to save yourself. But know you will die famous. As the investigation uncovers more and more, everyone will hear your story. How you stole the identity of a Kansas baby who died at birth, and obtained a Social Security number for it. How you wound up in Kanner Lake, then killed Edna San for no more reason than revenge over an argument. How you, abused as a child, lonely and guilt-ridden, hung yourself when you knew you would be caught." He sighed with satisfaction. "See how perfectly these pieces fit together?"

He smiled again, as if reveling in his brilliance.

Abruptly he reached down and yanked her arms, streaking her shoulders with renewed pain. Paige cried out. Before she knew it, she was on her feet.

Sudden, gripping panic overwhelmed her once more. Her muscles firmed. One leg lashed out, aiming for Mamba's groin.

He jerked aside. Her foot met air.

Her knee snapped, weakened. Paige staggered backward. Mamba slapped both arms around her waist and hoisted her off her feet. She struggled to break free. He rotated and shoved her onto the chair. It slid backward, its legs scraping the floor.

The low noose jostled against her head. Paige flinched from it, arms punching wildly, legs churning. Mamba grabbed her throat and hung on, reaching for the noose with his other hand. She bucked and jerked, whipped her head from side to side, cries bursting from her mouth. Mamba held on tighter.

The noose slipped around her head. He grabbed both sides of the broom as if it were a barbell, yanked it up, cutting off her air. She gurgled, hands flying to the rope, scrabbling, scrabbling to loosen it.

Mamba raised the broom higher, increasing the pressure. Suddenly he let go. Disappeared behind her.

In the second of relief Paige sucked in oxygen.

Without warning the rope tightened again. Paige could hear the rope grinding against the rafters above her as Mamba pulled.

"Better stand up."

He pulled more, and Paige scrambled to her feet to loosen the noose, then up on the chair. The broom above her head teetered and knocked against her shoulder. She sucked in hungry breaths, the rope sliding across rafters until the noose tightened once more. It tugged at her body, separating her feet from the chair. Pain shot through her throat.

She lifted into space.

Paige struggled against death. The pressure on her throat was going to snap her neck in two. She flailed, desperately seeking ground. Odd sounds like the lurching scrape of rock over metal sputtered from her mouth. Dots coruscated in her eyes.

"Reach for the broom!" Mamba snapped.

The broom! Up flew her arms, seeking the wood. Her right hand found it, dragged that end down, tipping the other side from her reach. Her left fingers thrashed air.

"Even it out or you'll strangle."

Just as she started to lose consciousness, understanding trickled into Paige's brain. She thrust up the right side of the broom, caught the left side. With both arms she lifted herself toward the handle in a trembling pull-up.

The slipknot loosed around her neck.

Paige clung to the broom and stuttered in air. Her chest heaved, her throat grating. The world narrowed into a tunnel, reduced to the drag of oxygen into her lungs. *Breathe, breathe, breathe.*

Slivers of pain punched into her injured shoulders. Her arms weakened. She couldn't hold herself up very long.

Noises behind her. Paige lifted higher. She sensed Mamba tying off the extra rope to the leg of the metal cabinet. He would leave her to her fate, pulling up, strangling, pulling up, strangling—the slow death he'd promised. Her gaze rolled downward. She hung about a foot off the chair.

Mamba slipped into her vision and picked up the chair, moved it away.

"Now." He posed before her, tongue flickering out to touch his lip. "How long do you suppose it will take you to die?"

SIXTY-NINE

Leslie reached the window, heart filling her throat. As she'd slipped down the side of the garage, she heard sudden movement. Bodies thumping, a woman crying out. Sounded like a fight. Paige was in serious trouble.

Flattening her stomach against the garage, Leslie gripped the window frame with her left hand for steadiness. Slowly she leaned over until one eye peered through the glass.

The sights hit her like bolts of lightning. A man fighting with Paige. Her whipping body. A *noose* hanging from the rafters.

Leslie jerked back, nerves scalding. Denials and stunning reality trounced her brain until she could barely reason. For a moment she could only hang there, pressed and shivering against the wood, her feet motionless, hands cupping her mouth.

A new sound, like chair legs shoved across a floor.

She peeked inside again.

From a chair beneath the noose, Paige battled for her life. The man slipped the deadly loop over her head, pulled on a broom tied above to tighten it.

Leslie shrank away from the window, air hiccupping from her throat. Paige was going to die before her eyes. And *she* would die too, if the man spotted her. Hung from the ceiling, her lungs bursting for air ...

God, what am I supposed to do?

Leslie turned and ran.

Down the side of the garage back toward the road, arms flapping. At the end of the garage, she avoided the noisy driveway, flying over the grass until she pulled up even with the Accord.

Chest heaving, she yanked her cell phone from her pocket and pried it open. Punched three numbers with shaking fingers.

"Nine-one-one, what is your emergency?"

"I—" The raw whisper snagged on her tongue. "This is Leslie Brymes. I'm at thirty-six ninety-two Lakeshore. A woman's being killed. She's about to be *hung*." Tears flooded Leslie's eyes, and her throat clogged up. She bent over the phone, explanations tumbling. "I just looked through the garage window and saw it. There's a man and he's fighting with her. Her name's Paige Williams, and the police were just here. Call Chief Edwards at the Kanner Lake station—he'll tell you. I think this has to do with Edna San, and I don't know who the man is, but he's *killing* her, and they have to get here right now!"

"Okay, ma'am, we'll put out the call. You just stay on the phone so we—"

"I can't stay on the phone; I have to *do* something!" A sob tore from Leslie's mouth. "We don't have time, don't you understand? There's no *time*. She'll be dead before anyone arrives, and I'm the only one here!"

"Ma'am, if you'll just calm—"

A weak cry filtered from the garage. The desperation in that sound hurled a sudden, fierce anger through Leslie's veins.

She flung down the phone and raced over the gravel toward the Accord.

SEVENTY

Paige's arms and shoulders blazed. She raked in gulping breaths, even as her fingers loosened from the broom handle.

God, please, if You're real, give me strength.

Mamba moved around her in a slow, wide circle, arms crossed and a cruel smile playing at his mouth. "If you had died tonight in your jail cell, it would have gone quickly. This is your pay for playing me."

Paige struggled for the power to hang on. A tremble started in her hands, moved to her wrists. Edged up her arm.

Mamba moved again into her line of vision. Her eyes strained left, following as he circled in front of her. "Do you know what you did to me, taking off with that money?" The words spat from him. "I'd slaved for years to work my way up. I was the number two guy, right under Mr. Drug King himself. But when that money was lost on my watch, he was ready to *kill* me. The only chance for my life was to promise him I'd hunt you down and make you pay—creatively. In some fashion that would prove my skills remain." He chuckled. "He'll be so impressed to read all about it." Mamba glided toward the front garage door, fading from her sight.

Paige's elbows shuddered, then her upper arms. Every back muscle burned.

Hold on, just hold—

Her fingers slipped off the broom. She sank—and the noose snapped tight around her throat.

Her legs kicked with abandon, arms beating air. Weakly she reached up, up, brushed the broom with her fingers, but her muscles turned to water. Her hands fell away.

"So soon?" Mamba tsked. "But then, it's for the best. I do have details to ... *tie up* before I leave town." He laughed at his joke.

Paige kicked and choked and gagged. The world dimmed ...

"Come on, reach for the br—"

The garage door exploded.

Wood caved in with a roar, splintered with the crackle of a thousand bonfires. Glass shattered and sharded and tinkled upon the cement. The gun of an engine filled the air. Through a darkening cave, Paige saw Black Mamba's body fly against the wall with a sickening *thud*. Something big and solid loomed to her right.

Paige's legs churned. Wildly she struggled for the broom.

The something lurched forward. Jerked to a stop. Lurched again.

Paige's calves smacked against metal.

The object heaved a third time. Her feet scrambled over the top of it, seeking footing. She slipped, her knees giving way. Her feet scrabbled again.

She stood. The rope loosened.

Her jaw hinged open. Sputtering air sucked down her raw throat.

Paige's fingers grappled with the rope at her neck.

A sound like a door opening. Paige's vision began to clear. A car hood materialized beneath her. Running footsteps. A shout—"I'm untying the other end!" Paige locked her weakening knees, fighting to hold herself upright, the slackened rope hanging into her face, broom knocking against her head ...

"Got it!"

A young blonde woman jumped to Paige's side, her face crimson, cheeks hollowed in fright. She leaned against the front of the car hood, held out her arms. "It's Leslie. Come on, I'll help you down."

Dazed, Paige lifted the noose over her face, her head. Let it go. It thumped onto the car hood. The broom clattered on metal, then bounced to the garage floor.

"Come on." Leslie's tone pulsed. She motioned with her fingers, glancing with terror at the body of Black Mamba.

He stirred and groaned. Struggled to rise.

Leslie pulled at Paige. "Hurry!"

Paige leaned down and sagged against her. Both knees gave way and she crumpled off the car, knocking Leslie backward. "Oof!" Leslie grabbed her arms, tried to keep her upright. But the velocity of her tumbling body proved too much. Paige fell to her knees, dragged Leslie down with her. The room spun. Paige sank to the floor and laid her head down, fighting the dizziness, knowing it would win. Her eyes slipped shut.

Distantly she heard Leslie push to her feet. A moment of silence—then a choked-off scream. Hissing curses from a male voice. The thumps and heavy breathing of a struggle to death.

Paige fought to open her eyes.

Strangling sounds, someone gasping for air.

Paige's eyelids weighed a ton.

God, help.

Her eyelids lifted halfway. Sight blurred and wavered, fixing on the wide-straddled feet of Black Mamba inches from her reach, and on the other side of him Leslie's blue-jeaned legs. Paige looked up. Mamba's back loomed above her, his arms raised. She couldn't see Leslie in front of him. No need. Paige knew he was killing her. And Paige had no strength to stop him. She tried to lift her arm. It refused to budge.

Paige was too weak to cry.

Then ... something. A trembling inside. With split-second viv-idness the helpless moments of Paige's life paraded before her. Beatings her mom doled out. Abuse Rosa's boyfriends inflicted. The night of murder that left her fleeing her own identity. Edna San's floating body.

Now the death of someone who had come to help.

From deep within Paige anger rumbled. Like the long-awaited eruption of a menacing volcano, it shook her being, then exploded.

Hot lava flowed out of Paige's soul, through her limbs. Flamed down her arms and fingertips. Paige's right hand lifted from the floor. Her legs scissored against cement, sliding her within reach of Black Mamba. Her clawlike fingers brushed pant leg, then grabbed the man's ankle.

Paige pulled.

Black Mamba grunted in surprise. Stepped back. The chok-ing sounds stopped and he pivoted. As his gripped foot lifted from the floor, Paige yanked again. Leslie screamed and pushed him. Mamba stumbled, cursed—and fell. His arms shot out to break the impact. Too late. His chin hit the cement with a sick-ening *crunch*.

Mamba lay still, moaning.

Paige's fury receded from her limbs, clumped in her chest, then fizzled. Her fingers sank away from Mamba's ankle. She could move no more.

Leslie swayed and sobbed but stayed on her feet. She stag-gered from Paige's line of fading sight. Paige heard the metal cabinet door squeak open, objects rattle. Leslie appeared again, a hammer clutched in white-knuckled hands. She approached Black Mamba, a vicious expression darkening her face. Raised the hammer.

Paige's eyes weighted shut.

She heard a *thwap*, like the sound of tenderizing mallet against meat. A second. Third. Mamba made no sound. Leslie emitted a teeth-gritted, vindictive cry. "Move again, and I promise you will *never* wake up."

Silence. Save for the heavy sound of her own and Leslie's breathing. Paige couldn't move.

Leslie erupted into fresh tears. She hacked and sputtered, the noises loud and jarring, and music to Paige's ears.

Leslie, whoever you are, keep strong. We can make it.

In time the sobs thinned. Lightened in tone. Then slowly morphed into the relieved and off-key laughter of one escaping the grave.

Paige's head swam. The sounds faded. Her last second of consciousness recorded shaky words she could not understand.

"So *there*, Milt Waking. I did it. Leslie Brymes got herself a story."

PART FOUR

Released

SEVENTY-ONE

Vince shivered as he stepped inside his house and closed the door, newspaper tucked under his arm. "Ooh, it's cold out there." He stomped his feet, loosening bits of snow onto the large mat in the entryway.

"Did you get it?" Nancy called from around the corner.

"Yeah." Vince followed the enticing aroma of fresh-brewed coffee into the kitchen. Nancy was already pouring his cup. She set it on the table, anticipation brightening her face. "Well, come on, let me see it."

Vince gave her a piqued look, even as his heart sparked at her animation. Her blue eyes were wide, her face fresh from sleep. In her luminescence she reminded him of the Nancy he'd fallen in love with. The Nancy before Tim's death.

Tim. The familiar knife stabbed his heart.

Vince pulled the paper out of its plastic bag and laid it on the table. The article took the entire front page, with a "Continued on page 2" at the bottom. Its headline was two inches tall.

JURY ACQUITS BRANDT ON ALL COUNTS

Nancy sank into a chair to read.

Vince shook his head. As if she didn't know every word the article would say. For the past three weeks his wife had succumbed to the fascination of trial-watching along with the rest of Kanner Lake. He pulled up a chair beside her. "You crazy lady."

She batted him with one hand, not taking her eyes from the article.

Vince leaned toward her, tilting his head to read as well. Nancy angled the paper so he could have a better view.

Centered on the page was a photo of a shell-shocked Rachel Brandt—Paige, as she was still affectionately and stubbornly called—coming out of the courthouse. Microphones aimed at her face, but as usual one of her hands was raised in a keep-away gesture. Briefly Vince wondered if she would now break her silence for the many television news shows offering her money. He doubted it. She might finally be safe from her threatening past, but clearly she still harbored an aversion to publicity.

Nancy's chin slowly sank, then bobbed up to follow the article to a second column. "This is a long story," she murmured. "Probably takes the whole paper."

"Yeah, well, Leslie likes to hear herself write."

"Oh, Vince." She tossed him an exasperated look. "Don't you think you've nursed that grudge long enough? If Leslie hadn't called Paige about the lawyer, if she hadn't offered to drive out there and pick Paige up—Paige would be *dead*."

He sniffed.

Nancy firmed her mouth. "And how about the fact that all those murder cases being linked to Black Mamba would still be cold? *And* that huge drug ring in Florida, including those dirty cops, would still own the streets."

Vince spread his hands, eyes widening. "*And* no land would be settled west of the Mississippi."

Air seeped from Nancy's throat. She gave him a playful shove and turned back to the paper.

Leslie Brymes. Vince frowned. That annoying kid had sure made hay with the story. She'd gotten herself interviewed on countless national shows. He sniffed again. At least she'd been too busy to hound him for information on every petty crime in Kanner Lake.

Nancy read on. Vince's gaze skipped across the article, landing on a paragraph recounting the Edna San investigation.

> The bullet recovered from the body of Bravo, San's Dober-man, matched the gun found in the cabin newly rented to Rick Forter (a.k.a. Black Mamba), and hairs found in the San house were consistent with his. Forter, under the false name Sidney Rykes, had gained employment as a shelf stocker at IGA, biding his time as he sought a headline-grabbing way to "make Rachel Brandt pay" for abscond-ing with the money he owed Florida drug king Tommy Landersing. The mounting evidence against Forter, plus Brandt's testimony about San's body, led authorities to charge him for the murder of the actress ...

Vince reached across the table for his cup of coffee, then sat back in his chair. Forget the article; he'd read it later. For now he was content to watch his beautiful wife devour every word. Vince laid a hand on her shoulder and rubbed.

One thing he had yet to decide—how did he feel about Paige's acquittal? She'd clearly broken the law, which Vince had dedicated his entire career to uphold. Felony obstruction, felony failure to report, and felony destruction of evidence were among her myriad charges. Francesca Galvin, now a retiree in southern California, had certainly wanted to see Paige punished. On the witness stand the woman hadn't hidden her feelings of resent-ment in the least. But like the townsfolk, who'd rallied to Paige's side after the whole sordid tale came out, Vince couldn't help but sympathize with her plight. And in part he had lying Paige Williams to thank for saving his marriage. The loneliness in her eyes had jostled his own soul to better nurture the family God had given him.

He glanced at Paige's photo in the paper. She'd grown out her hair and let it go back to her natural light-brown. Good choice. She was even prettier than before. Frank West sure seemed to notice, Vince thought sardonically. Although the kid would deny it till doomsday.

Vince sighed. He wouldn't admit it was just as well the feds hadn't prosecuted for the identify theft of the name Paige Williams. Rachel Brandt had been through enough. And one could argue she'd harbored no criminal intent in assuming a false name for her own protection. Besides, she'd earned the bargain. With her information on the huge interstate drug ring— including handing over the thousands of dollars she'd hidden away—the feds had been able to bust it apart.

"Hmm." Nancy tapped a finger against the paper. "It says they're thinking yet another murder case is linked to Black Mamba. This one's in Las Vegas."

"Guy got around."

"He evidently confessed to that one too." Nancy's brow creased. "Why would somebody who's gotten away with so many crimes do that? Why not just keep his mouth shut?"

Vince set down his cup, remembering the utter coldness on Rick Forter's face as the man had lain under guard in his hospital bed. Complete lack of remorse, mixed with arrogance. Vince shrugged. "Now that his name is known, he wants credit for all his creativity. He's a sick mind."

Nancy shuddered. "To think he was here in Kanner Lake." Her face hardened. "I don't care what state tries him first; I hope he gets the death penalty."

Vince raised his eyebrows. "Oh. Now we *want* people to pay for their crimes, do we?"

She huffed. "Honestly, Vince. You can't possibly compare Paige to that man."

"I'm not, I'm not." He held up both hands. "Truce, okay?"

Nancy pursed her mouth, as if considering his offer. "Truce." She leaned over and kissed him. A warm, wonderful Nancy kiss.

SEVENTY-TWO

At ten a.m. a brisk knock sounded on Paige's apartment door. She heaved a sigh. She was exhausted. Why did Leslie have to be on time? Why did she have to come at all?

Reluctantly Paige opened the door.

Leslie stood in the hall, bundled in a puffy pink jacket and matching gloves. Yellow sequins outlined the embroidered daisies on her jeans. She spread her hands in a *ta-da!* gesture. "Here I am, girl; let's go!"

Paige swallowed. "I have to get my coat and stuff. Come on in."

Leslie breezed inside, her face flushed from the cold. "If you dress warmly enough, we can walk the three blocks." She grinned. "Or is this Florida girl not macho enough for the cold?"

"I'll be fine." The words came out pinched.

Leslie looked at her. "What's the matter?"

Paige turned away and sauntered to the couch. Lowered herself onto the edge of a cushion and stared at the carpet. "I don't want to go, Les."

Leslie blew out air. "Of course you do. Paige, we've been through this. You're acquitted, you're clear and free as a bird, and it's time to start making a life for yourself. Besides,"—she pointed a pink-gloved finger—"you *promised* me you'd do this."

"I know." Paige clasped her hands, focused on her feet. What was the matter with her anyway? This was no big deal, just a

310

trip down to Java Joint. But in truth it was so much more. It was her venture into the Kanner Lake community after all the months of hiding. Since July she'd done nothing but work at the store—thanks to Sarah Wray's bigheartedness, she hadn't been fired—then scurry back to her apartment. She hated all the whispers in the store, the looks on the street. She was in the town news, the Pacific Northwest news, the national news. Her story and her face and ultimately her trial had become the fascination of the country. Now the nightmare was over, but everyone everywhere still knew her face. Paige just wanted to crawl into a cave.

Leslie sighed. She slipped off her gloves and coat and sank beside Paige. They studied the floor together.

"Look, Paige. You need to do this for your own good. You're the one who told me how much you want friends and a family. Well, Kanner Lake folks are *like* family. And you know they like you. Think of all the cards you got. The people who came to the store just to tell you how sorry they were about all you'd gone through. People in this town even pitched in to pay your bail! And Pastor Hank and other church members helped you move your stuff to this apartment. So come on ..."

Paige's throat tightened and her eyes burned. She blinked back tears. The people from the church *had* been good to her, especially the pastor. He'd called several times to reassure her, telling her that Jesus loved her and was willing to forgive her for everything. Telling her Jesus would make her life new if she would only ask. Pastor Hank had sent her a card with a Bible verse—Psalm 68:6: "God makes a home for the lonely." The pastor couldn't possibly know how much those words meant to her. Especially when she thought of her mother.

"It's not that I'm ungrateful, Leslie. It's just that ..." She squirmed, straining to form the words. "Everyone knows how much I lied about *everything*. My whole past, where I was from, how old I am, even my name. And they know every detail about all the horrible things I did. Even though they seem to forgive me, looking them in the face is so *mortifying*. Plus, I don't know if I can give them anything back. I haven't had much practice." Paige raised her head to look at Leslie. "You know?"

Leslie's eyes grew bright. She grasped Paige's arm. "You gave back to *me*, didn't you? You forgave me for looking at you as just a story."

Paige shrugged. "It was kind of easy after you saved my life."

"Yeah, well, you saved mine too, so we're even."

Paige had to smile. She bumped Leslie's shoulder with her own. "Besides, you got everything you wanted, Miss Famous TV Personality."

"Oh, really." Leslie bumped her in turn. "I also waged some mighty hefty news campaigns to encourage sympathy for you, if you'll remember. Enough to have ol' Jared Moore lecturing me about objectivity in journalism." She wagged her head at the words.

Paige pretended to consider her argument. She was loving this girl banter. She and Leslie had fallen into it naturally, even with the pressure of the last few months. Leslie had been there for her every day. "Yeah, I guess you did help me out."

Out. There was a play on words. If things hadn't gone Paige's way, she'd be sitting in jail right now. Since yesterday's verdict, some of the jury members had spoken to the media about why they'd acquitted her. They'd thrown around newly acquired lingo like "totality of circumstances" and "criminal intent." Paige wasn't sure if they'd turned the law on its head or not, but one thing was clear. For whatever reason, they hadn't wanted her punished for the crimes she committed. In fact, two jury members said she'd been "punished enough."

"Well then." Leslie bounced to her feet. "Let's go grace Java Joint with our presence. No use wasting all this beauty and talent on your apartment." She grabbed Paige's wrists and pulled her up. "They're waiting for you to come say hi."

"You mean you *told* them I was coming?"

Leslie's hand fluttered. "Oh, good grief, so what? I wanted to make sure the regulars would be there in this cold weather. And it's the last Saturday morning you can go. After this weekend you'll be back working on Saturdays."

Sarah Wray could have demanded Paige come back to work immediately after the trial, but she had wanted to give Paige the weekend to "get her head back together." Leslie was right—today was the day.

"Okay, okay." Paige fetched her coat and gloves from the closet.

"Besides,"—Leslie slipped her jacket back on, a mischievous expression stealing over her face—"you deserve that free drink Bailey's promised you. Shoot, with all the people tramping through this town to cover your story in the past seven months, she's never had more business."

Paige gave her a weary look. "Nice to know my infamy helped *somebody* out."

They stepped from the apartment into the hall. Paige made sure to lock the door.

Outside Leslie tucked her arm through Paige's as they crunched through the snow to Java Joint, their breath puffing tandem streams in the cold air. "I really like your hair longer," she remarked. "And the brown's such a nice shade."

"Yeah." Paige wanted to say more but was too embarrassed. She'd never liked the dyed black very much. And never before had she worn her hair that short. Now that she at least didn't have to worry about the past chasing her, it felt good to return to her natural color.

They reached Java Joint. Paige hadn't set foot inside the café since that day last July, when she was paranoid of every glance.

Through the windows she could see the cheery walls and Bailey behind the counter. Three tables had occupants. Tourists for the ski season? Paige peered at the four counter seats. All taken. The locals were waiting. She drew a deep breath.

Leslie opened the door and they stepped inside, warm inviting air wafting around their cheeks. "Hey, folks!" Leslie called. Every head in the place turned. Paige cringed. A chorus of greetings sounded from the three men and one woman in their counter stools. Paige recognized Pastor Hank.

"Well, *there* you are." Bailey stepped away from her machine, placing the backs of her hands on her hips. Her face held that ever-sweet friendliness. Remorse twinged through Paige. She shouldn't have held Bailey at arm's length these past few months. Every time the woman had stopped into Simple Pleasures to invite her for a free coffee drink, Paige had put her off. Now Bailey was smiling as if she'd never been rebuffed. "Come on in and get a hot drink."

She and Leslie stopped to shrug out of their coats and gloves. Leslie dropped them on an empty table, then nudged Paige toward the counter. Pastor Hank slipped off his stool. "Sit here, Paige. I've been parked too long anyway."

She managed a smile as she took the seat. "Thanks."

Momentary silence. They all looked at her as if wondering what to say, the atmosphere shimmying with her self-consciousness.

Leslie moved behind Paige, hands falling on her shoulders. "I think you may have met some of these other folks a while back." She pointed to the attractive black-haired woman on the far end, clad in a maroon turtleneck and slacks. "That's Carla. In real estate. She's the listing agent for the Edna San property, all three million dollars' worth of it."

Carla raised her cup with a grin. "And I can't wait to sell it to the right person. Cheers, Paige."

"Hi." Paige gave her a little smile.

"This here's Jake, sitting next to you." Leslie tapped her fingers on the dingy baseball cap of a sixtyish man with a thin face and buggy eyes. He touched a hand to the brim of his hat. "And on the other side of you" — Leslie pointed to the gray-whiskered man on Paige's left — "is Wilbur."

"Watch out, Paige; he bites." Carla aimed a warning glance down the counter.

"Who asked you?" Wilbur shot a mean look back at her.

Leslie sighed. "Don't mind them, Paige; neither one has an ounce of manners."

"Hey, Ted." Bailey focused on a table near the wall, where a dark-haired man frowned at his laptop, lips silently moving. At Bailey's call his head jerked up and he gazed around blankly. Bailey crooked her fingers at him. "Come out of Sauria for a minute and join us." She turned to Paige. "Ted used to be in logging, but he suffered a bad leg break and couldn't continue. He's going to be Kanner Lake's famous science fiction writer."

Ted pulled in a slow breath. His eyes roamed before landing on Paige, and recognition filtered across his face. "Oh yeah. Right." He pushed out of his chair and limped over. "Hello there, Paige." He nodded to her, unsmiling, yet Paige sensed an unassuming acceptance. As if she had no salacious history, no baggage. As if she were a normal newcomer to town. Just ... Paige Williams.

Warmth flushed through her body. She smiled in gratitude. "Hi."

As their eyes held, a realization struck deep within Paige, unfolding like a blossom in time-lapse photography. Pastor Hank was right. She'd been released. God was offering her a second chance in life. What a fool she'd be not to grasp His hand — and accept it.

"So." Bailey pressed her palms on the Formica. "What'll you have, girls? It's on the house."

Paige blinked away from Ted, refocusing her mind. She ordered a biggie mocha, and Leslie, a nonfat biggie latte. Bailey turned with a grin to make the drinks.

To her left Paige felt Wilbur's eyes burning a hole right through her. She glanced over to find the old man openly staring. Hadn't he done the same thing last July? She forced herself to look him in the eye ... and a second moment of truth gripped her: There was no need to be anxious about this man, or any of the others. This was just Wilbur. He was probably like this to everybody. So he didn't hide his curiosity; at least there was no pretense about him. The tightness in Paige's chest loosened further.

Wilbur pulled the sides of his mouth down and looked her over good. Then bobbed his scruffy chin with satisfaction. "You're one gutsy gal. I *like* that in a woman."

Paige searched for an appropriate response. "Well, um. Thank you."

Something akin to pride flickered across the old man's features. "I'm a pretty tough ol' bird myself." He moved his hands to the bottom of his thick wool shirt and—to Paige's dismay—started to pull it up.

The others groaned. Carla choked, "Oh, Wilbur, *please*. She'll never come back."

Wilbur paid them no heed. He wagged his head and the shirt rose further, exposing a rotund belly and white-haired chest. "So, Paige Williams. Whadya think of my scar?"

ACKNOWLEDGMENTS

I owe a few folks some mighty big thanks for helping me with this story:

Tony Lamanna, Spirit Lake, Idaho, chief of police, in law enforcement since 1969, answered many questions, and most important, read the manuscript to catch my errors regarding police procedure. He was wonderfully, unselfishly helpful. If you find a mistake in this area, mea culpa. (Or perhaps I fictionalized with intention.)

Gary Johnston, lieutenant with the Bonner County Sheriff's Department, also answered questions regarding some rather strange law enforcement scenarios — with a straight face.

Sherry Ramsey, writer for the *Priest River Times*, led me to Tony and Gary in the first place and offered information about a small-town newspaper.

Terry and Marilyn Cooper, owners of the *real* Simple Pleasures, at 221 Sherman Avenue in Coeur d'Alene, Idaho, allowed me to feature their beautiful store. All the merchandise mentioned in this story is sold at Simple Pleasures. Visit their website at www.simplepleasures-cda.com.

A few of my blog readers, affectionately called BGs, suggested quirks for the various characters that hang out at Java Joint. They are: Lynette Sowell, Ron Estrada, Evelyn Ray, Grady Houger, C. J. Darlington, Kelly Klepfer, Sherry Stewart, and Dineen Miller. Special thanks to BG Stuart Stockton for allowing me to use his

science fiction novel *Starfire* for S-Man. All of S-Man's characters, his Saurian world, and the Saurian language are straight
from Stuart's manuscript (still seeking a publisher as this book
goes to press).

To one and all, thank you from the bottom of my heart.

BRANDILYN
COLLINS

KANNER LAKE SERIES

CORAL
MOON

BOOK 2

PROLOGUE

Kill tonight—or die.

The words burned. Through his retinas, into his brain, back, back, to the innermost center of neurons and synapses. There they bubbled and frothed like hot acid, eating away at his soul.

Only a crazy person would follow their command.

He slapped both hands to his ears, cradled his head. Pushed in, squeezing, until the pressure battled the pain inside. His eyes screwed shut, mind pleading for the horrific message to be gone when they reopened. He hung there, cut off from the outer world, attention snagging on the life sounds of his body. The whoosh of breath, the beat of his heart.

Their words boiled.

The pressure grew too great to bear. He pulled his hands away, let them fall to his sides. The kitchen spun. He edged to a chair and dropped into it. Bent forward and pulled in air until the dizziness passed. Clutching hope, he turned his gaze once again to the table.

The note still lay upon the unfolded Kanner Lake Times newspaper, each horrific word against the backdrop of a coral crescent moon.

How did they get in here?

His shoulders slumped. What a stupid question. As if they lacked stealth, as if mere walls and locked entrances could keep them out. He'd been down the hall in the bedroom watching TV, door wide open, yet had heard nothing. Hadn't even sensed their presence as he pushed off the bed and walked with blithe ignorance to the kitchen for some water.

A chill blew over his feet.

His eyes bugged, then slowly scanned the room. Over white refrigerator and oak cabinets, wiped down counters and empty sink. To the threshold of the kitchen, leading into the hallway. There his gaze lingered as the chill worked his way up to his ankles. It had to be coming from the front of the house. His skin oozed sweat, sticky fear spinning down over him like the web of a monstrous spider. Trembling, he pulled himself out of the chair. For a moment he clung to the smooth table edge, ensuring his balance. Then slowly, heart beating in his throat, he forced himself across the floor, around the corner, through the hall and toward the front door.

It hung open a few inches.

They were taunting him.

Slowly he approached, hands up and fingers spread, as if pushing through phantoms. Sounds of the night outside wafted upon the frigid air—the rustle of breeze through tree limbs, distant car tires singing against pavement. He reached the door, peered around it into blackness, knowing he was a fool to seek sign of them. The air smelled crisp, tanged with the purity of pine trees. The last vestiges of snow dusted his porch, bearing the tracks of his footprints alone.

He closed the door and locked it. As if that would do any good. Shivering, he sagged against the wall, sickened defeat puddling in his chest. How naive he'd been to think they would leave him in peace.

But hadn't he seen this coming? All the events that had occurred in the last few months ...

Minutes ticked by, the death shroud of reality settling over his being.

Shoulders drawn in, he made his way back to the kitchen and his inevitable fate. Each footstep drew him away from the life he'd built, reasoning and confidence seeping from him like blood from a slow but fatal wound. His conscience pulsed with repugnance at what he must do. His inward ear sought that rhythm, desperate to embrace its beat. But it proved too faint amid the drumming terror of the consequences of disobedience.

Unyielding, the message sat on his table, beckoning like an executioner to the noose. Was it only a half hour—and a lifetime—ago when it hadn't been there? He fell once more into the chair, wiped his forehead with the back of his hand. His reluctant gaze landed upon the words, and nausea roiled anew. No misunderstanding their directives. He knew they had a chess score to settle. Who else would they choose as their pawn?

He pushed back against the chair, arms crossed and hugging himself, the way he used to do as a boy. Dully, he stared at the window, seeing only his own pitiable reflection. For a long time his form transfixed him, blinking back first in fright, then with the slowly evolving expression of self preservation.

He need only pursue this one piece of business, and his debt would be paid. Surely, then, they would leave him alone.

For another hour … two, he sat, willing his queasiness to fade as he brought his mind into focus. How to do what he must do? He considered details, possible repercussions. Laid stealthy plans.

By the time he rose shortly before midnight, he felt nothing but the desperate pull of his perfection-demanding task.

Gathering the necessary items, shrugging on a coat, he slipped out into the cold and soulless night.

Brink of Death

Brandilyn Collins

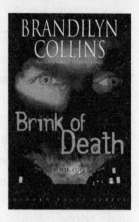

The noises, faint, fleeting, whispered into her consciousness like wraiths passing in the night.

Twelve-year-old Erin Willit opened her eyes to darkness lit only by the dim green nightlight near her closet door and the faint glow of a street lamp through her front window. She felt her forehead wrinkle, the fingers of one hand curl as she tried to discern what had awakened her.

Something was not right . . .

Annie Kingston moves to Grove Landing for safety and quiet —and comes face to face with evil.

When neighbor Lisa Willet is killed by an intruder in her home, Sheriff's detectives are left with little evidence. Lisa's daughter, Erin, saw the killer, but she's too traumatized to give a description. The detectives grow desperate.

Because of her background in art, Annie is asked to question Erin and draw a composite. But Annie knows little about forensic art or the sensitive interview process. A nonbeliever, she finds herself begging God for help. What if her lack of experience leads Erin astray? The detectives could end up searching for a face that doesn't exist.

Leaving the real killer free to stalk the neighborhood . . .

Softcover: 0-310-25103-6

Pick up a copy today at your favorite bookstore!

ZONDERVAN®

GRAND RAPIDS, MICHIGAN 49530 USA

WWW.ZONDERVAN.COM

Stain of Guilt

Brandilyn Collins

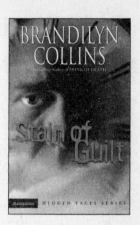

As I drew, the house felt eerie in its silence. . . . A strange sense stole over me, as though Bland and I were two actors on stage, our movements spotlighted, black emptiness between us. But that darkness grew smaller as the space between us shrank. I did not know if this sense was due to my immersion in Bland's face and mind and world, or to my fear of his threatening presence.

Or both . . .

The nerves between my shoulder blades began to tingle.

Help me, God. Please.

For twenty years, a killer has eluded capture for a brutal double murder. Now, forensic artist Annie Kingston has agreed to draw the updated face of Bill Bland for the popular television show *American Fugitive.*

To do so, Annie must immerse herself in Bland's traits and personality. A single habitual expression could alter the way his face has aged. But as she descends into his criminal mind and world, someone is determined to stop her. At any cost. Annie's one hope is to complete the drawing and pray it leads authorities to Bland—before Bland can get to her.

Softcover: 0-310-25104-4

Pick up a copy today at your favorite bookstore!

ZONDERVAN®

GRAND RAPIDS, MICHIGAN 49530 USA

WWW.ZONDERVAN.COM

Dead of Night

Brandilyn Collins

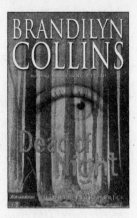

All words fell away. I pushed myself off the path, noticing for the first time the signs of earlier passage—the matted earth, broken twigs. And I knew. My mouth turned cottony.

I licked my lips, took three halting steps. My maddening, visual brain churned out pictures of colorless faces on a cold slab—Debbie Lille, victim number one; Wanda Deminger, number three . . . He'd been here. Dragged this one right where I now stumbled. I'd entered a crime scene, and I could not bear to see what lay at the end. . . .

This is a story about evil.

This is a story about God's power.

A string of murders terrorizes citizens in the Redding, California, area. The serial killer is cunning, stealthy. Masked by day, unmasked by night. Forensic artist Annie Kingston discovers the sixth body practically in her own backyard. Is the location a taunt aimed at her?

One by one, Annie must draw the unknown victims for identification. Dread mounts. Who will be taken next? Under a crushing oppression, Annie and other Christians are driven to pray for God's intervention as they've never prayed before.

With page-turning intensity, Dead of Night dares to pry open the mind of evil. Twisted actions can wreak havoc on earth, but the source of wickedness lies beyond this world. Annie learns where the real battle takes place—and that a Christian's authority through prayer is the ultimate, unyielding weapon.

Softcover: 0-310-25105-2

Web of Lies

Brandilyn Collins,
Bestselling Author
of *Brink of Death*

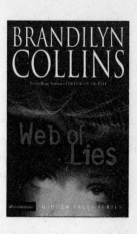

*She was washing dishes when her
world began to blur.*

*Chelsea Adams hitched in a
breath, her skin pebbling. She knew
the dreaded sign all too well. God
was pushing a vision into her consciousness.*

*Black dots crowded her sight. She dropped a plate, heard
it crack against the porcelain sink. Her fingers fumbled for
the faucet. The hiss of water ceased.*

God, I don't want this. Please!

After witnessing a shooting at a convenience store, forensic
artist Annie Kingston must draw a composite of the suspect. But before she can begin, she hears that Chelsea Adams
wants to meet with her — now. Chelsea Adams — the woman
who made national headlines with her visions of murder.
And this vision is by far the most chilling.

Chelsea and Annie soon find themselves snared in a terrifying battle against time, greed, and a deadly opponent.
If they tell the police, will their story be believed? With the
web of lies thickening, and lives ultimately at stake, who will
know enough to stop the evil?

Softcover: 0-310-25106-0

Pick up a copy today at your favorite bookstore!

ZONDERVAN®

GRAND RAPIDS, MICHIGAN 49530 USA

WWW.ZONDERVAN.COM

Cast a Road before Me

Brandilyn Collins

A course-changing event in one's life can happen in minutes. Or it can form slowly, a primitive webbing splaying into fingers of discontent, a minuscule trail hardening into the sinewed spine of resentment. So it was with the mill workers as the heat-soaked days of summer marched on.

City girl Jessie, orphaned at sixteen, struggles to adjust to life with her barely known aunt and uncle in the tiny town of Bradleyville, Kentucky. Eight years later (1968), she plans on leaving—to follow in her revered mother's footsteps of serving the homeless. But the peaceful town she's come to love is about to be tragically shattered. Threats of a labor strike rumble through the streets, and Jessie's new love and her uncle are swept into the maelstrom. Caught between the pacifist teachings of her mother and these two men, Jessie desperately tries to deny that Bradleyville is rolling toward violence and destruction.

Softcover: 0-310-25327-6

Pick up a copy today at your favorite bookstore!

Color the Sidewalk for Me

Brandilyn Collins

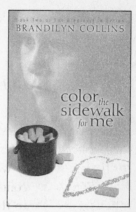

As a chalk-fingered child, I had worn my craving for Mama's love on my sleeve. But as I grew, that craving became cloaked in excuses and denial until slowly it sank beneath my skin to lie unheeded but vital, like the sinews of my framework. By the time I was a teenager, I thought the gap between Mama and me could not be wider.

And then Danny came along. . . .

A splendidly colored sidewalk. Six-year-old Celia presented the gift to her mother with pride—and received only anger in return. Why couldn't Mama love her? Years later, when once-in-a-lifetime love found Celia, her mother opposed it. The crushing losses that followed drove Celia, guilt-ridden and grieving, from her Bradleyville home.

Now thirty-five, she must return to nurse her father after a stroke. But the deepest need for healing lies in the rift between mother and daughter. God can perform such a miracle. But first Celia and Mama must let go of the past—before it destroys them both.

Softcover: 0-310-24242-8

Pick up a copy today at your favorite bookstore!

ZONDERVAN®

GRAND RAPIDS, MICHIGAN 49530 USA

WWW.ZONDERVAN.COM

Capture the Wind for Me

Brandilyn Collins

One thing I have learned. The bonfires of change start with the merest spark. Sometimes we see that flicker. Sometimes we blink in surprise at the flame only after it has marched hot legs upward to fully ignite. Either way, flicker or flame, we'd better do some serious praying. When God's on the move in our lives, he tends to burn up things we'd just as soon keep.

After her mama's death, sixteen-year-old Jackie Delham is left to run the household for her daddy and two younger siblings. When Katherine King breezes into town and tries to steal her daddy's heart, Jackie knows she must put a stop to it. Katherine can't be trusted. Besides, one romance in the family is enough, and Jackie is about to fall headlong into her own.

As love whirls through both generations, the Delhams are buffeted by hope, elation and loss. Jackie is devastated to learn of old secrets in her parents' relationship. Will those past mistakes cost Jackie her own love? And how will her family ever survive if Katherine jilts her daddy and leaves them in mourning once more?

Softcover: 0-310-24243-6

Pick up a copy today at your favorite bookstore!

ZONDERVAN®

GRAND RAPIDS, MICHIGAN 49530 USA

WWW.ZONDERVAN.COM

Eyes of Elisha

Brandilyn Collins

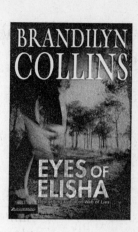

The murder was ugly.
The killer was sure no one
saw him.
Someone did.

In a horrifying vision, Chelsea Adams has relived the victim's last moments. But who will believe her? Certainly not the police, who must rely on hard evidence. Nor her husband, who barely tolerates Chelsea's newfound Christian faith. Besides, he's about to hire the man who Chelsea is certain is the killer to be a vice president in his company.

Torn between what she knows and the burden of proof, Chelsea must follow God's leading and trust him for protection. Meanwhile, the murderer is at liberty. And he's not about to take Chelsea's involvement lying down.

Softcover: 0-310-23968-0

Dread Champion

Brandilyn Collins

Chelsea Adams has visions. But they have no place in a courtroom.

As a juror for a murder trial, Chelsea must rely only on the evidence. And this circumstantial evidence is strong—Darren Welk killed his wife.

Or did he?

The trial is a nightmare for Chelsea. The other jurors belittle her Christian faith. As testimony unfolds, truth and secrets blur. Chelsea's visiting niece stumbles into peril surrounding the case, and Chelsea cannot protect her. God sends visions—frightening, vivid. But what do they mean? Even as Chelsea finds out, what can she do? She is helpless, and danger is closing in . . .

Masterfully crafted, *Dread Champion* is a novel in which appearances can deceive and the unknown can transform the meaning of known facts. One man's guilt or innocence is just a single link in a chain of hidden evil . . . and God uses the unlikeliest of people to accomplish his purposes.

Softcover: 0-310-23827-7

Pick up a copy today at your favorite bookstore!

ZONDERVAN®

GRAND RAPIDS, MICHIGAN 49530 USA

WWW.ZONDERVAN.COM

Three ways to keep up on your favorite Zondervan books and authors

Sign up for our *Fiction E-Newsletter*. Every month you'll receive sample excerpts from our books, sneak peeks at upcoming books, and chances to win free books autographed by the author.

You can also sign up for our *Breakfast Club*. Every morning in your email, you'll receive a five-minute snippet from a fiction or nonfiction book. A new book will be featured each week, and by the end of the week you will have sampled two to three chapters of the book.

Zondervan *Author Tracker* is the best way to be notified whenever your favorite Zondervan authors write new books, go on tour, or want to tell you about what's happening in their lives.

Visit *www.zondervan.com* and sign up today!

ZONDERVAN®

GRAND RAPIDS, MICHIGAN 49530 USA

ZONDERVAN.COM/
AUTHOR**TRACKER**